Also by Paige Tyler

WOLF
UNDER FIRE

PAIGE
TYLER

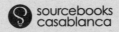
sourcebooks
casablanca

Published by Sourcebooks Casablanca, an imprint of Sourcebooks
P.O. Box 4410, Naperville, Illinois 60567–4410
(630) 961-3900
sourcebooks.com

Printed and bound in the United States of America.
OPM 10 9 8 7 6 5 4 3 2 1

With special thanks to my extremely patient and understanding husband. Without your help and support, I couldn't have pursued my dream job of becoming a writer. You're my sounding board, my idea man, my critique partner, and the absolute best research assistant a girl could ask for. Love you!

CHAPTER 1

London

JESTINA RIDLEY MOVED THROUGH THE DARK, DIRTY alley, careful to avoid the broken glass and occasional uncapped syringe, praying something useful would come out of this little visit to the seedier side of Stockwell. But after sidestepping one especially wet and smelly patch of asphalt, she rephrased that thought, deciding this particular part of southwest London was pretty much all seedy. Definitely not the kind of place tourists flocked to after midnight.

Good thing I'm not a tourist.

"I've got nothing," Jaime Wilkerson grumbled through the tiny radio bud wedged in her ear. "I told you this was going to be a waste of time. That guy we talked to doesn't know squat about this kidnapping."

"In all fairness, he never said the kidnappers were holding the girl here," Neal Goodwin, the other member of their Special Threat Assessment Team, pointed out, his gravelly voice rough over the radio. "He said the people who grabbed the kid used one of these abandoned buildings to stage their equipment and plan the job. He didn't say they'd still be here."

Jes stifled a groan. Neal was right, but she'd hoped they'd get lucky all the same. She and the other two members of her STAT team had been in London for three days checking out a kidnapping with clear supernatural indicators, and so far, they'd come up with nothing.

A week ago, someone had snatched fourteen-year-old Olivia Phillips out of her bedroom on the eighth floor of her apartment building. Her father was a high-level official in MI5, the British Security Service, which meant the place where they lived had better security than most, including watchdog monitors on all the elevators and doors, as well as cameras along every corridor and a handful of roving guards.

None of it had mattered. Olivia had gone missing in the middle of the night and whoever kidnapped her had left the two men guarding the building dead, their throats torn out. The way the men had been killed—along with the mystery of how the kidnappers had gotten into the apartment—had immediately put the crime on STAT's radar, since it looked like the handiwork of supernatural creatures.

After seeing autopsy photos of the guards' bodies, Jes had no doubt some kind of paranormal was involved in the kidnapping, but that didn't make it any easier to track down the thing. Especially since Olivia's parents had stopped cooperating with law enforcement within twenty-four hours of the girl's disappearance, claiming they were doing it on the advice of legal counsel. Jes thought it was more likely because the kidnappers had contacted them to negotiate a ransom and warned them not to involve the cops. Considering the father worked for MI5, it was also possible he was freezing out the locals and letting the British version of the FBI handle the investigation.

Not that it mattered who was running the case for the Brits. Jes and her team were here for one reason—to determine if there were supernatural elements at play and deal with them accordingly. Because that's what STAT did:

figured out what scary thing they were dealing with and made it go away.

"All right, let's call it a night. Wrap up whatever you're doing and meet back at the car." She sighed. "We'll come back tomorrow and check out the area again, this time in the daylight. I doubt we'll find anything, but maybe we'll get lucky and someone might remember seeing something."

Jaime and Neal agreed, sounding as frustrated as she felt. Both of the guys had been with STAT for over a year and knew how bad it could be in the real world when things that went bump in the night targeted their prey. Olivia had been missing for so long, even one more night could mean the difference between getting the girl back alive or not.

Jes continued along the alley, checking out the rear entrances to a series of low-cost government housing buildings that looked like they hadn't seen a legitimate tenant in years. The doors were nailed shut, the windows boarded up, and there wasn't a single light to be seen inside or out. If there was a place in this neighborhood where a supernatural creature might hang out, it'd be here. But when she stopped every so often and peeked through the cracks between the wooden slats over the windows, shining her small flashlight inside, she didn't see anyone.

She was heading toward the grassy side of the apartment building to meet up with the rest of her team when she heard a low, menacing growl over her earpiece that chilled her to the core. It was immediately followed by gunshots, then shouting.

Jaime and Neal.

Crap!

Pulse pounding, Jes pulled her Sig 9mm with her free

hand, clicking off the safety with her thumb as she raced across the scrubby grass in the direction of the sound. She rounded the corner of the building to find herself face-to-face with construction equipment, trash-filled dumpsters, and a handful of big, metal storage pods. As she weaved her way through the maze, she realized the growls and gunfire had ceased and all that was left was an eerie silence. She fervently prayed that meant Jaime and Neal had taken down whatever the hell they'd come across.

But if they had, why hadn't they called out *all clear* over the radio?

"Jaime? Neal? Do you copy?"

No answer.

Double crap!

Jes smelled the blood before she saw the two bodies lying motionless on the ground near one of the dumpsters. She ran toward them, her heart in her throat. If she could pick up the odor of blood, there had to be a bucketload of it.

There was.

Dark red pools of it that looked black even in the glow of her flashlight.

Damn, she hated being right.

Knowing her teammates were almost assuredly dead but needing to check all the same, she crouched beside Jaime when movement near one of the storage containers caught her attention. She jerked her head up to see something big and hulking in the darkness less than fifteen feet away. That same low growl she'd heard before rumbled from its chest as it gazed at her with glowing yellow eyes, and a chill ran along her spine.

Jes brought up her weapon, resting it on the hand that held the flashlight, and pulled the trigger in quick succession, knowing there was no way she could miss at this distance. But the creature disappeared before the bullets could find their mark. One moment, it was there, and the next, it was gone. Before she'd even gotten a good look at it.

As fast as the thing moved, it could easily come at her from a dozen different directions, but she couldn't worry about that. One or both of her teammates might be alive. All that mattered was helping them.

But when she turned her flashlight on Jaime and Neal, she realized it was too late. Whatever had killed them had savagely torn out their throats. They had been dead before they'd hit the ground.

She swallowed hard and pulled out her phone, thumbing the speed-dial button for the STAT emergency operation center in Washington, DC as she scanned the area around her for the creature that had killed her teammates.

"This is Agent Ridley," she said. "Two agents are down and I need a cleanup team out here ASAP. Tell McKay we have confirmed supernatural involvement. I'm going to need backup."

Washington, DC

Jake Huang cursed silently as he strode down yet another hallway on the fourth floor of the J. Edgar Hoover building. How the hell was he going to find the conference room where he was supposed to meet with his new boss in this damn maze? He supposed he could ask one of the other FBI agents who zipped past him in their perfect professional clothes with their perfectly styled hair and perfectly shined shoes, but ultimately, he couldn't bring himself to admit he didn't know his way around the place yet. He was a federal agent now. Shouldn't he know this kind of stuff?

Then again, maybe he should cut himself a break. He'd only been in DC for less than a week and had spent most of that time trying to find a place for him and the twins to live. His boss, Nathan McKay, had given him a quick whirlwind tour of the huge FBI headquarters, then told him to focus on getting settled before worrying about the job. Of course, that was before McKay had called this morning telling him he had thirty minutes to be at the office.

So much for getting settled in.

If it were just him, Jake would have grabbed the first apartment he could find close to work and called it a day, but he had other people in his life now, namely Zoe and Chloe Haynes, the eighteen-year-old beta werewolves he'd rescued from a vampire coven and recently become responsible for. Bringing teenage werewolves who'd gone through their first change barely two months ago to a city as big as Washington, DC was crazy to say the least, but that's what it meant when an alpha stumbled across betas who needed him. They became a pack and a huge part of each other's lives.

When McKay had offered him a position on the joint FBI/CIA Special Threat Assessment Team—aka STAT— the first thing he'd done was ask Zoe and Chloe what they thought. If they'd been against the idea, he would have walked away from the once-in-a-lifetime opportunity. Even though it meant uprooting the life they'd just started in

Dallas, the twins had urged him to take the job. The girls were thrilled at the idea of living in the nation's capital, while he was excited to have a job that would let him openly reveal his werewolf nature and use the abilities that came with it.

Jake turned down another long hallway, sure he'd covered every square foot of the floor he was on, when he picked up a familiar scent—werewolves. One female alpha. One male omega. Doubting there could be many people like him wandering around the building, he let his nose lead him in the right direction.

He chided himself for not thinking of using his keen sense of smell before this. Then again, he'd only recently started embracing his werewolf side. Ever since he'd first turned four years ago, he'd done his best to forget what he'd become.

He half closed his eyes, letting his sense of smell take over and guide him in the right direction. That not only let him shut out a lot of the external distractions so he could focus on the two scents, instead of everything going on around him, but it also kept anyone from freaking out if they noticed his dark eyes were now bright golden yellow. Having someone see him walking the halls like he was stoned wasn't ideal, but it wasn't as bad as them realizing his eyes were glowing like some sort of creature on Halloween.

Fortunately, nobody seemed to notice one way or the other.

A few moments later, he walked into a small conference room to find Harley Grant and Caleb Lynch waiting for him. McKay, thankfully, was nowhere in sight. At least Jake wasn't late.

"Either of you have any idea what McKay wants to see us about?" Jake asked as he sat down across the table from the two werewolves he was somehow supposed to form a pack with even though they'd just met a few days ago.

As if all it took was shoving the three of them in a small room together and waiting for magic to happen.

Jake wasn't an expert on the subject, but from what he'd heard, werewolves were normally drawn together naturally, finding each other without having to work at it. Kind of like him with Zoe and Chloe. But McKay had hired him and the other two werewolves with the expectation that they'd form a pack. Probably because McKay had recently worked with another pack of werewolves—namely the Dallas PD SWAT Team—and seen how impressive the results could be when people like them worked together.

"No clue." Caleb leaned back in his chair, casually propping the sole of his boot on the edge of the table. Tall, with dark eyes and a perpetual smirk, his shaggy, dark blond hair looked like it hadn't seen a brush in a week. "McKay said it was something urgent, but it's been an hour since he brought us in here, so I guess it can't be that urgent."

Jake winced. "That's probably my fault. He called me forty-five minutes ago, but it took me a while to get here. All I know is that he's got a mission for us."

Caleb looked like he couldn't care less about Jake's excuse or the mission. Actually, he didn't look like he gave a damn about anything.

That was par for the course with omega werewolves. And Caleb was a prototypical omega. Big, strong, and as fast as any alpha, he was barely able to keep his inherent werewolf nature under control, not to mention he was nearly incapable of caring about anybody but himself. Loners by choice, omegas rarely formed pack bonds. Jake could only imagine how much fun it was going to be trying to get the man integrated into the team.

To make matters worse, Caleb was a convicted criminal. The only reason he wasn't in jail right now was because he'd agreed to work for STAT. One screwup and the man would go straight back to prison. Jake didn't know exactly what the other werewolf had done to get him tossed in a cell or why the commander of the Dallas SWAT Team had vouched for him, but he had, and now, Caleb was Jake's problem.

Jake glanced at the third member of their dysfunctional pack to see if she had anything to add to the discussion. From the disinterested look on the pretty blond werewolf's face, Harley didn't seem to care any more than Caleb did about the meeting.

He wished he could say he was surprised, but he wasn't. While he'd only talked to the female alpha for a while the first day they'd met, Jake could already tell gaining her trust wasn't going to be easy. From the little she'd said about her werewolf abilities, he got the feeling she'd yet to accept her inner wolf. He couldn't shake the sensation that Harley didn't like what she was. It made him wonder what the hell McKay had said to get her to agree to the job.

Jake opened his mouth to ask if either Caleb or Harley had found a place to live yet—because the silence was starting to get uncomfortable and it seemed like a safe thing to talk about—when the door to the conference room opened and their boss walked in. Brown hair sporting a touch of gray at the temples, McKay appeared every inch the federal agent, right down to the black suit and wire-rimmed glasses.

Harley sat up a little straighter.

Caleb didn't even have the good sense to take his foot off the table—nice to confirm he did indeed have the social graces of a sea slug.

Two other agents were with McKay, a man and woman, both of whom were probably in their mid- to late-twenties. Six feet tall with dark hair, a square jaw, and blue eyes that looked like they didn't miss a thing, the guy looked like someone central casting would give you if you asked for a standard-issue FBI agent, dark suit and red power tie included.

The woman, on the other hand, was different. In fact, the only thing "standard issue" about the petite agent was the navy-blue pantsuit she wore. And while Jake wasn't an expert on the FBI or CIA, he was pretty sure her vivid purple hair wasn't the norm. But that wasn't the only thing unique about her. Nope. Her eyes were purple, too. Lavender, actually. At first, he thought she was wearing contacts but then realized the color was real.

Considering STAT had recently recruited werewolves, it wasn't surprising to think they hired other supernaturals. Maybe the unique-looking woman was more different than she appeared.

"Sorry I'm late," McKay apologized.

He closed the door, then flipped a switch on the control panel beside it. A moment later, a high-pitched hum filled the room, making Jake wince. On the other side of the table, Harley and Caleb mirrored his reaction. Shrill noises and keen hearing didn't mix, but the meeting must be seriously classified if McKay was going with a frequency jammer to keep anyone else from picking up their conversation.

"Jake Huang, Harley Grant, Caleb Lynch, meet two more members of the team—Forrest Albright and Mistal Swanson." McKay pulled out the rolling chair at the head of the table and took a seat. "Forrest was FBI for almost five years before joining STAT a year and a half ago. Misty has been with the organization a little less than that."

While McKay fiddled with the keyboard on the table in front of him, trying to boot up the computer connected to the huge screen on the front wall, Misty sat down in the empty chair next to Jake. Forrest sat beside her.

"What about you, Misty?" Caleb said, casually eyeing the woman across from him. "McKay didn't say where you worked before joining STAT."

Mistal flipped her long, colorful hair over her shoulder and turned her gaze on the omega. "McKay recruited me after I graduated from college because of my unique abilities."

That was cryptic, Jake thought. Harley seemed just as curious. "What abilities are those?"

At the far end of the table, McKay finished tapping on the keyboard as the STAT organization's logo filled the screen, along with several warnings about protecting classified information and sensitive sources.

"Misty is a technopath," their new boss said, as if that explained everything. When Jake and his fellow werewolves continued to stare at him, McKay added, "She's similar to a telepath, only she reads electronic equipment, not people."

Jake had no idea what the hell McKay was talking about. At least Harley and Caleb seemed equally confused.

"Okay," Jake said. "But that doesn't really answer my question."

McKay looked at Misty. "Want to give them a demonstration?"

Lips curving, Misty held her hand out to Jake. "Give me your cell phone."

He'd just upgraded his phone before moving there, so he didn't want Misty blowing it up or anything. But he had to admit he was curious, so he dug it out of his pocket and handed it to her. Before his eyes, Misty's lavender irises went completely white, making her seem even more supernatural.

"Your pass code is 1-2-3-4? Seriously?" She laughed. "Not that there's much in here to protect. A contact list with a dozen names and a handful of photos, all of them with the same two kids—twin girls. You're in some of them. And you're smiling." Misty's eyes returned to their normal lavender as she handed the phone back to him. "You should smile more often. It's a good look on you."

Jake stared at her, not sure what to say to that. Hell, he didn't even understand what he'd heard.

"I can access any electronic device I touch," she explained. "And since the Internet connects everything and everyone, that means I can get into pretty much anywhere and anything if I want to."

"So you're basically a hacker?" Caleb's voice was casual as usual, but Jake got the feeling he was impressed.

Misty gave him a smile. "Yes. Although I prefer the word *technopath*."

"How is that even possible?" Harley asked, a stunned expression on her face.

Misty opened her mouth to answer, but McKay interrupted.

"I understand you all have questions, and any other time, I'd have the whole team get to know each other, but unfortunately, that's not an option right now. We have a situation in London. Two STAT agents are dead. I need to get your team up to speed and on a plane ASAP."

Jake sat up straighter.

Shit just got real.

Fast.

And they were going to have to learn how to be a team and work together—fast.

He shoved his phone in his pocket. "What do we have?"

McKay pushed a button on the keyboard. The moment a photo of a red-haired teen girl with freckles appeared on the screen, their boss went into briefing mode, telling them fourteen-year-old Olivia Phillips had recently been kidnapped and that the security guards for her apartment building had their throats ripped out.

"At approximately 0200 this morning London time, our STAT team was attacked by an unknown supernatural." McKay flipped to another slide, this one of two men lying on the ground with their throats torn out, blood soaking their ragged clothes.

He moved to the next slide, a photo of a beautiful woman with full, pouty lips, long dark hair, and even darker eyes. Jake was so locked on the picture he barely heard what McKay was saying until he realized the woman was the third member of the team in London. Which meant she was soon going to be *his* teammate. His heart suddenly hammered in his chest at the thought.

What the hell?

"Senior field agent Jestina Ridley didn't get a good look

at the creature but took several shots at it. The thing is so fast it disappeared in a blur before she could even hit it."

Jake frowned, dragging his gaze away from the photo, getting his head back in the game and wondering if that was an exaggeration on Agent Ridley's part. The creature couldn't actually be that fast. Then again, she could also have been so rattled by the brutal death of her teammates, she'd been confused about what had happened afterward. It wouldn't be the first time he'd seen someone do that in a stressful situation.

McKay must have seen the doubt on Jake's face because he gave him a pointed look. "Don't downplay Jes's observations. She's got more field experience with supernaturals than any other agent in STAT. If she says the creature was so fast it was a blur, then it was a blur. You're the lead agent for the team—that was part of the deal when we recruited you. And while you have a load of tactical expertise, Jes has been dealing with supernatural creatures for a long time. Make good use of her experience with them."

"Understood," Jake said.

He didn't have a problem working with someone more experienced in the field. He might have been a Navy SEAL and a cop in his former life, but this agent thing was new. Although he couldn't imagine she'd be thrilled to work for someone so lacking in seniority as far as time in STAT was concerned. Hopefully, it wouldn't be an issue.

"For reasons we haven't fully worked out yet, Olivia's parents are no longer cooperating with the police, which makes it difficult to determine exactly what the current situation is and how these supernaturals are involved," McKay continued. "It could be a vampire, a werewolf, or something completely different."

While Jake wasn't thrilled at the idea of facing more vampires—he'd had his fill of them weeks ago out in Los Angeles—the possibility of going up against other were-wolves sucked even worse, and he hoped the supernaturals who'd kidnapped Olivia and butchered those four men were anything other than his own kind.

Across from him, Harley and Caleb looked like they were thinking the same thing.

"When you get to London, you'll hook up with Jes at the American Embassy, confirm what kind of creatures we're dealing with, and figure out how to stop them." McKay looked at each of them in turn. "This goes without saying, but don't let anyone else know what you're in the UK for or what you're doing. The world isn't supposed to know super-naturals exist, much less that we have some working for the U.S. intelligence community."

McKay didn't have to worry about Jake saying anything to anyone. Like most werewolves, he was good at hiding what he was. His gut told him Harley and Caleb were no different.

Jake's gaze went to the computer screen at the front of the room and the photo of Jestina Ridley again. While his human side was already focused on the importance of the mission, his inner wolf was eager to get to London for a completely different reason—the gorgeous STAT agent he'd be working with.

Jake sprinted up the steps to the eighth floor of his apart-ment building. He had thirty minutes to tell the twins where he was going, pack a bag, and catch an Uber to the airport. Taking the stairs was faster than waiting for the elevator.

He yanked open the door to the stairwell, his head still spinning from the mission briefing. In a perfect world, he and his teammates would get to know each other's strengths and weaknesses before going into the field. Not only was he still figuring out this werewolf thing on a daily basis, but Harley and Caleb were both carrying enough baggage to fill a cargo plane. It was going to take a while for them to become a team, much less a pack.

Then there were Forrest and Misty. McKay had hand-picked them for the team, so they must obviously be able to handle themselves. Even so, there was no way to tell how they were all going to gel.

And that wasn't even counting Jestina. He knew even less about Jes than he did any of his other teammates. Other than that she made his inner wolf sit up and take notice—and that her previous teammates had been killed by a creature that might or might not have been a werewolf.

He cursed as he strode down the hallway. This mission was going to be like a HALO jump from twenty thousand feet—without a parachute.

The door of his apartment was open when he got there. If he hadn't picked up Zoe's and Chloe's scents inside, he would have gone into full-werewolf mode for sure. But their hearts were beating evenly, which meant they were safe.

He was halfway inside when he picked up two other scents that made him stop in his tracks. The twins weren't alone. There were a couple of guys in there with them. Suddenly, his heart started thumping harder and his fingertips began to tingle, a sure sign his claws were about to make an appearance.

Jake hadn't lost control of his inner werewolf for a long time, but right then, he had the urge to kill someone—slowly.

He strode through the entryway, his boots as silent on the tile as they were on the carpet of the adjoining living space. Zoe and Chloe were standing side by side in the middle of the room, their long, straight, platinum-blond hair practically floating in the gentle breeze of the air-conditioning. Identical twins, they were tall, slender, and graceful. His anger faded as he realized the girls were fine.

Although the twins were half turned away from him, Jake had no doubt they knew he was home. Even if they hadn't yet caught a glimpse of him out of the corners of their eyes, they would have undoubtedly picked up his scent. Then again, betas were attuned to their alphas in ways beyond the normal senses. It was just as likely they'd known he was home before he'd walked into the apartment building.

Neither girl turned to look at him. But that was because they were too busy staring at the two guys on the other side of the room, moving furniture. A few years older than the twins, both men had dark hair and wore jeans and T-shirts.

"I think it needs to go a little more to the left," Zoe said, motioning for the guys to move the couch they'd been patiently holding a foot off the floor.

The two men shifted the couch to the side as directed, then looked at the twins expectantly.

"How about that?" the wirier-built guy asked.

This time, it was the usually shy, reserved Chloe who answered. "A little to the right again."

Not that the girls seemed to be paying any attention to

the actual position of the leather sofa. Instead, their focus was on the flexing, bulging biceps of the two men.

Jake groaned silently. He had four older brothers but had always thought it would be cool to have a younger sister or two. Now that he had them, he realized maybe it'd been a good thing he didn't have sisters when he was growing up. Something told him he would have ended up in a lot of fights.

"The couch looks good right where it is," Jake said firmly, walking into the room. The sofa was one of the last pieces of furniture they'd been waiting to get delivered. "I'm sure these guys have someplace they'd much rather be than moving furniture for two eighteen-year-old girls."

Jake might have been talking to the girls, but he was looking straight at the two men, who went pale beneath their tans at the expression on his face. As one, they set the couch down.

"Oh hey, Jake." Flipping her hair over her shoulder, Zoe turned to give him a smile. "We didn't hear you come in."

Yeah right.

"This is Austin Dunn and Colt Holland," Chloe said, mirroring her twin's smile. "They both work with us at the FBI and were nice enough to come help with the furniture that was delivered today. We didn't even have to twist their arms."

Jake resisted the urge to roll his eyes. Chloe was scary smart, but sometimes he worried about how naive she could be. She had to know why these two guys had jumped at the chance to help her and Zoe. And it wasn't to get out of chasing down forgers or whatever they did at the FBI.

He needed to make it clear Zoe and Chloe were

off-limits. Since they weren't STAT, Austin and Colt didn't know he was a werewolf, but they'd quickly learn he wasn't someone to piss off if they messed with the twins.

McKay had gotten the twins part-time jobs at the FBI headquarters building while they attended college. Though he'd done it as a favor, Jake suspected McKay hoped to recruit Zoe and Chloe into STAT. McKay didn't seem to know a lot about betas, so to him, one werewolf was probably as good for covert work as the next, but there was no way in hell Jake would ever let the twins do anything dangerous.

No more than he'd let them hang out with two guys who were way too old for them—and not nearly good enough.

"Then I guess thanks are in order. I appreciate you helping them out," Jake said, moving past the twins to shake both men's hands in turn, squeezing hard enough to make sure Austin and Colt got the message. "I'm Jake Huang, the girls' legal guardian. Zoe and Chloe are more important to me than anything, by the way," he added, lowering his voice. "Which is why if I heard someone did something to make them unhappy, I'm not sure there's a limit to what I'd do to that person."

Jake had no doubt the twins heard him but didn't care. As long as Austin and Colt got the message. From the fear in their eyes, he was pretty sure they had.

Before either man could respond, Jake chuckled and good-naturedly slapped them on their shoulders, telling them they should grab a beer sometime.

"Anyway," he added with a grin, "it's been a long day and I'm sure you two need to get out of here."

Austin and Colt exchanged looks before nodding.

"Um, yeah." Austin looked at the twins. "We'll see you tomorrow at work."

Colt echoed the sentiment, giving Zoe and Chloe a nervous smile as he and Austin headed toward the door. Jake followed, closing the door behind them. When he turned around, it was to see both girls standing there, Zoe with her arms crossed, Chloe with her hands on her hips, disapproval obvious on both their faces.

"Was threatening them really necessary?" Zoe demanded. "They were just helping us move furniture. They didn't try anything."

"I'm sure they didn't, but believe it or not, I was once those guys' age." He walked back into the spacious living room, ignoring the synchronized eye roll they gave him. "I know what they were thinking when they volunteered to help."

Zoe and Chloe opened their mouths to argue, but he spoke before either could get a word out.

"Look, I'd love to stand here and discuss in detail why all men are pigs, but that's not why I came home early. I'm going on a mission."

The twins both tensed.

"Already?" Chloe asked, her blue eyes widening in obvious trepidation.

He sighed. "I know. I didn't think I'd be in the field this soon either, but unfortunately, I have to leave immediately." A glance at his watch had him adding, "In fact, I need to be downstairs to catch my ride in fifteen minutes."

Chloe chewed on her lower lip. "Where are you going? Is it dangerous?"

Jake carefully schooled himself before answering. Betas

could sense when their alpha was anxious, angry, scared—
everything. The girls would freak out if he gave away even a
hint of how dangerous this mission might be.

"I'm going to London. And no, it's not dangerous," he
said.

The twins relaxed a little at that, although Chloe was
still regarding him with an expression that suggested she
knew he was holding something back.

"How long will you be gone?" she asked quietly.

He opened his mouth to tell them a couple days, but it
would only make them worry more if it took longer.

"I don't know," he finally admitted. "But I promise I'll
Skype as often as I can."

Zoe and Chloe exchanged looks, then laughed.

"You don't even know how to Skype," Zoe pointed out.

He chuckled. "Okay, you got me. But I'll figure it out."

"We'll hold you to that," Zoe said. "Or we'll start burning up your phone with text messages, and we know how
much you hate typing with those monster-sized fingers of
yours."

Running over, Zoe and Chloe hugged him, telling him
to be careful while he was in London.

"Do you want us to wait for you to get back to go pick out
our puppy?" Chloe asked when she and Zoe pulled away.

Damn. He'd completely forgotten. They were supposed
to go to the shelter and adopt a rescue tomorrow. It was all
the girls had talked about since they'd moved there.

Jake shook his head. "I don't want you and the cute little
furball to wait on me. You two go and pick him—or her—
out." He glanced at his watch again. "Crap. I have to pack."

Crossing the living area, he headed down the short

hallway that separated the bedrooms from the rest of the apartment. His was the one at the farthest end and also the biggest of the three. Painted a light sand color, there were two dressers in addition to the king-size bed and two night tables.

Grabbing his weekender from the closet, he stuffed it with a little of everything, not exactly sure what he'd need. Before he'd left the office, McKay mentioned he and his teammates would get weapons once they got overseas, but beyond that, he wasn't sure if they'd be running the mission in tactical outfits or business suits. He'd just grabbed his toiletry kit and toothbrush, trying to think if there was anything he was missing, when his werewolf hearing picked up hushed voices from the kitchen.

"What do you think about inviting Austin and Colt over for dinner tomorrow night?" Chloe asked softly, as if she thought that would keep him from hearing. "We could order pizza or cook them something. As a thank-you for helping with the couch and stuff."

"They say the way to a man's heart is through his stomach," Zoe pointed out. "And since Jake won't be home, the guys would definitely be cool with it."

Jake shook his head as he picked up his bag and headed out of the bedroom. "You two know that I'm still here, right? And that I can hear every word you're saying?"

Zoe and Chloe were leaning back against the granite-topped island that separated the kitchen from the living room, grinning like they were the funniest people in the world.

"Yeah, we know," Zoe said.

"And that you could hear us," Chloe added. "We just wanted to give you a reason to Skype a lot while you're gone."

He snorted and dropped his bag on the floor, then walked over to wrap his arms around them in a group hug.

"Be careful while I'm away, okay?" he said. "And don't do anything crazy."

"We will," they promised in unison.

"You be careful, too," Chloe said.

"And come home soon," Zoe added.

Jake picked up his bag but didn't head for the door. Instead, he stood there wondering if working for STAT was a good idea. Because right then, the alpha werewolf in him didn't like the notion of being separated from his pack.

But then Zoe and Chloe were hurrying him out the door so he wouldn't miss his ride, and all he was left with were doubts.

CHAPTER 2

London

WHEN HER NEW TEAMMATES WALKED IN THE DOOR OF the small medical clinic in the basement of the American embassy in London, Jes immediately knew which one Jake Huang was. When she'd talked to Nathan McKay on the phone earlier, he'd described Jake as a charismatic man who commanded any room he stepped into. McKay was right.

Asian American with jet-black hair and dark eyes, Jake was easily six five. It was obvious he was extremely well built under that leather jacket, muscular more in that lean Tarzan kind of way than the bulky look of someone who lifted a buttload of weights. As he crossed the room, Jes couldn't help noticing the graceful way he moved.

Like an animal—a predator.

Then again, he was a werewolf.

He extended his hand. "Agent Ridley. Jake Huang." He glanced at the other people with him—two more were-wolves; a tall, dark-haired guy; and a woman with lavender eyes and hair to match. "Harley Grant, Caleb Lynch, Forrest Albright, and Misty Swanson," he said, pointing to each as he introduced them before turning back to her. "It's nice finally meeting you, though I wish it could have been under different circumstances."

Jes had worked with Forrest on a few other missions and got along well with him. She knew Misty by reputation and had heard a lot of good things about her but had never been in the field with her. The technopath would be a good addition to the team.

"Likewise," she said.

Jake's hand was warm, his grip firm, and while Jes knew it was stupid, she couldn't stop herself from peeking at his fingers, half expecting to see claws. There weren't any, but when she lifted her gaze to his, the expression there made her wonder if he'd somehow picked up on her thoughts. What if werewolves could read minds? She supposed it was possible. They wouldn't be the first supernaturals she'd run into with that talent.

Jes had been stunned when McKay told her he was sending a pack of werewolves to help find the creature that had killed her teammates. Then he'd really blown her mind by adding she was being assigned to the team permanently.

She'd heard rumors for the past several weeks that STAT was considering bringing in more supernaturals. She supposed it made sense. Saving the world from monsters was a nearly impossible job to start with, but after discovering a little while ago that vampires and werewolves existed, STAT realized they were in over their heads and needed an assist.

Jes never thought that assistance would come in the form of a pack of werewolves.

Part of her understood the people STAT was recruiting weren't like the monsters she'd spent the past couple years chasing. That said, she wasn't thrilled at the idea of working with Jake and his friends, especially after her former teammates might very well have been killed by werewolves.

"I'm surprised you came here straight from the airport," she said, releasing his hand, a little uncomfortable thinking about what Jake's claws actually did look like. She'd seen photos STAT had taken when they'd first encountered werewolves. She knew what he and his friends looked like when they wanted to. "I know flying from DC to London can wear you out."

"We wanted to get here as fast as possible, so we could take a look at the bodies of your teammates and get them back to their families for a proper burial," Jake said.

Jes opened her mouth to reply, then realized she wasn't sure what to say. Jake was right. She didn't know Neal and Jaime all that well, but she did want to get them back home. They deserved that. It was nice Jake thought the same, even though he'd never even met the two men.

She nodded. "Okay. They're back this way. The embassy has a cold storage room for when they need to repatriate deceased American citizens."

The two Marine Corps embassy guards who'd been stationed at the door outside the room eyeballed her and her new team but didn't say a word as they walked inside. They already knew Jes was an agent and probably assumed the people with her were the same.

Not quite a freezer, the room was cold enough to see your breath. Jes led them over to the metal tables in the center and wordlessly pulled the sheets down to the waist, revealing both men's upper bodies. They'd been stripped of their blood-soaked clothes and cleaned up as much as possible, but there was only so much that could be done with jagged wounds as vicious as theirs. Even though she'd already seen the bodies, she couldn't keep from cringing at the sight. Around her, everyone else flinched, too. She was a little surprised to see Jake and the other werewolves react that way. Surely, they must be used to seeing stuff like this.

"The embassy doctor did a preliminary exam," Jes said as Jake moved around to stand across from her. "There was no saliva in the wounds, which made her think they were caused by claws instead of fangs. Based on the similarity of the wounds, the directionality, and the depth, she believes Neal and Jaime were killed by the same creature—or creatures."

"Did you see more than one of them at the scene?" Forrest asked.

She shook her head. "No, but my gut tells me there were more than the one I saw. I didn't get a really good look at it, but I know it had glowing yellow eyes."

Jes glanced at Jake to see his reaction to that bit of info. She was disappointed when he didn't so much as blink.

"That rules out vampires," he said. "Their eyes are flat black, like a shark."

"I was thinking they might have been werewolves," she murmured, trying to keep an eye on all three of those particular supernaturals as she waited for some kind of response.

"If it was a werewolf, it damn sure wasn't an omega," Caleb said casually from his place over by the wall. She hadn't missed the way he'd separated himself from the rest of the team when they'd come in there, hovering on the edges of the room, like he didn't want to be a part of the team. Or maybe he simply liked his space. "If an omega lost it and started slashing up people like that, his eyes would glow blue, not yellow."

Jes had no idea what that meant. Maybe an omega was a type of werewolf? Before she could ask, Harley spoke.

"It wasn't a female alpha or beta werewolf, either. Her eyes would have been vivid green."

Unlike Caleb, Harley didn't seem to need her space. But

at the same time, Jes noticed she stood closer to Forrest and Misty, like she didn't want to be associated with her fellow werewolves.

Okay, obviously this werewolf thing was a lot more complicated than Jes thought. "Okay, if it wasn't an omega or a female werewolf, what kind was it?"

When Harley and Caleb turned their gazes on Jake, she had her answer.

Whatever kind of werewolf he must be.

"If it was a werewolf, then it had to be an alpha," Jake said softly, like it hurt him to admit it, and Jes almost felt bad for dragging it out of him. "Our eyes glow yellow gold."

Folding her arms, she locked eyes with him. "*If* it was a werewolf? The creature's eyes glowed yellow and it slashed my teammates open. What else could it be?"

At least Jake the werewolf was man enough to not flinch at the accusation she slung his way. Not that she thought he'd done it himself, of course. He'd obviously been a whole continent away at the time. But one male alpha werewolf was pretty much the same as the next as far as she was concerned. Hell, all werewolves—regardless of their silly designations—were the same to her.

"One way to find out, I guess," he said.

Stepping closer to the table, he leaned over Jaime, his face mere inches from the man's gaping neck wound.

For one horrified moment, Jes thought Jake was going to actually bite him, then she heard the sound of sniffing. He was smelling the body of her dead teammate.

She wasn't sure if that grossed her out any less.

Straightening, Jake walked to the other table, where Neal's body was laid out and repeated the same repulsive process. This time he stood there a longer while, eyes closed as he inhaled more deeply. It would have been fascinating if he wasn't doing it over the bodies of two men she'd known.

Frowning, he stood and looked at Harley. "Take a sniff and tell me what you smell."

Harley did as he asked but didn't look happy about it. In fact, she closed her eyes completely before leaning in to sniff the wound on Neal's neck. Jes didn't blame her. Being so close to something like that would have been too much for her.

It took Harley a lot longer to do whatever Jake had done, but when she finally stood up, she threw a confused look at him. "There's something weird about the scent. It's not...right."

Curious as to what the hell that meant, Jes glanced at Caleb, expecting Jake to ask him to smell the bodies, too.

"Omegas have a crappy sense of smell," Jake said, as if anticipating her question. "They can register strong scents, but they'd never pick up on something as subtle as this."

"As subtle as what?" Jes asked.

"As subtle as the scent lingering on the bodies," Jake explained. "At first, I thought it was an alpha werewolf, but there's something odd about it. Like the werewolf part of the scent is a cover for the one underneath it."

Now, she was even more confused. "What does that mean?"

"It means that whatever killed your teammates wasn't an alpha werewolf, but instead can assume the scent of one," Jake said. "At least on the surface."

Did he really expect her to believe that?

"A creature that can mimic the scent of a werewolf." Glaring at him, Jes flipped the sheet back over Jaime's body, then Neal's. "Isn't that freaking convenient."

Jake flinched at her words.

And for some reason, that made Jes feel like crap.

Drinking coffee in the middle of the night probably wasn't the smartest thing to do. Especially when she hadn't slept in almost twenty-four hours. Something the clock on the built-in microwave on the other side of the kitchen in the bed-and-breakfast where Jes and the rest of her teammates were staying seemed to take great pleasure in reminding her. But how could she sleep when, every time she closed her eyes, all she saw were Jaime and Neal lying in their own blood on the street with their throats torn out?

Hence the whole mainlining-caffeine-at-three-thirty-in-the-morning thing.

Jes took another sip, savoring the taste of the rich, creamy, dark blend. Saying the first meeting with her new team that afternoon had been a catastrophe was an understatement. The three werewolves seemed to instinctively know she didn't trust them. The tension in the monster SUV when they'd left the embassy had been so thick even a knife wouldn't have cut it.

It would have been much easier if they were staying at a hotel, instead of this charming country house on the outskirts of London. At least then they wouldn't be in each other's personal space 24/7. But it was where she and her former team had been staying so it didn't make sense to move. Maybe McKay had purposely left them at the B&B, figuring it would help them bond.

She snorted. *Fat chance of that.*

Jes glanced down at the coffee left in her mug, debating whether to get a refill, when she heard soft footsteps behind her. She looked over her shoulder to see Jake standing there.

Crap, for a guy who was six five and 250 pounds, he was light on his feet. Then again, he was a predator.

He gazed at her for a moment, an unreadable expression in his dark eyes, before motioning toward the coffeepot. "Mind if I have a cup?"

Jes had a momentary urge to lay claim to the whole damn pot—she'd made it after all. But that would be childish, not to mention hell on her relationship with her new teammate. Besides, sharing was the professional thing to do. They did have to work together. Whether she liked it or not.

"Go ahead," she said. "Cream is in the fridge, and there's sweetener in the cabinet beside the microwave."

Jes studied him over the rim of her mug as he moved around the island and to the counter on the far side of the room. Jake wore a pair of black running shorts that showed off long, muscular legs and a red T-shirt with "Property of Santa Fe PD" on the front that was tight enough across his broad chest to make her think he was seriously built under it. She might not trust him as far as she could throw him, but she had to admit he looked damn good.

Grabbing a cup off the rack on the counter, Jake filled it to the brim with coffee, then opened one cabinet after another until he found a box of shortbreads. Cookies and mug in hand, he came over to the island, setting them down before hooking a bare foot around the leg of the stool next to hers and dragging it his way, putting some distance between them. Did she smell that offensive to his oh-so-sensitive werewolf nose?

Opening the box of cookies, he took out half a dozen, then pushed the container toward her.

Goody, a peace offering.

Jes was tempted to ignore the gesture, but the square cookies were too tempting to pass up. Taking one, she slowly nibbled on it. Buttery and delicious, the shortbread paired perfectly with the coffee left in her mug, so she helped herself to another.

"Sorry about earlier," Jake said, his deep voice quiet in the small kitchen.

Jes looked up from her coffee to study him. She liked the dark scruff on his square jaw. It made him look dangerous.

Wait. What?

Why the heck was she even noticing things like that? Jake was her teammate—a fur-covered supernatural one to boot. She shouldn't be thinking of him as a man, handsome or otherwise. He wasn't a man at all, but a werewolf. She needed to remember that.

"Sorry about what?" she asked.

"That crap Caleb said." Jake gave her a sidelong glance. "About the luggage in his room."

Jes had to bite her tongue to keep from saying something nasty. Well, something else nasty. She'd seriously unloaded on Caleb earlier when the jackass had started bitching about some piece of crap leaving their stuff in his bedroom. She'd almost kicked him in the balls as she informed him that the piece of crap who'd left stuff in his room was a guy named Jaime Wilkerson.

"Yeah, the guy lying on a slab in the embassy morgue with his throat ripped out," she'd snapped. "So you're going to have to excuse him for not cleaning up for you."

Caleb's jaw tightened and his eyes flashed gold, but the werewolf hadn't said a word. Instead, he'd simply walked from the room, down the steps, and out the front door. He hadn't come back until well after dark.

"It's not your place to apologize for him," she said to Jake.

He shrugged. "I feel like someone should, since I doubt he ever will."

Jake was probably right about that. Caleb struck her as the type who'd rather chew off his own tongue than apologize for being a jackass.

"I'll help you pack up the stuff if you want," Jake said. "If we get it to the embassy in time, they'll be able to send it home with the bodies. There are probably some personal possessions their families will want."

The offer was so thoughtful and unexpected that Jes couldn't think of anything to say. So instead, she nodded and reached for another shortbread. Jake got there first. Taking out a cookie, he handed it to her, then grabbed one for himself. She laughed as he bit into it with his perfect white teeth.

"What's so funny?" he asked.

"Nothing, really. It's just that I didn't take you for a cookie kind of guy."

He took a swallow of coffee. "What kind of guy do you take me for then?"

She shrugged. "I don't know. Raw meat, I guess. Since you're a werewolf and all."

Jes expected him to chuckle, but instead, Jake went visibly still. Setting his mug down, he turned his head to look at her, his dark eyes intense.

"So that's how it is. I'm a werewolf, therefore, I eat raw meat? Are you down here drinking coffee in the middle of the night instead of upstairs in bed because you're afraid one of us is going to slip into your room and attack you?"

While his voice was low and even, it was obvious Jake was pissed, and for a moment, Jes felt ashamed. She had no reason to think Jake or any of the other werewolves would actually attack her or the others. But then she remembered exactly how Jaime and Neal had died, and that it could have easily been a creature like Jake who'd murdered them, regardless of his assertions to the contrary.

"Isn't that how it works with your kind?" she snapped. "You bite people and turn them into werewolves. Or worse."

Jake's jaw tightened and the carefully controlled mask he wore slipped, revealing anger, along with something she hadn't expected—disappointment and disgust. Just as quickly, the facade was back in place and he was on his feet, heading for the door. But then he stopped.

"I doubt you care, but that's not even close to how it works with our kind," he said, not turning to look at her. "Werewolves are born, not made. A bite from a werewolf doesn't do anything except hurt like a son of a bitch."

Jes was already up and hurrying after him before Jake made it half a dozen steps. Catching up to him, she got in front of him and blocked his path. This close, she was reminded of exactly how tall he was.

"What the hell does that mean, werewolves are born, not made?" she demanded, tilting her head back to look at him.

"It means you can go to bed, Jes," he said softly. "My pack and I aren't going to attack you or anyone else."

She pulled her navy-blue cardigan duster more tightly around her, folding her arms. "That doesn't answer my question. You can't honestly expect me to believe you were running around with fangs and glowing eyes in elementary school. I think the world would have noticed that."

Jake was silent for so long she thought he wouldn't answer, but then he let out a tired sigh, like he'd come to the conclusion he wasn't getting past her until he did.

"People like me are born with a gene that turns us into werewolves."

She frowned. "That's it? You have a chunk of mutated DNA and poof you're a werewolf?"

That earned her a derisive snort. "Unfortunately, it's not that simple. It only turns us into werewolves when something…bad…happens to us."

"Something bad?" she echoed, though for some reason she wasn't sure if she wanted to know. The sudden knot in her stomach said she didn't.

He stared at something over her shoulder, his gaze far away, like he was remembering. Then again, maybe he simply couldn't stand to look at her anymore. Or maybe he couldn't stand her eyes on him.

"Something traumatic and usually painful," he said softly. "In my case, it was when the helicopter my SEAL team and I were on got shot down and we crashed in the mountains of northern Afghanistan. Seven of us flew into those mountains. Four of us crawled out of the wreckage. I broke both legs, my hips, back, and most of my ribs." He shook his head. "I don't even remember dragging myself away from the flames engulfing the chopper."

She shuddered despite herself as she visualized the scene he'd described. She'd always been empathic to the plight of others, but thinking about Jake lying on the side of a mountain in enemy territory that…shattered…made it hard to get a breath for some reason. "Is that when you turned?"

Jake nodded, glancing at her from the corner of his eye. "Taliban fighters found the crash site, so my teammates and I were forced to hide for three days until an Air Force Pararescue Team could get there. Lying there in the darkness, wondering if the shot I just heard was some asshole killing one of my best friends, is something I'll never forget for the rest of my life."

She knew the feeling. "Did anyone else make it?"

He shook his head, swallowing hard. "They all died. After that helicopter crash, all those broken bones and four gunshot wounds…I should have been dead, too. There's no reason for me to have lived when they didn't, but I did because I have a chunk of mutated DNA, as you call it."

Jake met her gaze, his deep brown eyes flaring gold. This time, Jes was the one who looked away. She hadn't said or done anything wrong, but it sure felt like she had. She opened her mouth to apologize, wanting to tell him she had her own reasons for being wary of anything—anyone—like him, but he cut her off.

"The things that killed Jaime and Neal were monsters," he said, his voice flat. "Not because they had claws and fangs, but because of how they chose to use them. We're not all like that. Most of us are simply people trying to deal with stuff the best they can. Like Caleb, Harley, and me."

Jake didn't wait for a reply but instead stepped around her and strode down the hall and up the steps, his feet silent on the hardwood floor.

Jes stood there long after she heard him close his

bedroom door. Finally, she walked slowly into the kitchen and poured what was left of the coffee into her mug, added cream and sugar, then she sat there, her head spinning. Jake had given her a lot to think about and something told her it would be a long time before she fell asleep that night.

CHAPTER 3

JAKE HEARD NOISE COMING FROM DOWNSTAIRS BEFORE he even stepped out of his bedroom the next morning. Curious, he jogged down the steps, following the sound through the hallway and into the living room. Forrest and Misty were over by the coffee table, pulling electronic gear out of big black heavy-duty plastic cases.

"What's all this?" he asked.

Forrest glanced up as he unraveled a cable. "Video equipment for the Skype call we've got with McKay this morning."

That was when Jake noticed the large computer monitor set up in front of the intricately carved sideboard on the far wall. Forrest and Misty had already unpacked the keyboard, speakers, microphones, and camera. Jake had been in enough classified briefings when he was a SEAL to recognize an encrypted videoconference rig. And just like the gear in the Navy, this stuff was top-of-the-line. Maybe even a little better.

"You have time to grab some coffee if you want." Misty grinned. "Unless you want to stand there and watch Forrest and me plug in cable connectors."

Jake chuckled. "No. I'll leave you guys to your toys. Coffee's a lot more my style in the morning."

Especially since someone had been nice enough to make a fresh pot. Then again, he was so exhausted, he would have settled for whatever was leftover from last night. Sniffing the air appreciatively, he headed into the kitchen. As he grabbed a mug from the rack on the counter, Jake tried to tell himself the reason he was so tired was due to the five-hour time difference between DC and London, but he knew that was BS.

Not wanting to think about the real reason behind his insomnia last night, Jake poured coffee into the mug, then snooped through the cabinets for some cookies. He'd hoped for more of those shortbreads but couldn't find any, so he went for the chocolate chip ones instead. He'd have breakfast after the videoconference with McKay.

Coffee and pack of cookies in hand, he went back into the living room and flopped down in a wingback chair, watching Forrest and Misty work. From the way they handed cables and connectors back and forth, he got the feeling the two of them had done this a lot.

As he wolfed down one cookie and took another out of the package, Jake caught the covert looks and secretive smiles Forrest and Misty gave each other. When Forrest moved closer to where Jake was sitting to reposition a camera tripod, he picked up Misty's scent on the man.

I'll be damned. They're sleeping together.

For a moment, he wondered how that might affect team chemistry but then quickly dismissed the concern. Based on the conversation with Jes last night—not to mention the bad attitude his fellow werewolves seemed to have— they were already the most dysfunctional team in existence. What could a relationship between Forrest and Misty hurt? At least they liked each other.

Thinking about last night made Jake's inner wolf suddenly restless. Jestina was the real reason he hadn't slept. Besides being uncomfortable around him and the other werewolves, she'd as much as said she considered them no different than whatever had killed her previous teammates. She thought they were monsters.

His fingertips tingled, and he tightened his grip on the mug. If he didn't get it together, his fangs and claws were going to come out. But it was damn hard. He was seriously pissed. More than that, he was disappointed.

Jake had taken the job with STAT because McKay told him he wouldn't have to hide what he was, that his coworkers would accept him as an equal. Instead, Jes thought of him as a freak.

When he'd first met her at the embassy, not only had she been more stunning than her photo, but she'd also smelled frigging amazing, and he'd wanted more than anything for her to like him despite knowing what he was. Instead, revulsion had rolled off her in waves.

Saying it sucked was an understatement.

Realizing he'd made a big-ass mistake getting wrapped up in STAT, last night as he lay in bed staring up at the ceiling, he'd seriously considered walking away several times. But when the sun had come up, he was still there. For one thing, he was a frigging Navy SEAL, and SEALs didn't run from a fight. For another, there was still a fourteen-year-old girl out there somewhere almost certainly scared out of her mind, waiting for someone to bring her home.

Thoughts of Olivia Phillips were still rolling around in his head when Harley and Caleb came into the living room, mugs of coffee in hand. Harley took a seat on the couch while Caleb commandeered the other wingback chair. Neither of them said a word.

Jes showed up a few minutes later, a mug nearly the size of a flower vase in her hand. Some part of Jake—the not-so-chivalrous part—was pleased to see she looked as exhausted as he felt. Obviously, she hadn't gotten any more sleep than he had.

Good.

And now he felt like shit for being happy about it.

Jes didn't so much as look at him. She went out of her way to sit as far away from him as she possibly could, too, joining Harley on the couch.

"Everyone ready?" Forrest asked.

When they all said they were, Forrest typed something on the keyboard. A moment later, a vivid yellow band appeared across the top of the screen, confirming they'd established an encrypted connection secure enough for top-secret information. McKay's face popped up on the screen. Despite the fact that it was a little after two a.m. back in DC, their boss didn't look tired at all.

McKay didn't waste time with pleasantries and launched into the briefing.

"As you know, we initially focused our attention on Olivia Phillips," McKay said. "Even with the supernatural aspects of the abduction, we wanted to confirm it wasn't some kind of human trafficking or kidnapping for ransom situation. Grabbing her out of a high-rise condo in the middle of the night didn't fit any known human trafficking profiles, and a deep dive into the girl's family revealed they don't have enough money to support the kidnapping angle. That's when we shifted our focus."

The image of McKay minimized and moved to the upper-left corner of the screen, making room for a photo of a man in his midforties, light brown hair already going gray at the temples to match his eyes.

"This is Jack Phillips, Olivia's father," McKay continued.

"He's a senior investigator for MI5. His specialty is domestic terrorism, but for the past eight months, he's been part of a joint task force with Interpol, tracking down several top-level threats throughout Europe. Apparently, Phillips is extremely good at his job."

Jes sipped her coffee, both hands wrapped around the enormous mug. "You think Phillips went after someone who decided to push back and kidnap his daughter to get his attention?"

McKay nodded. "Yes, though there's still some debate on whether the kidnapping was simply payback for damage already done or as a way of making Phillips back off from a current investigation."

"Do we know who Phillips and the task force are investigating right now?" Jake asked, wondering if STAT had that kind of reach.

Photos of various people immediately popped up on the screen. Some were of Middle Eastern descent while others weren't. Many of the pictures looked like they'd been taken from a distance, some on crowded streets, some on rubble-strewn battlefields. Most of the men wore some version of a military uniform, but a few wore suits.

"Phillips is loosely involved with investigations of several high-level threats, but he's personally heading up only one," McKay said.

The collage of photos disappeared to be replaced by one man. Midforties, he was lean and fit with dark hair and hazel eyes. Jake didn't know much about men's fashion, but even he could tell the perfectly tailored gray suit the man wore was probably worth more than Jake's entire wardrobe—maybe his SUV, too.

"Is that…?" Misty's voice trailed off.

"I think it is," Harley said.

"It has to be," Jes agreed.

Jake was amazed at the wide-eyed looks on their faces. Clearly, they knew who the guy was even if he didn't. At least Caleb and Forrest looked as baffled as he was.

"It's exactly who you think it is," McKay said. "Lord Arran Darby, sole heir to the multibillion-dollar Darby fortune, permanent fixture of the international jet-set crowd, and black sheep of the British royal family. He's close enough in the order of succession for the media to love following him around, but distant enough that no one holds him accountable for his behavior. Of course, that's only his public persona. What very few people in the world know is that, until recently, Darby was also the most effective deep-cover operative MI6 had ever employed. With his connection to Jack Phillips, he's currently our primary suspect in the Olivia Phillips abduction."

Jake was still trying to wrap his head around why Jes, Harley, and Misty knew who Darby was while he and the other guys didn't when McKay's comment about MI6 finally filtered through. Everyone else looked stunned, too.

"Wait. What?" he asked. "Arran Darby is a spy for the British equivalent of the CIA? How the hell does a billionaire playboy end up in MI6?"

McKay shrugged. "We don't know much about how he was recruited. While getting into the files at MI5 and Interpol was shockingly easy, the firewalls at MI6 are a bit tighter. All we can say for sure is that Darby was recruited about fifteen years ago. While it might seem counterintuitive, it turns out his playboy persona was the perfect cover for him as a spy. He's skiing in the Alps one week and partying in Shanghai the next. Showing up in Moscow for an oil magnate's wedding is considered so mundane the media doesn't even bother to report it anymore. Somehow, the man has become the most visible yet invisible person in the world. MI6 used that to their advantage. Based on the number of redacted files we found at Interpol, Darby is responsible for an unbelievable number of covert successes over the years." McKay gave them a small smile. "Trust me when I say the entitled-playboy routine he puts on is all an act. In truth, the man is dangerous as hell and probably responsible for more deaths than any other active covert operative in the world."

"Okay, I'm just gonna go ahead and ask because I know everyone else is too damn chicken to do it," Caleb muttered. "Are you saying Darby is some kind of James Bond—license to kill and all that crap?"

"Pretty much."

Jake frowned. "If Darby is all that and a bag of donuts, why is MI5 and Interpol investigating him?"

"Because Darby went rogue," McKay said. "About a year ago, he disappeared during an operation in South America. We don't know what happened, but by the time he resurfaced, Darby had gone from being MI6's best agent to someone they wanted to erase."

More photos popped up on the screen. This time there were dead bodies, blown-up vehicles, buildings with the doors torn off the hinges, and belongings scattered everywhere. Before Jake could ask what they were looking at, McKay continued.

"As far as the outside world and the media are concerned, Darby hasn't changed a bit. He continues to travel the world and is frequently seen with all the right people. He even holds the occasional charity event just as he's always done. In reality, he's actually dedicated a huge amount of his time and money building a major criminal organization. And with the contacts he'd developed over the years working for MI6, it's coming together fast. Darby has been connected to the assassination of several leading industrial figures. No one has any idea what his goal is, but it's put MI5 and Interpol on his trail, not to mention getting him sanctioned by MI6."

"Sanctioned?" Jes said in surprise. "MI6 put out a kill order on him?"

McKay nodded. "We think they're worried he'll leak secrets if he's caught. MI6 operatives have made multiple attempts against Darby in the past few months, though none have come close, even though Darby doesn't seem to go out of his way to make it difficult for them. He acts like he's not worried about anything."

"He's taunting them," Jake said.

"Seems like it," McKay replied. "MI5 and Interpol aren't aware of the kill order, of course. They've been going after him hard for some time with the intention of putting him in prison. Until recently, they were getting close."

Jake snorted. "'Until recently' meaning when Olivia Phillips was abducted."

"And Jack Phillips stopped going to work, yes," McKay confirmed. "The investigation against Darby has ground to a halt while Phillips has been sidelined."

"I can see why Darby's your lead suspect then," Forrest said from where he stood beside Misty. "Damn convenient how the case against him has fallen apart. Almost like it was planned."

McKay spent the next few minutes outlining everything else STAT had dug up on Darby and his connection to Jack Phillips. By the time he was done, there was little doubt Darby was the one behind Olivia's abduction.

"Okay, so Darby's our guy," Jake said. "Do we have any idea where he's holding the girl or even how these supernatural creatures are involved?"

McKay shook his head. "Short answer to both questions—no. Darby owns dozens of properties in the London area alone. Expand that out farther to the remainder of Britain and Europe, and the number quickly climbs into the hundreds, maybe even thousands. Finding the girl won't be easy. As far as how he got supernaturals working for him—if that's what's going on—it's anyone's guess. That's what your team is for. You'll need to insert yourselves into Darby's life and find out where the man keeps all his secrets. I have a support team on the way to London right now to provide any kind of backup you might need, but I expect your team to handle all the heavy lifting."

"What's the plan?" Jake asked.

"There's an event at Darby's manor in two days, which will get your team inside the door and allow you to get close to him."

Jes frowned. "And how do we do that when no one else has been able to?"

McKay smiled. "We're going to get creative."

Jes exchanged looks with Jake. Something told him they were thinking the same thing—that they weren't going to like whatever McKay was planning.

CHAPTER 4

"Okay, I knew Darby was rich and supposedly related to royalty," Forrest said in awe as he maneuvered their luxury Rolls-Royce SUV up the driveway toward the lavish house ahead of them. "But I never thought he lived in an actual castle."

Jes glanced out the window, ducking her head a little to try and see all the way to the top of the house…and failed. Even though the driveway to the Darby manor was well lit and every window was ablaze with light, she still couldn't see all the way to the peak of the roof. The place was immense. Forrest was right—with its rough, stone facade and turrets at intervals along the upper floors, it did look like a castle.

Forrest slowed the Rolls, getting in the long line of expensive vehicles that were dropping off guests for Darby's Hope for Darfur charity event. As each vehicle reached the broad flagstone steps leading up to the manor, flashes of light illuminated the night as the London paparazzi took photos and videos of the rich and famous arriving for the party.

"So, Ms. Howard, you ready for your close-up?" Jake murmured from beside her in the backseat of the heinously pricey SUV.

Rose Howard was an American socialite who frequently moved in Darby's social circle. She and her personal body-guard had arrived in London earlier today, coming to the country specifically for the event. Tricking her driver into pulling over several miles down the road so Jes, Jake, and

Forrest could assume their identities had been incredibly easy. Hopefully, tonight's mission would be as easy as taking Rose's place at the charity function. She and Jake definitely looked the part, and there would be hundreds of people here for them to blend in with, so it should be. If they were lucky, maybe they'd stumble over something that'd tell them what Darby was up to with these supernatural creatures and where Olivia Phillips might be.

It was a long shot at best. If Darby was as intelligent and careful as his file suggested, would he really leave incriminating information lying around his home?

She glanced at Jake. Between the impeccably tailored suit he wore and the hint of scruff covering his jaw, she had to admit he looked every inch the bodyguard. She could see herself putting her life in his hands. If she really were Rose Howard, of course. And if Jake really were her bodyguard.

Pushing those distracting thoughts aside, she nodded. "As ready as I'll ever be. I only hope I can pull this off. I've barely had two days to try and memorize every factoid of Rose Howard's life. If someone at the party knows her well, this could go bad really fast."

Jake scanned the crowd of photographers lining the red carpet, chocolate-brown eyes narrowing—like he was actually a bodyguard worried about her safety—before giving her an appraising look.

"If your talent for playing the part of Rose Howard is anywhere close to your ability with makeup, you'll be fine," he said. "I still can't believe you did all that yourself. Now I understand what McKay was talking about when he said we'd get creative."

Jes reached up and gently skimmed a finger across the

latex prosthetics she'd applied to give her higher cheekbones that were an exact match for the socialite, making sure the edges were super smooth. Then she did the same to the ones she'd used to widen the bridge of her nose and make the point of her chin sharper. They were all perfect. The blond wig was right where it needed to be, too.

She gave him a small smile. "I guess all that money my parents spent on two years of theater classes in college didn't go completely to waste then."

Jake gave her a curious look, like he was about to ask for details, but Forrest interrupted him.

"Game time," he said, slowing the Rolls to a stop.

Jake was already out and around the SUV by the time a tall, thin man in a suit opened her door. Jes took a deep breath and pasted a big smile on her face as she stepped out onto the red carpet. The ridiculously expensive blue evening gown she wore had a slit up the side, so it was impossible not to flash a lot of leg, but she made sure the plunging neckline didn't reveal too much cleavage to the cameras. While she'd never met Rose, she didn't think the woman would want a bunch of gratuitous boob shots floating around out there on the Internet.

The real socialite, as well as her bodyguard and driver, would wake up in a local hospital in a few days with no memories of tonight. The doctors would tell them their Rolls-Royce Cullinan had been found overturned in a ditch the morning after the charity event, victims of an apparent hit-and-run. Police reports and crime scene photos would fully support the narrative that Rose and the two men with her were lucky be alive. The STAT support team McKay had sent over would make sure of that.

Jes stopped worrying about what would happen to the

real Rose Howard as she moved toward the cluster of enter-
tainment reporters near the side of the receiving area, praying she got this right.

Out of the corner of her eye, she saw Forrest drive away.
He'd park the Rolls along the outer perimeter of the estate
along with the other drivers, where he'd meet up with
Harley, then stand by monitoring the radio in case they
needed backup…or an extraction. Jes hoped it didn't come
to that. Bailing out of a place like this with all the security
Darby was sure to have would be a nightmare.

As she made her way up the red carpet, Jake shadowed
her at a distance so he wouldn't be in the paparazzi photos
while still remaining close enough to protect her like any
good bodyguard would.

The journalists seemed to know Rose well enough to recognize her, but not well enough to notice the fake Chicago
accent Jes put on. Or maybe the accent was simply better than
she thought. Then again, the only thing the reporters seemed
to be interested in was how much money she intended to
donate and whether she could shed any light on the subject of
whom Darby might be sleeping with at the moment. When her
answers turned out to be too boring, they all quickly moved on.

Jake silently slipped up behind her when she reached
the wide-open doors of the manor, playing the part of a
dutiful bodyguard. The well-dressed man there eyed Jes for
less than a few seconds before checking her name off on his
iPad. The two security guards standing to either side of the
doors studied her a bit longer, but something told her that
had more to do with how much skin her gown revealed than
any concern that she might be a threat.

Appearances could be so deceiving.

The men eyed Jake even longer, taking in his height and build before running a handheld metal detector over him. They easily found and confiscated the two pistols he was carrying, telling him he could pick them up at the end of the night. She and Jake had expected that and weren't too worried since Jake came with weapons of his own—fangs and claws.

"That accent you put on another remnant of your college theater program, or are you originally from the Midwest?" Jake murmured as they stepped inside.

"I was born and raised in Pennsylvania," she said. "A girl I went to college with was from Chicago and I picked it up from hanging out with her."

Accents had always come easily for her, which had not only helped her get a lot of roles in her college productions, but had also been invaluable when she was with the CIA, since she'd done a lot of undercover work.

Jes paused for a moment in the foyer, her breath taken away by the grandeur of the space. She'd expected something opulent and maybe a little over-the-top. What she got was a three-level atrium big enough to fit a basketball court in—along with the stands. Two sweeping marble staircases led the way up, where a huge crystal chandelier hanging from the ceiling grabbed her attention and refused to let go.

A twelve-piece orchestra to one side of the foyer played soft music while hundreds of people stood in small groups, chatting over drinks and hors d'oeuvres. Something told her that if each of them sold the fancy clothes and jewelry they had on right now, Darfur and the rest of the Sudan would be set for years. She ignored the irony of people flaunting this much wealth at a charity event and moved farther inside while trying to act as if she'd spent her entire life among them.

At the same time, she kept an eye out for Darby. She had no idea what she was going to do when she ran across him. Working without a script was a little scary, but thanks to her time in the CIA, she was used to it.

"Would you like a glass of champagne?"

Jes turned to see Caleb standing there holding a silver tray with a half dozen flutes of bubbly golden liquid. The big werewolf was dressed in black pants and a matching vest over a crisp white shirt. She briefly wondered where the hell they'd found an outfit to fit him so well. He looked good.

"Veuve Clicquot, of course," he added, his expression giving absolutely nothing away as he held the tray out to her, like he was simply another bored waiter who served rich snobs for a living.

Jes was more than a little impressed. When McKay suggested getting Misty and Caleb into the manor as part of the catering staff, she hadn't thought the big guy would be able to pull it off. Clearly, she'd been wrong.

As for Misty, she was even more of a natural than Caleb, deftly moving around the room with her tray of hors d'oeuvres.

"Thank you. I think I will." Jes plucked one of the crystal flutes off the tray with a smile.

The omega werewolf shifted the tray a tiny fraction, maintaining the balance of the remaining glasses. Caleb didn't make a move to offer one to Jake, and her "bodyguard" didn't step forward to take one. Everyone was playing their parts to perfection.

She took a sip, then made a show of asking Caleb

questions about the champagne, just in case anyone nearby was listening. He discussed the age and type of grape it was made from like he actually knew what he was talking about. Although he could have been completely BS'ing her for all she knew. She was more of a rum-and-vanilla-coke kind of girl.

"Darby is in the great hall directly behind me," Caleb said softly in between comments on the expensive champagne. "I've seen him talking to dozens of people, but no one who looks like they're the kind who might be involved in kidnapping a kid. Though to be truthful, I don't know what a person like that is supposed to look like."

"Have you had a chance to snoop around yet?" Jake asked.

While he directed the question at Caleb, he leaned in close to Jes, like he was whispering something important in her ear. Jake's warm breath glided across the skin of her neck as the scent of his cologne surrounded her. Given that they were standing in the home of a rogue spy who'd already shown a willingness to kill those he considered enemies, she refused to think about how distracting those sensations were.

"I've covered the entire first floor since Misty and I arrived and haven't found anything worthwhile. Definitely no teenage girl, that's for sure," Caleb replied. "But considering this level is open to guests, I wouldn't expect to find anything. I talked to Misty right before you got here, and she hadn't gotten much beyond all the pass codes for the manor's security system."

Jes nodded. Having those codes might come in handy later, especially if everything ended up going to crap tonight. She was about to ask whether the manor had any interior surveillance, but Caleb was forced to move away to serve other partygoers. Jes cursed silently. Jake didn't seem thrilled, either. But it wasn't like they could follow Caleb around like a couple of groupies. He couldn't even covertly talk to them through the tiny microphone inside the collar of his shirt while he was serving other guests.

Thankfully, Caleb worked his way over to their side of the room again. Jes tipped her glass in his direction like she wanted a fresh drink, even though she hadn't even touched the first one.

"How about the second and third floor?" she asked when he stopped in front of her.

Caleb collected several empty glasses from a small table, taking his time balancing them on the tray. "The north wing of the second floor is open. There's a library, an art gallery, and a set of bathrooms in that direction. The south wing is roped off, but they don't seem to be keeping people away. The stairs leading to the third floor are the only ones that are actually guarded. Security won't let anyone go that way."

"Then that's where we need to check first," Jake said as Caleb walked away and disappeared into the crowd. "Misty," he added, knowing she was listening to their conversation in her earpiece even though she hadn't said anything, "head up to the second floor. If we can find a way up to the third, that skill of yours will come in handy."

Giving Jake a slight nod, Jes casually headed toward the stairs, exchanging niceties with a few people she passed along the way. It was almost funny the way everyone greeted her as a close friend, even though she doubted most of them knew anything more about Rose Howard than her name.

When she and Jake reached the second-floor landing, Jes glanced to her right to see a hulking guy in a dark suit standing at the foot of the stairs to the third floor. If the unmistakable bulge of a weapon under the man's jacket wasn't enough to keep people away, the stone-cold expression on his face would be.

Jes headed to the left, following several other people toward the library and art gallery Caleb had mentioned. She'd only gotten a few steps when a deep voice called her name. Well, Rose Howard's name actually.

Stopping, she turned, expecting to see yet another stranger with a fake smile pasted on his face, but instead found Arran Darby coming her way, an expression that could only be described as intrigue on his face.

"Rose," he said with a grin. "It's been a long time."

Putting one hand on her hip and the other on her shoulder, he leaned in to kiss her cheek, getting way too close to her lips for comfort. Then he was pulling back, leaving one hand on her waist as his hazel eyes locked on her mouth for a moment before continuing down to her exposed cleavage. Finally—after about five seconds too long—his gaze returned to hers.

"I must say, you look as beautiful as ever."

The weight of his words—not to mention the look in his eyes—hit Jes like a ton of bricks. Oh, crap. Rose Howard didn't merely move within Darby's social circles: they'd slept together!

Alarm bells went off in Jes's head as she fought to stay calm, worried Darby would see through her makeup job.

But when he didn't accuse her of being an imposter, she took a breath and gave him what she hoped was a warm smile.

"It has been a long time, hasn't it?" she murmured, resisting the urge to move away from him. The feel of his hands on her was making her skin crawl. "Thank you for inviting me tonight."

"Of course," he replied softly, and for a moment, Jes was afraid the man might try to kiss her—on the lips this time. But instead, he took a step back, one hand sliding down to capture hers.

The distance gave Jes the opportunity to assess Arran Darby. He seemed different than his photos. Bigger and more powerful. There was something about how he carried himself that didn't exactly meet with her expectations of a rich, entitled aristocrat.

Jes was still trying to figure out what it was about Darby that creeped her out when she heard Jake clear his throat. He was trying to look professional, but Jes noticed the tension in his shoulders. Something about Darby was making Jake uncomfortable, too.

If the way his mouth tightened was any indication, Darby didn't seem very happy about the interruption.

"Arran, let me introduce my bodyguard, Jake," she said before she realized her faux pas. Rich people didn't introduce their bodyguards. But the words were out, and she couldn't take them back. "Jake, Lord Arran Darby."

Jake and Darby stared at each other for a moment, distaste obvious on their faces as they shook hands. Jes didn't miss the way they tried to crush each other's grip. The alpha-male behavior would have been amusing if it wasn't for the fact that Darby was a trained killer who was almost certainly responsible for Jaime's and Neal's murders.

"Should I be concerned you felt the need to bring your bodyguard with you?" Darby asked, a curious expression on his face as he turned his gaze on her. "Is there a particular threat I should know about?"

For a moment, Jes thought maybe Darby might actually care for Rose and that she might be able to use it to her advantage. But then she caught the challenge in his eyes and decided it was probably more about male pride than anything else. Did he think she was sleeping with Jake, too?

Like I'd ever sleep with a werewolf.

"Nothing like that," she laughed. "But a woman can never be too careful. It makes no sense paying someone to be my bodyguard, then leaving him in the car like an umbrella. What if it rains?"

Darby regarded her thoughtfully, like he didn't really understand the comparison. Or maybe he did and couldn't come up with a witty response. Finally, he nodded and gave her a dashing smile that struck Jes as somewhat practiced. Ignoring Jake like he no longer existed, Darby slipped a hand behind her back, turning them toward the north wing of the manor.

"I was hoping to run into you tonight," he murmured as they walked. "There are several recent additions to my gallery I want to show you."

Jes glanced over her shoulder to see Jake following them, an unreadable expression on his face.

Darby must have picked up on her hesitation because he stopped and gestured at the man guarding the staircase to the third floor. "Damien can walk with us if you have concerns about your safety. Your bodyguard can take a break, or whatever it is he does when he's not guarding your body."

Jake clenched his jaw and he looked like he wanted to argue, but Jes motioned with her eyes at the set of stairs Damien had just vacated. She wasn't sure how long Jake and Misty had to get up there before the man was replaced by someone else, and this opportunity was too good to miss.

Giving Jake a nod—and hoping he'd picked up on her signal—Jes turned and allowed Darby to guide her down the hall toward the gallery, trying to ignore how creepy his hand felt.

Jake had no idea what it was, but there was something seriously wrong with Darby. Simply put, the man didn't smell right, and his inner wolf didn't like it. His inner wolf also didn't like the predatory look in Darby's eyes when he leaned in to kiss Jes. In fact, Jake had to fight the urge to rip the guy's face off.

What was it about the man that made his claws and fangs want to come out?

Darby wasn't physically intimidating. Six feet tall, he was maybe 190 pounds at most. But at the same time, there was something about the man that said he was dangerous.

That he was a killer.

In the end though, it was the man's smell that most made Jake's inner wolf wary. He'd never been around anyone who smelled like Darby. It was nearly impossible to define exactly what the man smelled like because he didn't smell like anything. Actually, that wasn't true. The guy had a scent, but it was muddy. Like someone had taken the scents from five or six people, mixed it all up in a bottle, and then dumped it all over themselves.

He was still considering if Darby had done something to mask his scent when he realized the man was still staying way too close to Jes—and that she didn't seem thrilled about it.

That makes two of us.

Jake stepped closer and cleared his throat, ignoring the glare Darby threw his way. The moment he felt the man's crushing grip as they shook hands, he realized Darby was a hell of a lot stronger than he looked. Definitely much stronger than anyone his size should be.

He was so wrapped up in wondering how that was possible that Jake barely heard the conversation going on between Jes and Darby. It wasn't until the big security guard over by the staircase joined them—his scent as strange and vacant as Darby's—that he realized Jes was on the move. Then he caught the discreet gesture she made toward the steps and realized she'd orchestrated things so he and Misty could search the third floor.

He was impressed by her quick thinking.

Jes disappeared down the hallway and around the corner with Darby and Damien, the sounds of her fake Chicago accent continuing to filter softly through his earbud. If Jes got into trouble, he'd hear it and get there before anything happened. Still, something about leaving her alone with Darby bothered him. So much so that his fingertips and gums tingled. Damn, he could already feel his fangs starting to extend.

The reaction surprised him, especially considering Jes didn't even like him. If he had time, Jake would have dug deeper into why his inner wolf was losing his shit, but he didn't. Jes had taken a risk to give him and Misty a chance to get upstairs. He'd be damned if he'd waste it.

Turning, Jake casually headed for the stairs like he had every right in the world to go up to the third floor. He half expected someone to stop him, but even though there were at least a half dozen people in sight, none of them said a word.

"Misty, I'm on my way up to the third floor," he said softly into his mic. "Meet me up there—and move fast. I don't know when another of Darby's men is going to show up to guard the steps."

There weren't any security cameras on the third floor and Jake's nose told him nobody was up there, either. That meant he didn't have to worry about being careful as he started to search the seemingly endless number of rooms.

The first three he came to were bedrooms. They were all large and lavishly decorated, each with a small office or reading area off the main space. He was tempted to snoop around, but he knew it would be a waste of time. He could tell within seconds of walking into them that the rooms hadn't been used by anyone in a while. That weird, muddy scent he associated with Darby was everywhere along the third floor, but faint enough in those rooms to make him think the man hadn't been in any of them for weeks.

Jake slipped into the main hallway to head for the next

room when Misty hurried toward him, glancing over her shoulder every few steps. Like Caleb, she was dressed like the other waitstaff, her vivid purple hair pulled back in a bun.

"Caleb is keeping an eye on the stairs," she said. "He'll let us know if anyone heads up here."

He nodded, gesturing to the rooms on his left. "You take that side."

Misty disappeared into the first room on her side of the hallway while he did the same on his side, finding a few more bedrooms and a study that stunk of old cigar smoke. The stench made his nose burn, and he moved out of there as fast as he could, onto the next room.

The whole time he searched, he heard Jes's voice in his earbud as she talked to Darby about art and his charity efforts. Jake tried to stay focused on what he was supposed to be doing but found himself standing in the middle of yet another bedroom, listening to her soft tones as if mesmerized.

It wasn't until Misty practically shouted his name that he snapped out of his daze. *Shit.* He shook his head, striding out of the room and across the hallway. He needed to get it together before he let something stupid happen.

Misty was in Darby's home office. Although calling it that was a disservice. The room was almost twice as big as the conference room at STAT. In addition to the immense antique desk near the back wall, there was a conference table with a dozen chairs on one end of the room, and four monster leather chairs around a coffee table on the other. Bookshelves lined the wall on the left, while several gigantic TVs filled the one on his right. The space reeked of Darby's scent, meaning he clearly spent a lot of time in there.

Misty pulled out the rolling chair behind the desk and sat down, her eyes almost glowing as she appraised the big-screen monitor and sleek keyboard in front of her. She seemed even more petite in the fancy leather chair. Younger, too. Jake absently wondered how someone like her had ended up in a covert organization like STAT. Outside of her unique talent, it didn't seem like a good fit.

"Darby's computer. Nice," he said, closing the door and locking it, then walking around the desk to stand beside her. In his earpiece, Caleb murmured there were now two guards stationed at the bottom of the steps on the second-floor landing. "Let's hope he left something incriminating on there."

Misty rested her hands on the keyboard. "Actually, it's a wireless access point to the server, so it's even better. As for him leaving something incriminating on it, I've learned people put far more of their lives into the digital realm than they ever realize. Even people like Darby, who are obviously extremely careful not to make mistakes. All I have to do is find it."

Jake hoped she was right. "What can I do to help?"

"Watch my back while I'm inside," she said, her voice distracted, like she was already lost in a world of her own. "A system like this is going to have a lot of security firewalls in place to keep me out. Once I'm in there, I'll be pretty much out of it, so if anyone comes in here, I'll be completely defenseless."

That sounded scary as hell.

"I got you covered," Jake assured her.

He would have asked her if there was anything he needed to know—like how long it would take her or what to do if there was an emergency—but before he could, Misty went still and her lavender eyes went completely white.

Okay, that's not creepy at all.

He stood there, not sure if he should stay close or give her space. After a moment, he decided to search the rest of the office. More to give himself something to do than because he thought he'd find anything.

While he rifled through the drawers of Darby's desk, he kept part of his attention focused on Misty, in case something went wrong, and the other part on the bud in his ear. Caleb occasionally gave him an update on the status of the guards downstairs, while Forrest checked in once to let them know everything was quiet outside, where he and Harley were stationed. The majority of the stuff on the radio was Jes talking with Darby.

While their conversation mostly revolved around the art in his private gallery, it didn't take long for Jake to figure out Darby was trying to talk her—or more precisely Rose—into his bed. Based on the things he said, it was someplace the woman had been before—many times. For some reason, the idea of Darby trying to get Jes into his bed—even if he thought she was someone else—bothered the hell out of him. Actually, it did more than bother him. It made his gums ache as his fangs fought to slide out.

Jake was so busy trying to understand why he'd react like that about a woman he'd known for a few days—one who was clearly disgusted by his very existence—he didn't even realize what Caleb was saying over the radio until he picked up the smell of the three men approaching from the end of the hallway.

"Jake! Do you copy?" Caleb's voice was urgent in his ear.

"Three of Darby's guards headed upstairs and are coming your way. You need to make yourselves scarce."

Shit.

Jake threw a quick glance at Misty, praying she'd heard Caleb's warning and had hopped out of the computer, but no such luck. Her eyes were still milk white, her body in the exact same position it had been in for the past fifteen minutes.

He darted over to the door, listening for a moment to confirm the men were definitely coming toward them. They were halfway down the hall, going room to room, conducting a slow security sweep. Jake silently cursed again, more colorfully this time, then hurried back over to Misty. He put a hand on her shoulder, gently giving it a shake. She wasn't as stiff as he thought she'd be. In fact, she was so relaxed she almost fell over and he had to catch her.

"Misty, we have to get out of here," he said. "Company's coming and we can't be here when it arrives."

Jake heard Jes's voice stutter a little in his earpiece. She'd obviously been listening in on what was happening as she continued to keep Darby occupied.

Out in the hall, the men were getting closer by the second.

Jake shook Misty again, a little harder this time, and leaned in close to hiss in her ear. "Dammit, Misty, wake up. We have about thirty seconds until those men get here, and then the shit is going to hit the fan."

"That's not going to work," Forrest said over the radio. "Misty can't hear you when she's deep in a computer like that. You're going to have to wait until she comes out of it on her own."

Effing great.

"We don't have time to wait for her to come out on her own," he growled. "I have no problem taking care of those three guards when they come in here, but there's almost certainly going to be some shooting, and Misty is positioned right in front of the door like a sitting duck. Can't I just…I don't know…yank her away from the computer? Disconnect her?"

"No!" Forrest almost shouted, his voice on the verge of what sounded like terror. "If you do that, you could trap her mind inside the computer with no way to get back. It'd be worse than killing her."

You've got to be kidding me. That sounded like something out of a screwed-up sci-fi movie.

"Then what the hell can I do?" he demanded, glancing at the door. The footsteps outside were getting closer.

"Delay the guards and give her more time," Forrest said. "She has to come out of the computer on her own."

Jake clenched his jaw, a rumbling growl building deep in his chest as he looked at Misty's defenseless form. "Caleb, I'm going to need a distraction—a big-ass one. Because when shit starts getting loud up here, I want the rest of Darby's guards heading in another direction."

"You have anything particular in mind?" Caleb asked casually, as if they had all the frigging time in the world.

Jake growled again. *Seriously?* Did the omega need to be told how to do everything or was he simply screwing with his pack's alpha?

"I don't care, Caleb. Feel free to be creative."

"Creative." Caleb chuckled. "I can do creative."

Jake didn't have much time to wonder if he was going to

regret giving Caleb so much freedom because just then, the doorknob rattled. A moment later, the door shuddered as whoever was on the other side tried to shove their way in.

Jake glanced at Misty and saw she seemed no closer to coming out of her trance than she'd been five minutes ago. She was so completely vulnerable right now that he didn't want to think how bad it would be if Darby's guards got past him.

He didn't have to think about it because he wasn't going to let that happen.

Jaw tight, Jake headed for the door when it burst open, swinging so hard on its hinges it bounced off the wall. It probably would have slammed shut again if not for the three big men shoving their way into the room.

They stared at Jake, clearly stunned to find him in there. All three of them held handguns, making Jake wish he had one of his own. He might have had fangs and claws, but that didn't mean he didn't like the comfort that came from holding on to a large-caliber automatic.

But as interested as they were in Jake, it was Misty—her hands still resting loosely on the keyboard, her eyes glowing white—that held their attention. The men seemed to realize at the same time that she was doing something to the computer because their weapons came up as one.

Letting out a low growl, Jake rushed the men, the muscles of his lower back and legs twisting and lengthening as he crossed the room. His claws and fangs ached to rip their way out too, but he forced them to stay where they were, praying he could get out of this without tearing the men completely apart. Yeah, they probably wouldn't have any problem killing him and Misty, and if he'd had a weapon, it might have been a different story. Despite that, Jake still wasn't keen on taking on the role of monster. Not unless he absolutely had to.

Jake was still a few feet away when the two men in front dropped to their knees and opened fire, while the one in the back took aim at Misty.

A bullet creased Jake's rib. He felt the sting sure enough, but it didn't slow him down. Ignoring it, he crashed into the middle of the three men. He expected them to stop shooting, but they didn't—even if that meant they were as likely to shoot each other as him.

Jake tried to keep control over his inner wolf, tried to use the animal's strength, speed, and agility without letting it take over. He succeeded for the most part. Snapping the wrist of the man who'd been aiming at Misty, Jake flung him on top of his buddy, then delivered a brutal punch to his throat before doing the same to the guy he'd landed on. A wrenching twist put the third man down with a broken neck.

It seemed like forever since the men had burst into the room, but it couldn't have been more than a few minutes. Still, there'd been a lot of gunshots, which meant there were probably more guards on the way.

Where the hell is Caleb and his distraction?

Jake turned to Misty, praying the noise had pulled her out of her trance. But what he saw dropped his heart into the pit of his stomach—actually, it was what he didn't see.

Misty was gone, the desk where she'd been sitting shredded and scarred from multiple bullets, the keyboard nothing but tiny pieces of plastic strewn over the antique wood.

Shit.

Shit.

Shit.

Jake raced around the desk, sliding to a stop when he saw Misty sprawled on the carpet. He didn't see any blood, but she was as pale as a sheet. Her eyes were even whiter and brighter than before, like two fluorescent bulbs.

He dropped down to her side, sighing in relief when he heard a heartbeat. But then he remembered what Forrest had said—just because she had a heartbeat didn't mean she was okay.

What if she's still in the computer?

"We have a problem," he said into his radio mic even as he heard the thud of leather shoes on marble steps. More guards were coming this way. "Misty's alive but she's down, and I don't think she was able to disconnect from Darby's computer before it happened."

Before Forrest or anyone else could reply, an explosion shook the entire manor. A split second later, a series of loud noises echoed through the house somewhere below him. Then the screaming started.

Caleb had finally caused a distraction.

Only Jake wasn't sure that was a good thing.

CHAPTER 5

JES WAS STILL WRAPPING HER HEAD AROUND WHAT Jake had said about Misty on the heels of those gunshots when the echo of an explosion bounced down the stairwell from the third floor and ricocheted around the art gallery. Even though she knew the noise had to be connected to the distraction Jake asked Caleb to create, she still jumped. Unlike the men and women around them, screaming and running for the exit in a stampede of panic, she played the part of a terrified socialite and cowered behind a god-awful sculpture so she could keep an eye on Darby and Damien. The two men didn't so much as blink at the noise. In fact, Darby looked irritated more than anything else.

"Check it out," he ordered Damien.

Like gunshots and explosions were completely normal at his parties. Then again, with the way MI6 had been trying to assassinate him over the past year, maybe it *was* common.

It was difficult pretending to be a damsel in distress when all Jes wanted to do was run upstairs to help Jake and Misty. From what she'd heard over the radio, it was obvious they were in trouble. Misty was locked in some kind of trance and Jake was fighting for his life. It didn't get more serious than that. Unfortunately, Darby had moved to stand in the doorway and was blocking her path. From the way he was calmly talking on his cell phone, it didn't look like he intended to leave anytime soon.

Jes was beginning to think the only way to get him to

leave was to take him down when the whole manor shook from a second blast.

Muttering a curse, Darby turned to her. "I need to check on what's going on out there and I think it would be safer for you to stay here, Rose." He must have thought that sounded alarming because he held up a hand in a placating gesture. "There's nothing to be concerned about, of course. I'm simply being careful."

When she promised to stay where she was, he gave her a nod, then turned and left the room, moving down the hallway at a rapid pace. She darted to the door to watch him go, breathing a sigh of relief when he headed downstairs, toward the explosion, instead of upstairs, toward Jake and Misty.

Jes silently counted to ten, then kicked off her high heels and took off running for the stairs.

"On the way, Jake," she said into the radio, praying she got there in time to help.

She hit the steps at a dead run, grateful for the long slit up the side of the gown that allowed her to move fast. When she got to the top, she slid to a stop.

The hallway was filled with a freaking army of Darby's guards, including that big bastard Damien. He and five other men were crowded around a room halfway down, and based on the flashbang grenades two of them were holding, they intended to charge inside.

"Flashbangs coming through the door, Jake," Jes said softly into her mic, hoping he heard the warning.

The words were barely out of her mouth before the men tossed the grenades into the room. There were two flashes of bright light, followed by two loud bangs, then all six of the men charged forward, guns blazing.

From the way some of them ducked, Jake had gotten his hands on a gun and was returning fire.

If she expected to help him and Misty, she was going to need a weapon, too.

Jes sprinted down the hall without giving it a second thought. Grabbing the last man through the door by the collar of his jacket, she yanked him backward, flipping him over her hip and slamming him to the floor before he knew what was happening.

Balling her hand into a fist, she punched him in the throat hard enough to stun him, then ripped his pistol out of his grasp while he was gasping for air. Refusing to think about the brutality of the situation, she placed the barrel of the large-caliber automatic against the man's chest and squeezed the trigger. In this position, the recoil of the big weapon was ferocious, but she ignored it—and the resulting blood—focusing instead on snagging the extra magazine from the man's underarm holster.

Getting to her feet, she approached the room carefully. The last thing she needed was to catch a stray round from one of the guards—or Jake.

Pressing her back against the wall outside the open door, Jes darted to take a quick look inside. The room was filled with acrid smoke from the flashbangs, but she could still see the dead bodies strewn across the floor. Jake and Misty were nowhere in sight and something told her they'd taken cover behind the heavy desk that was flipped over.

The piece of furniture was thick enough to stop the spray of bullets the men were popping off, but the gunfire was so intense Jake couldn't even try and get off a shot in return. Since the bad guys were already spreading wide to circle around and come at the desk from both sides, the situation was only going to get worse.

What if Jake had already been hit?

That thought scared the hell out of her. She'd heard a werewolf could absorb a lot of damage, but how much was too much?

"Backup's arrived," Jes announced loud enough for Jake to hear her in his earbud, even over the gunfire, then took aim and started shooting.

The moment the men realized someone was coming at them from behind, they turned their weapons on her. At the same time, Jake popped up from behind the desk and began blazing away with the automatic in his hand. Bodies started dropping under the combined effort.

Jes was sure they'd gained the upper hand, but then a flashbang came at her through the light haze of smoke still filling the room from the previous ones. Cursing, she leaped back into the hallway to keep it from blowing up right in her face. She hit the floor hard, the air getting knocked out of her. Ears ringing, she scrambled around and lifted her pistol, knowing a bad guy would be coming to finish her.

But no one did. A moment later, the shooting stopped. It was immediately replaced with a roar and a growl that seemed to echo through the house and make the entire third floor vibrate.

Jes quickly climbed to her feet, only to fall on her butt again as Jake and Damien crashed through the wall. Somewhere along the way, they'd lost their weapons and were now locked in hand-to-hand combat, like two enraged monsters. Jake wasn't the only one with claws, either. Damien had them, too.

Jake had been sure the creature that had attacked Jaime and Neal wasn't a werewolf, but seeing Damien fight, she was beginning to think Jake had been wrong.

Jes got up on one knee, trying to get a shot at Damien, but he and Jake were moving way too fast as they smashed each other into first one side of the hallway, then the other, fists slamming into their opponent so hard she could hear bones break.

She was about to say the hell with it and take a shot at Damien regardless of the risk, but then he slung Jake bodily across the hall, bouncing him off the wall. Even though it had to hurt, Jake immediately jumped to his feet and kicked Damien in the center of his chest, shoving him halfway down the hallway.

Jes didn't waste the opportunity. Lifting her weapon, she emptied the remainder of her magazine in the man's chest. Damien flew backward from the impact of all those rounds hitting, slamming into the floor so hard she felt it. She didn't give a crap if he was a werewolf. That many bullets through the center of his chest had to mean he was freaking dead.

Dropping the spent clip, she quickly slammed a new magazine in and chambered a round. The son of a bitch had killed Jaime and Neal and tried to do the same to Jake. It took everything in her not to put all the bullets in the fresh magazine into him. The only thing stopping her was the knowledge that she might need them if they had to fight their way out of the manor.

She was so focused on keeping her weapon trained on Damien where he lay on the floor, she didn't even realize Jake had disappeared back into the room until he ran out with a limp Misty in his arms. Jes's heart sank like a stone.

"We need to go," Jake said, striding past her and heading

down the hallway away from the steps. "We're about to have more company."

Jes didn't ask how Jake knew that. She simply chased after him.

The fight with Damien must have caused him some serious damage, but Jake carried Misty without slowing down. They were almost at the end of the corridor when she heard the thud of footsteps on the stairs behind them.

Jes glanced over her shoulder to see at least ten armed men reaching the third floor. That was bad enough. But then Damien sat up, shirt covered in blood and looking pissed as hell...and not nearly as dead as he should be. Suddenly, the group of armed men didn't seem like a big deal. Damien worried her way more.

Turning, she sprayed the men—and Damien—with half the rounds in the magazine just to make them duck, then ran after Jake again. She expected him to seek refuge in the last room along the hallway. Instead, he yanked open the french doors at the end of the corridor with one hand, exposing a small Juliet balcony.

What the hell were they going to do with that? It wasn't like they could hide out there. The balcony was too shallow. Besides, Damien and the rest of Darby's men had already seen where they were headed.

Jes was about to ask Jake as much when he gently placed Misty on the floor. Before she could question the move, he turned, put both hands on Jes's waist, then swung her over the metal railing of the balcony, holding her by one wrist and dangling her like a toy.

"When I let you go, grab the railing of the veranda below us," he said, dark eyes intent on hers.

Wait. What?

Jes opened her mouth to tell him he was insane—that she wasn't a werewolf with superstrength and animallike reflexes like him—but she was already falling. She released the pistol she didn't even realize she was holding, somehow miraculously grabbing the railing on the second-floor veranda before she fell to her death.

Crap. It felt like her shoulders were being ripped out of their sockets.

She was never doing that again.

Jes was still hanging there in midair when she felt as much as heard Jake leap past her. She looked down just in time to see him land on his feet on the lawn below her, Misty wrapped firmly in his arms.

He'd jumped from the third floor of a building—with someone in his arms—and landed on his *feet*.

Double crap.

Setting Misty on the ground, he scooped up the automatic pistol Jes had dropped, firing it at something above her. She flinched when the bullets struck the metal balcony, but then felt like cheering when the men up there grunted as other bullets struck flesh.

"Let go!" he shouted to Jes before shooting another volley at the floor above her. "I'll catch you."

That idea was even crazier than the first one, but Jes did it, falling at a dizzying speed. She opened her mouth to scream, unable to stop herself, but then strong arms snatched her out of the air before setting her on her feet. She barely had a chance to catch her balance before Jake grabbed her hand and dragged her away from the manor.

He scooped up Misty in one arm on the way even as

bullets kicked up the grass all around them. Seconds later, the big Rolls-Royce SUV was barreling across the lawn toward them, Harley at the wheel. The moment it skidded to a stop, Forrest jumped out of the passenger seat to take Misty from Jake while Caleb got out of the back and fired a MAC-10 machine gun at the remaining men on the third floor. Jes wasn't sure if he hit anyone, but they sure as hell ducked.

Jake led Jes past Caleb and practically shoved her into the backseat, then jumped in after her, deftly climbing over her to take the window. The big omega followed, sitting on the other side of her and yanking the door closed as Harley floored it, tearing the grass to all hell as they sped away. Bullets thumped into the metal around them, but nothing got through.

Jes glanced out the rear window to see Darby and Damien standing at the tiny third-floor balcony, the fury on their faces clear even at this distance.

Turning back around, she looked toward the front seat, where Forrest was cradling a still-unconscious Misty on his lap. Jes prayed she'd be okay.

Sighing, she relaxed into the seat to find Jake regarding her silently, his eyes glowing golden yellow, his jacket torn in numerous places, and the bruise on his jaw, along with the cut on his cheek, already fading.

For a second, her heart stopped at the sight of that golden gaze. Damien—she was sure it'd been him—had eyes like that the night he'd torn Jaime and Neal to shreds.

She immediately rebuked herself. Jake was nothing like Damien. He'd saved her butt—and Misty's—not more than sixty seconds ago.

Jes replayed the part of the aforementioned rescue when she'd let go of the railing and Jake had caught her, cushioning her two-story fall as if she were as light as a feather. It was nearly overwhelming to think about how strong he had to be to do something like that.

As she found herself being drawn deeper into those mesmerizing gold eyes, another thought occurred to her. When had she started trusting Jake enough to do something as certifiable as let go of that railing and take it on faith he'd catch her?

Jes had no answer to that question, and as the Rolls smashed through the gates of the manor and kept going, she wasn't sure she'd ever be able to answer it.

"Is Damien a werewolf?" she asked.

Jake shook his head. "No."

"But he has claws like you, and I heard him growl. On top of that, I put at least four bullets through his chest, and it barely slowed him down," she pointed out. "If he isn't a werewolf, what is he?"

"I don't know," Jake admitted. "But he smells like whatever killed Jaime and Neal."

"I knew it," she muttered. "I knew it was him the minute I saw those damn glowing eyes of his."

Beside her, Jake looked away for a moment. By the time he met her gaze again, the gold had faded from his eyes and they were once more their natural color. Part of her was almost disappointed.

"It could have been Damien," Jake said. "It could also have been Darby. He smells strange, too."

Jes blinked.

Darby didn't simply have a supernatural creature

working for him—he *was* one. Jes definitely hadn't seen that coming. From the look on her new teammates' faces, neither had they.

CHAPTER 6

JES CLOSED THE DOOR OF MISTY'S ROOM WITH A YAWN. Glancing at her watch, she saw that it was almost four o'clock in the morning. If she were smart, she'd walk her tired butt straight to her room and get a few hours' sleep before the next crap storm arrived. She'd been with Misty for the past hour—along with Forrest—and before that had sat in on a Skype call with Jake, Harley, Caleb, McKay, and the members of their backup support team who were staying in a B&B across town. She and her teammates had tried to explain what the hell they'd run into earlier that evening, but when you were limited to creatures that smelled strange, were strong as hell, and extremely hard to kill, it didn't result in a lot of useful conversation.

But as exhausted as she was, Jes knew there was absolutely no chance of getting any sleep tonight. Her mind was insistent on the fact that it was barely ten thirty back home in the States and, therefore, way too early to go to bed. Combine that with all the adrenaline still pumping through her veins from their misadventures at Darby's manor, and she wouldn't be ready for bed for another four or five hours. Which would be about the time she and the rest of the team would be going back to work again, so what the hell was the point?

Not having anything better to do, Jes turned and headed for the stairs. If she was up, she might as well eat. And food sounded really good about then, since the only thing she'd put in her stomach in the past eight hours was expensive champagne.

She was about halfway down the steps when she heard male voices coming from the kitchen. Since Forrest was in Misty's room watching the still-sleeping technopath like a hawk, that meant it had to be Jake and Caleb.

Jes wasn't sure why she came to a stop on the stairs, but even after everything that had happened earlier at Darby's, how they'd worked and fought alongside each other, it still felt like there was this distance between her and Jake. He and Caleb sounded like they were having a private conversation and walking in on them would be rude.

So instead, she stayed where she was, telling herself she wasn't eavesdropping. She was merely waiting for them to finish up. Once they did, she'd continue down the stairs and slip into the kitchen.

Of course, within five seconds, Jes realized Jake and Caleb were in fact talking about something intensely private—her and Forrest. Her first instinct was to turn around and go to her room, regardless of how hungry she was. But for some reason, she couldn't get her feet to move.

"You think they'll ever trust us enough for this team thing to work?" Caleb asked in that low, deep voice of his.

"I hope they will," Jake murmured softly. "We seemed to work well together tonight. At least when the bullets started flying."

Caleb snorted. "Don't tell me you didn't notice the way Forrest grabbed Misty from you the moment you got out of Darby's place. I don't think he trusted you with her, even after you saved her ass in there."

There was silence as Jake considered that.

"I get your point, but that doesn't mean it's because he doesn't trust us," Jake finally said, as if choosing his words carefully. "Maybe it's crazy, but I think it'll work out if we give it enough time. I mean, Jes risked her life coming upstairs when Darby's men had Misty and me pinned down in that office. She could easily have let us buy it. That's got to count for something."

Jes wasn't sure what made her feel like crap more—that Caleb didn't think she and Forrest trusted him, Jake, and Harley to work with, or the fact that, until a few hours ago, she wouldn't have said he was wrong. If that wasn't bad enough, her stomach flip-flopped when Jake said that stuff about her coming to his aid back at the manor. As if he'd actually thought she might let him and Misty die instead of helping them simply because they were supernatural creatures. Was that how bad it was for werewolves and other supernaturals? Did they naturally assume humans would stand by and do nothing while they got shot to crap?

She folded her arms and rested her shoulder against the wall. Maybe they had good reason to worry. She'd heard the mutterings around the STAT headquarters. There were a few people at HQ who didn't seem comfortable with the idea of working with supernaturals as dangerous as werewolves. Okay, maybe more than *a few* people. And if she was being honest, she'd be forced to admit one of those people had been her.

A queasy feeling settled in the pit of her stomach as the way she'd been acting sunk in. Jes had never thought of herself as prejudice against anyone for any reason, but it was impossible not to recognize that's exactly what she'd been. Simply because Jake and his friends were different.

She was so wrapped up in berating herself for being a crappy excuse for a person she missed most of what Caleb said in reply to Jake mentioning her backing him up at the manor.

"Yeah, but do you think Jes'll be so quick to run to your rescue the next time, now that she's seen you in werewolf mode and knows what you're capable of?" Caleb asked.

"I don't know," Jake admitted with a sigh. Though she had no idea why, it hurt somewhere deep in her chest to hear him say that. "I've never been in a situation like this before. When I was in the SEALs, I never had to worry about whether my teammates were there for me or if they were committed to the team. I guess what I'm saying is that I don't know how to make us a team when it's obvious Jes would rather walk away than be part of it."

Jes stiffened. Part of her wanted to be offended Jake thought she'd walk away from the team. She'd never walked away from anything in her life. Had she subconsciously been giving him those signals?

"I wouldn't hold the fact that she wants off the team against her," Caleb said. "Hell, I'd walk away myself if I could."

Jes would have liked to say she was surprised by Caleb's abrupt confession, but despite meeting him a few days ago, it was obvious he wasn't a team player. In fact, he struck her as a loner.

Jake didn't seem stunned, either. At least that's what it sounded like from the soft chuckle he let out.

"You don't have to sugarcoat it, you know," Jake said. "I know McKay pretty much blackmailed you into taking the job. I hadn't thought about it much until now, though. I guess I owe you an apology."

Caleb snorted again, and Jes imagined the big were-wolf shrugging his shoulders. "There's no reason for you to apologize. I was the one who made all the poor life choices, starting with the one that ended up with me becoming an omega instead of an alpha and ending with the one that landed me in that prison in Texas. I thought breaking out of the place was one of my better decisions, until I realized I'd be running for the rest of my life. When McKay made his offer, I figured spending the next three years risking my life for the feds would be worth it for a shot at a clean record and my freedom."

Jes's head spun. It was all she could do to keep from running down the steps and into the kitchen, demanding to know what Caleb was talking about. What did he mean about a poor choice resulting in him becoming an omega instead of an alpha werewolf? And what had he done to get tossed into prison? More importantly, if he'd escaped and been on the run, how had McKay found him?

"So, what you're saying is that while you don't really want to be here, you won't do anything to screw up your chance at redemption," Jake said.

"I'm not sure I'd call it redemption," Caleb muttered. "But back to the point I was trying to make about Jes earlier. Just because she has some reservations about being on the team that doesn't mean it can't eventually work out. I have my reasons to be wary and I'm staying. Maybe she will, too."

Jes almost fell off the step she was standing on, confused as to why Caleb was suddenly on her side.

In the kitchen, Jake let out another soft laugh. "Wait. Weren't you the one who just said Jes didn't trust us enough for this team to ever work out? Now you're saying I should give her a chance?"

"I never said Jes didn't trust us," Caleb corrected. "I

pointed out I didn't think Forrest did, then asked what you thought Jes would do now that she'd seen what you can do as a werewolf. Wherever your mind went after that is completely on you. Look, all I'm saying is that you might want to talk to her before you decide you know what's going on in her head."

Jake didn't answer, like he was thinking over what Caleb said. Before he could reply, a loud ping sounded from the kitchen, echoing in the silence.

"That must be the Skype call you've been waiting for," Caleb said even as Jes heard the stool he'd obviously been sitting on scrape along the floor. "I'm gonna try and get some sleep."

Jes pushed away from the wall, wondering if she could make it upstairs before Caleb caught her standing there, but she barely had time to form the thought before the big omega walked out of the kitchen and down the hall.

"I thought I heard someone on the stairs," he said, his gaze level with hers even though she was a few steps higher than he was. "Couldn't sleep?"

Jes's heart thudded faster. Was that Caleb's subtle way of letting her know he'd realized she'd been there the whole time he and Jake had been talking? But when he stood there regarding her curiously, she decided maybe that wasn't it.

"Yeah," she said. "I was sitting with Misty and thought I'd come down to get something to eat."

She walked down the rest of the steps and started past him when he gently caught her arm.

"Is Misty okay?" he asked, the concerned expression seeming almost out of place on his rough features.

Jes nodded. "She woke up a little while ago. Outside of a

major migraine and some concussion-like symptoms, she's fine. Or at least she says she is. Forrest is going to sit with her for the rest of the night just to make sure."

She thought she might have caught a quick smile slipping across Caleb's face, but it disappeared before she could be sure. Turning, he headed up the steps but then stopped, his heavily muscled shoulders visibly tense. Jes stiffened, too, sure he was going to confront her about why she'd been eavesdropping before.

"I'm sorry about that crap I said the other night about the bags in my room," he said quietly. "I didn't know they belonged to your teammate. If I had, I wouldn't have…"

"It's okay," Jes said, stunned at the apology, even if it was long overdue. "We were all tired and tense. I already forgot about it. You should, too."

Caleb looked over his shoulder and gave her a nod, then continued up the stairs, his heavy boots silent on the steps.

That left Jes alone in the hallway. She hesitated, torn between going to her room or heading to the kitchen. Surely, Jake had heard her and Caleb talking. Not going into the kitchen now would seem weird.

Taking a deep breath, she made her way in that direction.

Jake was sitting at the island when she walked in. He was focused on his laptop, a big smile on his face. She tried to ignore him as she went over to the coffeepot, but that proved more difficult than she thought. For some reason, Jes couldn't stop herself from looking his way. The urge to tell him he was all wrong about her bailing on the team and that he and the other werewolves could trust her was suddenly overwhelming, but then she caught sight of something on the laptop that completely fragmented her thought processes.

Two cute girls were wedged in tightly together on a Skype screen, soft features identical, long, straight hair so perfectly platinum Jes wanted to think it came out of a bottle but instinctively knew it didn't. They couldn't have been any more than eighteen years old at the most.

Jes concentrated on pouring coffee into a mug, then adding cream and sugar. She didn't want to eavesdrop on their conversation—she'd done enough of that already—but it was hard not to when they were barely four feet away from where she was standing. The discussion seemed to revolve mostly around what Jake had been doing in London and whether he'd gone sightseeing yet. It was impossible to miss the way he kept steering the conversation away from him and the work he was doing and focused on the two girls and what they were up to. He kept asking if they'd had any guys over, and from his tone of voice, it was obvious the answer better be no.

That's when it hit Jes.

The twins were Jake's kids.

Her mind immediately rebelled at the realization. No way was Jake old enough to have two teenage daughters. He couldn't be much older than she was, and at thirty-six, she couldn't have handled two kids who looked ready to be filling out college applications.

Then another thought poked her in the stomach hard enough to make breathing next to impossible. Wait...holy crap...was Jake married?

Jes tried to ignore what sure felt like jealousy—even though she knew it couldn't possibly be—forcing herself to breathe and replay every conversation she'd had with him. He'd never implied he had a wife waiting back in DC for him. If he was married, why wasn't the woman on the Skype call with the kids?

Maybe he was a single dad?

Jes—and the little green-eyed monster lurking in the back of her consciousness—decided that was a much better scenario. Although she couldn't imagine how difficult it would be raising two teen girls on your own while working for STAT.

Curiosity getting the better of her, Jes picked up her coffee and casually turned around, trying to be covert about sneaking another look as she sipped the hot beverage. Apparently, she wasn't as stealthy as she thought because the twins looked over Jake's shoulder and directly at her.

"Aren't you going to introduce us, Jake?" one of the girls asked.

Jake spun around on the stool so quickly he almost lost his balance. Crap, he hadn't even realized Jes was there. So much for those vaulted werewolf senses.

—————————

Jake was so stunned to see Jes standing there, it was all he could do to keep his jaw from dropping. Yeah, he'd heard her talking to Caleb on the stairs earlier, but then he'd gotten caught up in talking to Zoe and Chloe and assumed she'd gone back upstairs. Sneaking up on him shouldn't even have been possible, not with his sense of smell and keen hearing. But for some reason, his nose had been worthless ever since what happened at Darby's place. It had gotten so filled with her scent that she was the only thing he could smell in the whole house right now. His damn ears weren't much better. The steady beat of her heart, which normally would have been nothing more than a background noise, now drowned out nearly everything, including the sound of her footsteps.

Hand shoved in the pocket of the long cardigan she wore—which she looked good as hell in—Jes's gaze went back and forth between him and his laptop. He hadn't seen her since they'd gotten back from Darby's, when she'd headed straight upstairs to help with Misty. Now that he got a good look at her, he couldn't miss how exhausted she must have been. It made him wonder why she was down here in the kitchen, getting coffee, and not up in bed trying to steal a few hours of sleep.

It was only when she arched a questioning brow at him that he realized he'd been staring at Jes like an idiot…and the twins were still waiting for introductions. What was it about his teammate that got him off balance so easily?

"Jestina Ridley, Zoe and Chloe Haynes," he finally forced himself to say, pointing out each twin in turn as he said their names, knowing firsthand how difficult it was to tell the girls apart until you got to know them.

"And this is Sam," Zoe said, holding up the silky black puppy with white on his chest and floppy ears that was sitting on her lap.

"And Dean." Chloe held up Sam's identical twin with a grin. Seriously, it was as hard to tell them apart as it was the girls. "We were supposed to adopt one puppy from the shelter, but they're twins. There was no way we could separate them."

Jake shook his head with a chuckle. He'd always been a dog person, so he didn't mind. And the girls were clearly in love with them. "We couldn't have that."

"They are too adorable for words," Jes said, giving the twins and their dogs a smile as she perched on the stool beside him.

Jake couldn't help grinning as Jes, Zoe, and Chloe oohed and aahed over the puppies and talked about all the stuff the little furballs had gotten into already.

After a while, the twins steered the conversation away from Sam and Dean to Jes and how long she'd been in STAT—and whether she was *special* like Misty or an *ordinary* field agent like Forrest.

When Jes blinked at them over the rim of her mug, Jake could tell she'd been caught off guard by the question. She seemed to have no idea how to deal with the fact that Zoe and Chloe knew stuff the rest of their organization would have treated as classified. Thank God he'd gotten them out of the habit of saying the word *werewolf* over an unsecured Skype connection. Jes would probably have lost her mind over the release of classified information.

"As you have probably already figured out, Zoe and Chloe have a bad habit of speaking first and thinking later," he said drily, throwing a pointed look at the twins he was sure they'd ignore. "Please feel free to ignore their rude questions. I usually do."

Jes laughed, the sound soft and musical. "It's okay. I remember what it was like to be young and say the first thing that popped into my head. I don't mind admitting I'm more like Forrest than Misty."

On the other side of the Skype connection, Zoe and Chloe tried to hide their disappointment as they munched on handfuls of Peanut M&M's.

Beside him, Jes opened her mouth to say something to

him, then closed it again. After a moment, she took a deep breath and charged on. "I hope this doesn't come out the wrong way, but I never pictured you as a dad. Then again, maybe that's because I don't want to admit I'm old enough to have kids myself."

Jake chuckled. He'd gotten used to people wondering about his relationship with the girls since he and the twins had become a pack. "I'm not Zoe and Chloe's biological father, but I am their legal guardian and they're a very important part of my life. Which is why I'm still awake at four o'clock in the morning Skyping with them before they go to bed."

He expected the usual litany of questions that always followed an admission like this: How did you come to be the legal guardian to two teen girls? What happened to their parents? Don't they have any other family? Wouldn't it be better if they were raised by a woman? Why aren't they out on their own already? Since he'd started taking care of the twins, he'd heard it all and had his responses ready.

So, he was a little thrown when Jes didn't ask a single question. Instead, she looked at him like he was the greatest thing since free Wi-Fi, then turned to the girls and asked them whether they'd finished high school yet and what they were going to major in when they went to college.

Just like that, Jes and the twins were talking about stuff like they'd known each other for years. Jes didn't ask about how Jake and the girls had met or ended up as a family. Instead, their conversation revolved around college classes, driving, shopping, and what London was like.

"Please tell me you have pictures of Big Ben and the London Eye," Zoe said. "What about Buckingham Palace?

And those double-decker buses—you've ridden in one of those, right?"

"And those black taxis," Chloe added. "Did you ride in one of those?"

"What about those red phone booths?" Zoe interrupted, her blue eyes wide. "Do they still have those? And do they work?"

Jake shook his head with a laugh. Even after living with the twins, it still amazed him how fast they talked. When Jes looked at him with an overwhelmed expression, Jake decided it was time to step in and come to her rescue.

"You two do realize we're over here to work, not sight-see, right?" he interrupted before either of them could pepper him and Jes with more questions.

"We know that," Zoe said, rolling her eyes in the way only a teenager could. "But you've been over there for days. You haven't had any time off at all?"

"No, we haven't," he said.

"You haven't been doing anything dangerous, have you?" Chloe asked, her expression serious now, like she somehow knew how close his entire team had come to getting killed mere hours earlier. Then again, maybe she did know. Chloe was crazy intuitive like that.

Jake hesitated. He couldn't be honest without freaking the twins out, but he didn't want to sugarcoat the risk this job entailed, either. He never wanted to lie to the girls. But as he opened his mouth to try and find the right words, Jes nudged him in the ribs with her elbow.

"We definitely aren't doing anything dangerous," she told the twins, a bright smile lighting up her beautiful face. "In fact, we went to a big charity event tonight in a castle.

The kind with a red carpet, fancy waiters carrying trays of champagne, and lots of those puff pastries everyone oohs and aahs over. I'm pretty sure I saw Zac Efron there."

Jake had no idea who Zac Efron was, but the name grabbed the girls' attention, not to mention put a smile right back on Chloe's face. For no other reason than that, Jake was completely fine with his teammate stretching the truth a bit when it came to tonight's adventures. After all, Jes hadn't actually lied—except maybe about Zac Efron.

"Why didn't you tell us you went on a date?" Chloe demanded, her expression a mix of surprise and excitement.

It wasn't until a moment later when Chloe turned to share an all-too-knowing look with her sister that Jake realized where their minds were headed.

"It wasn't a date," he said quickly even as Jes shook her head. "It might have been a charity event in a castle, but we were there to work."

"With Zac Efron?" Zoe questioned, looking dubious. "And champagne?"

"What did you guys wear?" Chloe asked, her expression going from amused to calculating.

He didn't know where they were going with that question. Or more precisely, he didn't see the point. But the intent expression on both girls' faces made him think it important for some reason. "I wore a suit. Jes had on a dress."

Thinking about how stunning Jes had looked in the aforementioned gown with her shoulders bare, cleavage on display, and slit up the side to expose all that leg was enough to distract any man. Which was probably why he didn't realize Zoe and Chloe were staring at him like he was stupid. Shaking their heads in unison, they turned their attention to Jes.

"What kind of dress was it?" Chloe asked, her face as eager as her sister's.

"This crazy gorgeous Oscar de la Renta number in a shimmering blue color," Jes said, sounding almost as giddy as the girls. "I have no idea how STAT got their hands on the thing, but I'm pretty sure it was worth as much as my car back home in DC. And the Christian Louboutin heels they found for me? They were killer sexy and even more comfortable than my running shoes. I'm going to miss them."

"They didn't let you keep them?" Zoe squealed. "That's cruel!"

Jake was pretty sure those heels—which had admittedly made her calves look scrumptious—had never made it out of Darby's manor. She definitely hadn't been wearing them when he'd caught her coming off the balcony.

Of course, Jes didn't give that nugget of information away. Instead, she shrugged her shoulders with a sorrowful expression. "I guess it just wasn't meant to be. But that dress, those shoes, and I will always have that one night together. We'll never forget what we meant to each other."

Now it was Jake's turn to roll his eyes at all the fashion drama as Jes and the twins bemoaned the end of a relationship that could have apparently changed the world. They were talking about a pair of frigging shoes. He'd be the first to admit Jes had looked smoking in them, but still, they were just shoes. How could a woman get that attached to a bit of leather and some buckles in just a few hours? There'd been a particular pair of combat boots he'd worn every single day during a nine-month deployment to Iraq that he remembered being pretty fond of, but when the soles had split on one of them, he'd tossed them into the garbage without a second thought. Okay, he'd missed the old pair for a few days until he'd broken in their replacement, but that was the closest he'd ever come to developing feelings for his footwear.

"What did Jake wear?" Chloe asked, leaning forward to eagerly continue the interrogation about all things fashion.

Jake groaned silently. Christmas at their place was likely going to be much more complicated than he'd anticipated. Gift cards probably weren't going to cut it.

"I told you," he said. "I wore a suit."

"It was a Brioni," Jes told them. "A classic two-button style, perfect for the part he played tonight."

"Part?" Zoe prompted.

"I was a rich socialite and Jake was my tall, mysterious, menacing bodyguard." She gave him a sidelong glance. "He played his role to perfection and looked deadly in that suit."

The girls laughed at that, asking for details, which Jes was more than happy to provide. Jake had to admit he was impressed by the way she weaved the narrative of them having a thrilling time at the high-class charity event without ever mentioning the danger. She kept the twins riveted.

"Are you guys going out together again?" Chloe asked when Jes finished.

"I know where you're headed with this, Chloe, and it isn't like that," Jake said, jumping in before Jes could answer. He didn't want his teammate to tell them anything that was blatantly untrue or mislead the girls. Especially Chloe. Of the twins, she was the one who'd latched on to him the hardest after the death of their parents. She'd also been the one most worried about him working for STAT. She might support him in his desire to work there, but he knew it scared her all the same. "Yes, Jes and I went to a charity event last night, and while there were parts that were fun, we really were there for work. Going forward, that's what we're going to be focused on—work."

Zoe and Chloe looked at each other in that way they always did, their faces serious again.

"You won't be doing anything dangerous, right?" Zoe asked.

He hated lying to them, but there was no way the girls— especially Chloe—could handle the truth. So, he took a page from Jes's book and merely *stretched* the truth a bit.

"Nothing too dangerous," he said. "We're looking for a teenager who went missing a week ago. We're just trying to figure out what happened to her and how we can help bring her home."

The twins exchanged glances again, and Jake knew they were going to ask for more details. Which he wasn't going to give them even if he could. So, instead of going there, he changed the subject.

"What have you two been up to today?" he asked, taking a sip of coffee and trying to make the question sound as casual as he could. Which wasn't very casual, based on the way they both rolled their eyes. But thankfully, they let him slide.

"We worked until noon, then Mr. McKay gave us the rest of the day off so we could get some more furniture and stuff for the apartment," Zoe said.

Jake glanced over at Jes. "McKay offered the girls part-time jobs doing administrative work for STAT. They don't have security clearances, so there's only so much they can do, but he definitely keeps them busy."

"Austin and Colt came over after they got off work and put together the bookcases we got, then we all went out for pizza," Chloe added.

Jake scowled. To say he wasn't thrilled about two guys hanging around the apartment when he wasn't there was putting it mildly.

"Austin Dunn and Colt Holland?" Jes asked.

Zoe nodded. "Do you know them?"

"I've worked with them a few times." Jes glanced at him, as if she knew what he was thinking. "They're great guys— the kind you'd want keeping an eye on your family when you're out of town."

The twins smirked and Jake was waiting for them to stick out their tongues and tell him *I told you so*. Wisely, they refrained from doing that. Instead, they munched on more M&M's, cuddled their puppies, and asked Jes what she knew about the young FBI agents they clearly had crushes on. At least the guys didn't have criminal records. That was something, he supposed.

They talked for another half hour, and even though it was over a laptop screen and they were thousands of miles away, it was still good to talk to Zoe and Chloe and see that they were doing okay. It was difficult hanging up, but it was getting late back home, and he wanted the girls to get to bed, even if they swore they wouldn't be able to sleep for hours now that they'd talked to him and Jes.

"And remember to be careful," Chloe reminded him. "Both you and Jes."

He smiled. "I'll be careful and so will Jes."

Beside him, Jes smiled and nodded, then made a show of crossing her heart.

That seemed to make Zoe and Chloe happy, and they both grinned and waved before logging off. Jake closed the laptop with a sigh, wondering for the hundredth time if he'd done the right thing by joining STAT. Risking his life when he was a SEAL and even a cop was completely different when all he had to think about was himself. He had two people who depended on him now.

"You hungry?" Jes asked, pulling his attention away from his new family and how his choices were affecting them. "I'm making grilled cheese."

He lifted his head to see that Jes had gotten up and was taking a cast iron frying pan out of a bottom cabinet. There was a loaf of bread and a package of cheese already on the counter beside the stove. He considered pointing out it was five o'clock in the morning and that grilled cheese sandwiches were probably more of a lunchtime thing, but then decided melted cheese on bread was good anytime, day or night.

"Um, yeah," he said. "I could eat."

Setting the skillet on the stove, she turned on the gas, then took a knife out of the block that was big enough to take off someone's head and approached the wheel of Double Gloucester.

"How about I cut the cheese and you handle the bread and butter?" he murmured, moving across the kitchen.

"Okay. Thanks." She set the knife on the counter and opened the bag of bread. "How many sandwiches do you want?"

Jake considered that. "Four or five."

He cringed inwardly. That was way more than a normal human ate and he waited for Jes to say something snarky, but she made no comment about his crazy enormous appetite as she took out a dozen slices of bread.

The Double Gloucester wasn't as hard as he thought it'd be, but he made sure to concentrate on cutting the orange cheese so the slices would be even.

"If I'm being too nosy, feel free to tell me to back off, but I'm curious how you ended up as Zoe and Chloe's legal guardian," Jes said as she spread butter on the bread.

Jake paused in mid-slice, wondering if it was a good idea to reveal those kinds of secrets to someone like Jes. There was no reason not to. With the security clearance she possessed, getting into his personnel file wouldn't be that difficult. Then she'd know everything there was to know about him and the twins.

"About six months ago, several men broke into Zoe and Chloe's home in Utah," he said, cutting another slice of cheese. "The assholes murdered their parents right in front of them, then kidnapped the girls. They had no idea where the men were going to take them, but considering they were in Santa Fe when they were finally able to get away, there's a good chance the bastards were taking them to Mexico to sell them. Twins can fetch a lot of money in the human trafficking auctions down there."

He'd stayed focused on the cheese he was slicing, knowing if he didn't, his claws would come out. Every time he thought of what those sons of bitches did to Zoe and Chloe's parents and intended to do to them, his inner wolf wanted to do some serious damage. Jake didn't blame the beast. If he ever found those men, he'd tear them to pieces—with or without claws.

Jes gasped, butter knife poised above the slice of bread

in her hand, her face pale. "That's awful. What did they do after they got away?"

"They followed their instincts and ran."

She frowned as she reached over to grab a few slices of cheese and assembled the sandwiches. She loaded on the cheese, too. He liked that.

"What do you mean, followed their instincts?" she asked.

"The trauma of seeing their parents murdered and getting kidnapped turned them into werewolves," he said, not looking at Jes, afraid of what he'd see in her eyes. "The instincts they were following were their inner wolves nudging them toward their alpha, the werewolf who would protect and look out for them. In their case—me."

When Jes didn't say anything, he glanced at her out of the corner of his eye and saw her staring at him in shock as what he'd just said hit her.

"Zoe and Chloe are werewolves?" she asked. "I never would have guessed. They look so...normal."

Jake bit his tongue to hold back the growl that threatened to slip out. "What, I don't look normal? Is that what you're saying?" He glared at her, the tips of his fangs coming out. "So, tell me. What exactly does a werewolf look like to you anyway?"

Jes sighed, her shoulders sagging. The breathy sound somehow calmed him down even though he didn't want to.

"I didn't mean it like that," she said softly. "It's just that you, Harley, and Caleb are all physically intimidating. There's no mistaking that the moment you walk into a room. But Zoe and Chloe are nothing like that. They're so cute and precious and the complete opposite of intimidating. You can't blame me for noticing they aren't like you."

Jake let out a breath, his fangs retracting as the tension drained from his body. On some level, he knew he'd overreacted, seeing slights and insults that probably weren't even there. But for some ridiculous reason he didn't understand, he wanted Jes to accept him for what he was. Whenever it seemed like she rejected his werewolf side, it bothered the hell out of him.

"The twins aren't like me," he said softly, slicing the rest of the cheese. "They aren't like Harley or Caleb, either. They're beta werewolves, which makes them smaller and less...outgoing...than the rest of us. They have the fangs and claws like we do, but they're less likely to use them except in extreme situations. Instead, they depend on the strength of their pack—and their alpha—to keep them safe. As you probably picked up during our conversation, Zoe and Chloe are pretty much the same as any other eighteen-year-old girls out there. They care about guys, music, college, shopping...guys. The only difference is they went through something traumatic and became werewolves."

Jes was silent as she put together the rest of the sandwiches. "You said instinct brought you together, but how did you and the twins actually find each other?"

"Before I joined STAT, I was a cop in Santa Fe. After my shift one night, I stopped at a diner to grab something to eat before I went home. The moment I walked in, I smelled Zoe and Chloe. They had been there right before I was. I couldn't have missed them by more than half an hour." He shook his head. "I can't explain it, but something told me they were in trouble. I used my badge to get the manager to show me the security footage, and as soon as I saw the twins on camera, I knew they were in trouble and that I had to find them. Luckily, my inner wolf led me right to them."

Jes didn't say anything as she placed three of the sandwiches she'd prepared in the frying pan, letting them sizzle there for a while before squishing them flat with a metal spatula. A savory aroma immediately filled the kitchen, making his mouth water.

"Did you ever figure out who murdered their parents and kidnapped them?" she asked, focusing all her attention on the sandwiches.

He shook his head. "Unfortunately, no. McKay is looking into it for us, but if I'm right about the human-trafficking angle, they're probably not even in the States any longer."

"You said you're their alpha." She glanced at him. "Does that mean you're like their adoptive father?"

He grimaced. "I'm definitely not old enough to be their dad. I'm more like an older brother, I guess you'd say."

Jes nodded. "It's still pretty cool, though. There aren't a lot of people out there who'd step up like that. It says a lot about you."

He shrugged, not sure why it felt so nice to have her compliment him like that. "I'm their alpha. It's something you'll come to understand about werewolves in time. It might be complicated, but there are some connections out there that can't be ignored."

Jes looked over at him, her expression unreadable. Jake found her dark eyes drawing him in, and he realized he liked the way it made him feel when she gazed at him like she was right then. Like he wasn't the monster she thought after all.

Giving him a half smile, she turned her attention back

to the sandwiches, setting the finished ones on a plate and adding the uncooked ones to the skillet.

"What does your family think of you taking in two teenagers?" she asked, smashing the sandwiches down with the spatula until the orange cheese melted and started to ooze out.

He leaned back against the counter, resting his hands on either side of him. "I kind of had to lie to them a little. I told them that Zoe and Chloe are the daughters of a Navy SEAL friend and his wife, who'd both gotten killed, and that they didn't have any other family. My mom and dad were sorry to hear about what happened, but they're thrilled to have two granddaughters. I have four married brothers who all have boys. While my parents love them like crazy, they're ecstatic to have two girls to spoil. Not only that, but they're twins, which is like some kind of extra credit as far as my mom is concerned."

While Jes transferred the remaining sandwiches to the plate, Jake headed to the fridge for ketchup.

"Can you grab mustard, too?" she asked.

He glanced at her over his shoulder. "On grilled cheese? That's disgusting."

She laughed and carried the plates over to the table. "Don't knock it until you try it."

Jake wasn't too sure about liking it even if he did try it—which he wasn't going to—but took out the bottle of Dijon mustard all the same. Sitting down opposite her, he squeezed half the bottle of ketchup onto his plate and dunked the corner of his first sandwich in the puddle, then took a bite. The bread was buttery and crispy, and the cheese melted in his mouth. Damn, it was good.

"Since you said you had to lie to your family about the

twins, I'm guessing that means they don't know what happened to you," she said quietly, like maybe she didn't think she should ask, as she bit into her sandwich.

"That I'm a werewolf?" He let out a short laugh. "No. There was a time right after I turned when I wanted to tell them, but ultimately, I realized I couldn't. There are some people in the world ready to know about the existence of things like me, but unfortunately, my family isn't among that group. It's safer to leave them comfortable in the world they know."

"That must be tough, not having anyone you can talk to."

He smiled. "I have people I talk to. The twins are just a Skype call away. And I even had a conversation of sorts with Caleb right before you came down, so there's potential there. I'm getting the feeling that Harley isn't big on the whole talking thing, but I'm holding out hope for her."

Jes laughed, a light sound of real amusement. "Two out of four ain't bad."

"And there's you now," he added, though he had no idea where the hell those words had come from. "For some reason, I find myself telling you more than I probably should."

Jes smiled, and once again he was taken in by those deep, dark eyes as they locked on his. "Well, I do have a top-secret security clearance," she murmured, dipping her sandwich in mustard. "Your secrets are safe with me, so feel free to share anytime."

Jake knew a line when he heard one, but it still made him laugh. At the same time, he also couldn't ignore the little zip of electricity that surged through him at the thought of having someone like Jes he could actually talk to about stuff. Yeah, he had Zoe and Chloe, but there was stuff he couldn't tell them. And Caleb or Harley...just no.

"Are your brothers in the military, too?" she asked.

He picked up his second sandwich and dipped it in ketchup and took a bite. The Double Gloucester was pretty good for grilled cheese. It had sort of a smoky favor.

"All four of them were in," he said. "Dad, too. For our family, the military was a way to gain experience so we could come back home and get a job in law enforcement. All of my brothers either went in the army or the navy and became military police of one form or another. Then they came back and became cops in the Santa Fe area, either for the city or county."

"But you became a SEAL." She regarded him curiously. "Why?"

He finished the second sandwich and picked up another. "I wanted to do something different. I loved being a SEAL, but then that helicopter went down, and I became a werewolf, so I went back to Santa Fe and into law enforcement like the rest of my family."

"Why didn't you stay in the SEALs?"

He shrugged. "I was so busted up that the navy figured I couldn't be a SEAL anymore and I didn't fight them on it. All I could think about while I was lying in that hospital bed were the guys on my team who were gone."

Jes nodded like she understood. Maybe she did. She'd lost her own team just a few days ago.

They ate in comfortable silence for a little while before Jes asked him more about his family and what they were like. So he made her laugh with stories about his brothers and their wives and his nephews that ranged in ages from five to fifteen. Then he completely blew her mind with the fact that his mom and dad had known each other since they were in kindergarten and dated all through high school and while she'd been in college and he in the military.

"Sometimes, I'm still amazed they knew it was the real thing all the way back when they were teenagers," he said. "Can you believe they've never even held hands with anyone but each other?"

"That is pretty crazy," she replied with a laugh. "What did your mom and dad think about you leaving Santa Fe to come work for STAT? Since all your brothers stayed in the area, I get the feeling your family is close."

"We are," he said. "Dad was disappointed I didn't stay with Santa Fe PD, my brothers are jealous, even though they try to hide it, and my mom hates that her new granddaughters and I have to live all the way across the country. DC might as well be on a different planet as far as she's concerned."

"I feel you there," Jes groaned. "I grew up in Pennsylvania, barely four hours away from DC, but my mom acts like it's the other side of the world. She's always wondering why STAT can't transfer me somewhere closer."

Jake opened his mouth to ask Jes about her family when footsteps interrupted him. He looked up to see Forrest and Harley coming into the kitchen.

"We heard voices." Harley eyed their empty plates with blatant interest. "Then smelled food and figured we should come down to see what you guys were up to."

"We just had grilled cheese sandwiches," Jes said. "Jake and I can make you and Forrest some if you want."

Harley looked longingly at their plates again. "Are you sure you don't mind?"

"Of course not." Jes got to her feet. "Sit."

Harley took a seat beside Jake while Forrest pulled out a chair near the one Jes had just vacated. Finally getting the team—at least most of it—together for something completely unrelated to work like eating a meal was a win as far as Jake was concerned, and he jumped up to help with the sandwiches.

"How's Misty?" he asked over his shoulder as he handed the loaf of bread to Jes and reached into the fridge for more cheese.

Forrest ran his hand through his hair and leaned back in his chair. "Finally sleeping comfortably, which is why I thought it'd be okay to leave her alone for a while. As soon as I eat, I'll go back upstairs to check on her."

That was a relief. After what happened at Darby's, Jake had been worried about her. While it'd be great if she'd learned something helpful from Darby's computer, her well-being was more important right now.

While Harley and Forrest ate, the mission was put on the back burner and they all simply chatted about regular stuff. Like Forrest wanting to someday own his own Rolls-Royce SUV like the one he'd driven tonight, Jes's fear of heights and addiction to cherry Dr Pepper, and Jake's trials and tribulations of finding an affordable three-bedroom apartment in DC. Even Harley shared a little bit of herself, telling them about growing up in the mountains of Colorado.

It was almost like they were an actual team.

Before Jake knew it, two hours had passed and the sun was coming up. Forrest and Harley offered to help clean up, but Jake waved them off. It was obvious Forrest wanted to check on Misty, and Harley still looked a little tired, despite getting a few hours' sleep when they'd gotten back last night. Jake was ready to fall into bed, too, but no way was he leaving the dishes for Jes.

Even though he'd already accepted the house was going to smell like her while they were staying there, the scent of jasmine and fresh laundry enveloped him as she went up on tiptoe to reach over his shoulder and put a glass in an upper cabinet. It was all he could do not to groan in appreciation.

As if sensing the effect she had on him, Jes paused only inches away, her gaze meeting his. If either of them leaned in a little closer, they'd be kissing.

He took a step back, clearing his throat. "Thanks for the sandwiches. And for coming up to the third floor when I got into trouble at Darby's place."

Jes stood there silently, gazing up at him for the longest time. Part of him wondered if a woman like her could ever kiss a werewolf.

Shoving her hands in the pockets of her long cardigan, she backed away, then turned and headed for the door without a word. Just before slipping out of the kitchen, she stopped and looked back at him, her brown eyes warmer than he'd ever seen them.

"Thanks for catching me when I let go of the railing," she murmured. "That was a long fall."

Then she disappeared, heading down the hallway and upstairs before Jake could tell her it wasn't a big deal. That anyone would have done the same. But then he remembered what Jes felt like in his arms when he'd caught her. She was firm in all the right places and soft and curvy in others.

Maybe it was a bigger deal than he'd realized.

CHAPTER 7

JES GLANCED COVERTLY AT JAKE OUT THE CORNER of her eye as they drove through the city. Since they were supposed to be playing the part of London Metro detectives today, he was dressed in a suit and tie again, with a crisp white shirt underneath. She'd come to the realization last night she was a sucker for him in clothes like that. Not that he didn't look good in his usual jeans, T-shirt, and leather jacket, too, but as the song said: every girl's crazy about a sharp-dressed man. Her included.

She realized abruptly that she also liked watching him drive. It sounded crazy, but she'd always thought you could tell a lot about a person from how they drove. In Jake's case, it was obvious he was in total control of the vehicle even though they were driving on the opposite side of the road in traffic that rivaled New York City's. She especially enjoyed watching the way his hand flexed as his fingers lightly gripped the wheel. She liked his hands. They were strong. Which made her suddenly wonder what it would feel like to have them caressing her body.

Her face flamed.

Okay, stop thinking stuff like that right now. You're a federal agent, not a lovesick teenager.

"So, who's the last person on our list again?" Jake asked, dragging her out of her daydream as he weaved the rental through the heavy traffic along this particular stretch of A206.

At least Jes was pretty sure they were still on the A206.

Between the gathering gloom of evening, the absolutely crappy road signs, and her wandering mind, it was entirely possible they'd turned onto a completely different road at some point. She glanced at the map on her phone, relieved when it assured her they were still south of the Thames. That was the important part.

In the front passenger seat of the Audi four-door, Jes turned her attention to the collection of notes on her lap to check the name, but before she could reply, Forrest answered from the backseat.

"Evie and Henry Robinson," he said, holding up a sheet of paper so the passing streetlights would illuminate it in the dusk. "Evie is the one on the list. They live right across the river in the Poplar neighborhood. She's a concierge at the Lanesborough, an upscale, five-star hotel located at Hyde Park Corner. He's a construction contractor who specializes in building restaurants. They have one kid, a four-year-old boy."

Jake frowned. "Fifty bucks says Evie Robinson has no connection to Darby, just like everyone else on that damn list."

Jes didn't take that bet. Neither did Forrest. She understood Jake's frustration, though. They'd spent the better part of the day driving back and forth across London, tracking down a collection of people who had no obvious connection to each other or Arran Darby. The only noteworthy thing about them—other than Misty had found their names on a list in Darby's computer—was that they all seemed to be hiding the fact that someone in their family had been kidnapped. But what the hell any of the people had to do with Darby or why he might want to kidnap a member of their family was anyone's guess.

Misty had woken up around nine that morning and immediately come downstairs asking for a pen and pad of paper. Forrest had pleaded with her to get some more rest or at least eat breakfast first, but Misty insisted she needed to write down everything she'd seen in Darby's computer.

So while Forrest cooked Misty breakfast, Jes, Jake, Harley, and Caleb had crowded around the kitchen table, watching as Misty scribbled what seemed to be random numbers and letters on the page. As she continued, the randomness was replaced with peoples' names, addresses, bank accounts, names of chemicals, and mathematical formulas.

In addition to being able to wander through electronic equipment, Misty also had a photographic memory. As that first page became two, then three, then a lot more, all Jes could do was shake her head. No wonder Misty had been slow to come out of the computer during the midst of the fighting. She'd been stealing the place blind.

Every time Jes or anyone else tried to ask Misty questions, she'd wave them off. "Don't interrupt. I'm downloading."

That was when Jes realized Misty's eyes were completely white, which made her wonder if the technopath even realized what she was writing. It was amazing to see, but to be honest, it had also been kind of creepy.

By the time Misty was done writing, there was a mountainous stack of pages but one particular list of names that had attracted her attention the most.

"What's so special about this one?" Jake had asked, looking at the page with nine names listed on it.

"Well, for one thing, this list was all by itself behind a Fort Knox of firewalls, encryption algorithms, and counter-hacking protocols," Misty said in between bites of scrambled eggs and cheese. "For another, Jack Phillips, the MI5 agent with the missing daughter, is number five on the list."

That got Jes's attention, as well as everyone else's. They didn't recognize the other names, but with Phillips on the list, it was difficult to believe any of it was a coincidence.

It had taken McKay and the intelligence people in STAT—working with the support team there in London— less than an hour to come up with a background sheet for each person on the list. From there, it was a matter of splitting up the team and the list into two groups and heading out to do a little investigating. Jes had gone with Jake and Forrest, while Caleb and Harley had gone with Misty.

Since Jake couldn't do a British accent to save his life, Jes suggested he let her and Forrest—who was something of a natural when it came to accents—do the talking. Pretending to be detectives with the Metropolitan Police there to talk to them about a string of break-ins in the area had been Forrest's idea.

Not that it helped very much in the long run. By the time they'd talked to the third family on their list, it was obvious these people were all hiding something from them. The first family had shoved them out the door within the first five minutes, while the other two had put on polite faces but said nothing of value.

Jake had noticed the people's heart rate and breathing were elevated, and at the third house, he'd picked up the scent of blood. Forrest had noticed small pieces of glass near the back door of the cottage, too, a sure sign of forced entry. Combining that with the fact that Jes had seen a few kids in the family photos on the walls but the kids themselves were currently nowhere to be seen, it wasn't difficult to figure out Darby's people had already been here and kid-napped them. It was equally obvious nothing she or Forrest said would get the families talking. They probably believed if they whispered a word to the cops, their kids would be at risk. Jestina couldn't say she blamed them.

"Head north toward Blackwall Tunnel," Forrest said. "It should connect to the A12 and take us straight into the neighborhood where the family lives. The Robinsons' house should be pretty easy to find."

The drive through the narrow two-lane tunnel was soothing, and Jes felt her eyelids growing heavy as she was lulled by the droning sound of the vehicles moving around them. Her screwed-up sleep cycle was probably finally catching up to her. Not exactly a good time for it.

As she hovered in that place halfway between sleep and awake, Jes found herself replaying what had happened in the kitchen last night over and over in her head. The first thing she'd thought about when she'd woken up that morning was how close she and Jake had come to kissing. There'd been a minute or two when she thought maybe she'd dreamed the whole thing, but all it took was the memory of how good Jake had smelled as they'd stood there, and all of the emotions of that moment came flooding right back. She'd wanted to kiss him, and she was certain he'd felt the same.

But then he'd pulled back and the moment had been lost. Embarrassed, she'd turned and gotten the hell out of the kitchen so fast she'd almost fallen out of the thick, fuzzy socks she wore whenever she was hanging out at home. She'd barely remembered to stop and tell him thanks for catching her when she'd let go of that balcony, sure Jake would be able to hear her heart thumping in her chest.

The crazy part was that she had no idea where the whole idea of kissing him had come from. One minute they'd been sitting in the kitchen, laughing and talking about themselves with their teammates, and the next, her pulse had been racing and the urge to be in Jake's big, strong arms had been damn near overwhelming.

Jes had dated since high school, but she couldn't remember ever having this kind of response to any of the men she'd been with. Not even the ones she'd thought were special enough to sleep with.

"There's the A12 straight ahead," Forrest announced, jerking her out of her introspection as they emerged from the Blackwall Tunnel. "It should be less than a mile before we get there."

The sun had completely set by the time Jake parked in front of the Robinson's house. He made no move to get out of the car after he shut off the engine, but instead gave her and Forrest a look. "Assuming we find out the Robinson kid has been kidnapped, I think we need to push harder this time."

Jes couldn't argue with that idea. If they didn't get anything more from the Robinsons than they'd gotten from the three previous families, they'd be no closer to knowing what Darby was up to, which meant the entire day had been a waste. From the text updates Misty was sending, she, Harley, and Caleb hadn't had much luck, either.

"What do you have in mind?" Jes asked Jake.

"Let them know who's behind the kidnapping and see if that shakes them up enough to tell us something."

Putting Darby's name out there was a big risk. STAT was digging deep into the background of all the people on the list Misty had found, looking for connections to something that would interest someone like Darby, but there was a good chance they might not find anything. If she and her teammates didn't come up with something, the best they could do was put surveillance on the people on the list and see if that led anywhere. There had to be some reason Darby selected them, kidnapped their loved ones, and terrified them so much they wouldn't even consider talking to the police. Money definitely didn't seem to be the motive. Mentioning Darby sounded like a good idea to her.

She nodded. "Okay, let's do it. Forrest?"

He nodded, too.

Getting out of the car, they made their way to the closest row house, with its bay window and cute front porch. They'd just reached the steps when there was a crash from inside the Robinson residence. It was immediately followed by a high-pitched cry of a little boy in full-on freak-out mode, then a woman screaming in terror.

Reaching behind his back, Jake pulled his Glock .40 caliber with a curse. Unlike the weapons he'd carried to Darby's charity event, this one was legitimate, registered with the FBI as an issued weapon for special access programs. "I smell blood."

Running up the steps, he kicked in the front door so hard it flew completely off its hinges, bouncing loudly down the hallway of a short entryway before coming to rest against a coatrack.

"Stay behind me," Jake ordered.

Jes pulled her Sig, more than ready to tell him what he could do with his misplaced chivalry, that she was a federal agent the same as he was, but before she could get a word out, Jake was already heading toward the sounds of a struggle.

"Damien is here," he said calmly over his shoulder, as if he were simply pointing out the air outside was a bit nippy. "Remember—he's hard as hell to kill."

Jes wasn't likely to forget that.

She and Forrest followed Jake through the hallway and into the living room. A middle-aged man lay sprawled on the floor unconscious, blood pouring from a nasty gash on his head while a red-haired woman who couldn't have been more than a hundred pounds dripping wet fought ferociously to protect him even as she tried to hold on to the little boy Damien cruelly dragged away from her.

At their entrance, Damien shoved the boy into the waiting arms of one of the men with him, then aimed a large-caliber gun at Jake, pulling the trigger as the guy with the boy ran through the living room, into the kitchen, toward the back door. The second man stayed to back up Damien, turning his weapon on them too.

Jake spun around faster than Jes thought possible, shoving Forrest to one side of the room at the same time he scooped her up and dived to the other. Before Jes had a chance to take a breath, she was flying through the air, hitting the floor once before Jake rolled both of them behind a heavy, upholstered couch. He lay on top of her, protecting her with his body as bullets ripped through the couch and chewed up the hardwood floor.

As fast as it started, the shooting stopped. Jes heard the thud of booted feet as Damien and his buddy made their escape.

Jake was up and running after them in a flash. Jes followed, racing past where Evie was huddled over Henry, crying, through the kitchen, and out the back door. As she leaped off the back step onto the well-manicured yard, she heard Forrest tell the Robinsons they were Metro Police and to stay where they were.

Jes was a fast runner, but Jake easily outpaced her, reaching the wrought-iron gate leading out of the garden a good ten strides before her just as the roar of an engine filled the alley behind the row houses. Her heart sank when she sped out of the gate and saw Jake standing there staring at a dark gray SUV barreling away from them, a little boy's panic-stricken face pleading with them from one of the side windows. A part of her wanted to shoot at the fleeing vehicle and try to take out a tire, but with the boy in there, she couldn't take the chance.

She wanted to scream in frustration. By the time they got back to their car, the SUV would be long gone. And so would that poor little boy.

Knowing they had to try, Jes shoved her pistol in its holster. She was about to race back to the Robinsons' when she heard the purr of another engine somewhere farther down the alley. It was immediately followed by a thud and a yelp of complaint. She stopped and turned to see Jake climbing on a motorcycle that was already running, the man who'd apparently been riding it a moment earlier standing there beside him, his mouth hanging open in shock.

"I'll bring this right back—promise!" Jake shouted over his shoulder at the guy as he pulled the bike up beside Jes and slowed to a stop. "Hop on."

Jes barely had time to wrap her arms around his waist before he was gunning it, speeding down the alley so fast the cars parked along the side of it were nothing more than a blur.

"You know how to drive this, right?" she shouted over the roar of the bike's engine.

"We're going to find out," he shouted back, pulling out onto the main road and racing off after the rapidly disappearing rear lights of the SUV.

CHAPTER 8

IT TOOK A FEW SECONDS FOR JAKE TO FIGURE OUT THE Triumph motorcycle's gear shift pattern, but once he had it down, he was able to really put on the speed. The cars around them honked their horns and more than a few people leaned out their windows to shout obscenities at him, but he didn't give a damn. Catching up with that SUV and the little boy those assholes had kidnapped was the only thing that mattered.

"How are we going to find them in all this traffic?" Jes yelled from behind him, squeezing him so tightly he could hardly breathe. "They could have gone anywhere."

Every time she moved her body with his as they zipped from lane to lane, he felt her muscles flex and tighten. He'd be lying if he didn't say it was distracting as hell, but he forced himself to focus.

"Every car has a unique scent, based on age, what kind of fuel it uses, how well maintained it is, and what kinds of fluids are leaking out and how much. As long as they don't get too far ahead of me, I should be able to track them."

"Seriously?" she asked, the amazement obvious in her voice.

Jake chuckled and twisted the accelerator, steering the motorcycle down the middle of two lanes of traffic that had come to a near standstill. As he followed the vehicle's scent almost directly south, it occurred to him that they were heading back toward the Blackwall Tunnel. Good. The traffic in there would slow down the SUV for sure, giving him and Jes a chance to catch up.

As they sped along the A12, Jake replayed the shootout at the Robinsons' in his mind. The way Damien and that other jackass had sprayed bullets around the place without any concern about where they might end up was cold-blooded. Clearly, they weren't concerned about collateral damage. The way Damien had ripped that little boy right out of his mother's arms confirmed they were only interested in getting what they wanted.

Jake couldn't believe how close he, Jes, and Forrest had come to being shot. Although, if he was being honest, he'd mostly been worried about Jes. That's why he'd scooped her up and protected her with his own body and pretty much left Forrest to fend for himself. It was a shitty thing to do, and luckily Forrest was okay, but his inner wolf had taken over, and there was nothing he could have done to stop the beast.

Not that he would have changed anything about how he'd reacted. Protecting Jes had felt like the right thing to do. Sort of like the way it felt to have her arms wrapped around him right then.

"Is that them?" Jes yelled, pointing over his right shoulder. "Just now going into the tunnel?"

He looked and saw she was right. The gray SUV was about two hundred yards away, casually traveling in the right lane…as if they hadn't shot up the Robinsons' house a few minutes ago.

"That's them," he confirmed.

"What's the plan?" Jes shouted.

"I'll slip up beside them, and you put a couple rounds through their rear tire," he shouted back over the echoes as they entered the tunnel only a couple car lengths behind the SUV. "Hopefully that will put them into the wall of the tunnel, and we'll be able to smash in the window and grab the kid while they're still shaken from the crash."

Jake was glad he couldn't see Jes's face right then, so he wouldn't have to see the doubt there. Because yeah, the plan was lame AF. He could think of half a dozen ways it could be done better. A sniper round to the driver's head, a truck positioned just ahead to block in the SUV, another vehicle T-boning the SUV just as it left the tunnel. But all of those options required people and coordination time they didn't have.

He stayed to the left of the SUV as he moved closer, tucked in behind a small panel van so Damien and his buddies wouldn't see them. They were only a single car's length back when he felt Jes reach for her weapon.

Then everything went to hell.

Jake didn't know they'd been spotted until the rear window of the SUV exploded and automatic weapon fire sprayed the unsuspecting van in front of them, a BMW sedan to the right, and asphalt all around them.

Shit.

Jake slammed on the brakes—nearly putting the big bike in a nose stand—just in time to avoid the panel van that swerved to the side and bounced off the tunnel wall in a shower of sparks and concrete chips. Too close to even attempt an evasive maneuver, he held his breath, waiting for the careening vehicle to spin around and smash the motorcycle and them like a bug—or for one of the vehicles following behind to run them over in a blind panic.

But fate stepped in at the last second as a bullet from the depths of the SUV found the driver of the sedan near them.

The BMW swerved out of its lane, ramming into the panel van so hard the van went up on two wheels and started to go over. The recoil from the impact had the BMW ricocheting back to the road, and for a fraction of a second, there was a gap between the two vehicles. It was insane as hell, but he twisted the accelerator hand grip anyway and prayed this would work.

The bike surged ahead so fast under them, he was worried Jes was going to fall off. But somehow, she held on to him—and her weapon—and a moment later, they were through the gap and in front of the two vehicles that continued to smash themselves to pieces.

That left them completely alone behind the SUV, with no one to hide behind and no way to protect themselves short of giving up the chase. For a second, Jake considered it—for Jes's sake more than his own—but then he caught sight of the four-year-old boy scratching and fighting Damien inside the vehicle, and he knew they couldn't desert the kid.

Jake zigged and zagged back and forth across the narrow two-lane tunnel, both to avoid getting shot and to try to set Jes up for a shot at the SUV's rear tires. It wasn't an easy shot in the best of situations. Jes couldn't take any shot that might put the Robinson boy at risk. Unfortunately, Damien and his buddies didn't have that same restriction. The guy in the backseat with the automatic weapon blazed away as if he had an unlimited supply of ammo, while the driver seemed to take great joy in smashing the big SUV into the vehicles ahead of him, bouncing them off the walls and right into Jake's path.

When they finally exited the underpass a few minutes later, Jake decided he could go the rest of his life without seeing another tunnel, even if that one had been less than a mile long.

The road opened up a lot more, and the SUV was able to go faster, still swerving all over the road to keep Jake and Jes from getting too close. Half a mile later, a Metro Police vehicle pulled up beside the SUV and gestured for it to pull over. The poor cop got run off the road for his trouble, coming to an abrupt stop on a concrete guardrail.

They needed to end this now before someone else got hurt.

Jake accelerated, pulling up beside the SUV and setting Jes up for a clean shot at the back tire, but as she pulled the trigger, the big vehicle veered off the road, taking an exit that headed into a more residential part of the city.

Cursing, Jake followed the SUV as it took turn after turn in an effort to shake him. Several more police vehicles showed up to put a stop to the chase, but after the second cop car got shot to pieces by the guy in the back of the SUV, the rest dropped way behind.

Jake had about given up hope of finding a place to take down the SUV when a sign for Greenwich Park flashed by and the area to the left of the road opened up onto a carefully manicured lawn, while the right was populated by little clusters of trees.

"Get ready!" he yelled over his shoulder.

"They're going too fast!" Jes protested.

"I know, but we might not get a better chance." Revving the bike, he swung up on the left side of the SUV, beside the rear tire, keeping pace with the vehicle as it sped up. "Now!"

Keeping one arm tightly wrapped around him, Jes took aim at the back tire a few feet away from her and fired her

9mm three times in rapid succession. A split second later, the tire exploded into pieces.

His gut clenched as the SUV fishtailed a couple times, then slid gracefully off the road and into the tree-lined area to their right. For a moment, he thought they'd nailed it, but then the right tire dug into the soft shoulder of the road and the big vehicle flipped once...then twice...then a third time before finally coming to rest back on all four wheels. Smoke and steam immediately whooshed out of the engine compartment.

Jake slammed on the bike's brakes so hard Jes nearly slid right up and over his back. The moment the motorcycle came to a stop, she was off and running for the wrecked vehicle. Jake dropped the bike on its side and followed, terrified the boy had been killed in that horrific crash.

But then one of the back doors swung open and Damien stepped out, a crying, struggling little boy in his arms. There was blood on the kid's forehead and hands, but he was alive and kicking.

Thank God.

The other bad guys crawled out of the vehicle more slowly. They looked a little disoriented but undamaged— unfortunately. Damien tossed the kid to the driver, muttering something Jake couldn't make out. Without a word of comment, the man took the kid and headed for the woods, while Damien and the last guy hung back, obviously planning to keep Jake and Jes from getting anywhere near the boy.

Sirens echoed in the distance but they were getting closer. The local cops would first set up a perimeter of some kind before moving in. Jake knew they couldn't wait for help.

"Stick close," he murmured to Jes. "As soon as I engage them, you go for the boy. I hate to leave you on your own, but we don't have a choice. Remember how hard it is to kill these things, so focus on doing what you have to, to rescue the kid and get away."

She threw him a quick glance. "What about you?"

Jake let his fangs slide out. "Don't worry about me. I'll be right behind you."

Pulling his Glock, he charged Damien and the other man, popping off one round after another as he methodically closed the distance between them. He hit what he aimed at, but the bullets had little effect on them. Not surprising since the three rounds Jes had put in Damien's chest not too long ago had obviously failed to slow the man down very much. Still, his assault momentarily put both men back on their heels, which was all he was going for. All he needed was a little distraction so he could get close. Then he could use the other weapons he had at his disposal.

Damien and his buddy returned fire, and Jake winced as he felt at least two rounds hit him, one digging through the meat of his left thigh, the other grazing the right side of his rib cage. Ignoring the pain, he slipped his gun in its holster and surged forward with a growl. The muscles in his legs, back, and shoulders became bulkier as he shifted, long claws extending in preparation for the coming fight.

As he tensed for impact, he realized he was almost happy his bullets had done little damage to Damien and the other man. He was actually relishing the chance to physically tear into them. He considered that, especially since he'd never even used his werewolf-given abilities like this before, much less looked forward to the prospect.

Why now?

The revelation came to him faster than he thought possible: it was because Damien and the other man had tried to kill Jes back at the Robinson's place. These...things... had the nerve to actually go after someone who was quickly becoming incredibly important to him.

Jake had only a fraction of a second to ponder the significance of that epiphany before the time for thinking was past. Lunging into the air, he leaped past Damien and slammed into the other man—the one with the automatic assault weapon. He might want to kill Damien deader than dirt, but he needed to get rid of the guy with the assault rifle first. While he could absorb multiple hits from a weapon like that, Jes couldn't.

Jake felt as much as heard the crack as bones broke when his shoulder connected with the man's chest. He was fairly sure at least one of those bones was his, but he deemed the pain worth it when the man flew backward like he'd been hit by a truck, the M4 in his hands tumbling into the woods along the side of the road.

Out of the corner of his eye, Jake saw Jes peel away and chase after the man with the kid. Jake wanted to track her progress through the woods, but he couldn't allow himself that luxury. Before the man he'd rammed had even hit the ground, Jake spun around, sure Damien would make his move.

He barely got halfway around before catching sight of the pistol aimed at his head. Jake absently wondered if it was pure chance or whether Damien actually knew a bullet to a werewolf's head would kill him.

Either way, he brought his arm up, blocking Damien's and knocking his aim off just as the asshole pulled the trigger. The gun went off so close to Jake's head it felt like someone had driven a spike straight into his skull. His ears rang like crazy and his vision blurred, but it didn't matter. Damien was already lining up his next shot. And the first guy Jake had knocked down would be getting up. As much as Jake wanted to cradle his head in his hands and drop to his knees until the pain faded away, there wasn't time.

Grabbing Damien's gun hand even as he shook his head to clear his blurry vision, Jake pushed the weapon to the side, then brought his knee up and smashed it into the man's crotch hard enough to lift him off the ground. Before Damien could recover, Jake reached up with his free hand and grabbed a fistful of hair, dragging him close and head-butting him.

The crunch of breaking bone had Jake's inner wolf growling in satisfaction. But a glimmer of movement to the side reminded him the other guy was still out there, so he settled for slashing his claws across Damien's face before ripping the pistol out of his hand and tossing it on the ground, where it slid under the SUV. With a snarl, he shoved Damien aside, then turned to face the other guy, who was presently coming at him at a dead run.

Luckily, the guy hadn't bothered to look for the assault rifle Jake had knocked out of his hand earlier. But just because he wasn't carrying a gun didn't mean he wasn't armed. On the contrary, he had short, jagged claws like Damien. Even though Jake knew Darby and the men who worked for him were supernaturals of some type, it was still a little weird to see them sprouting claws. It seemed unfair that creatures other than werewolves got to have weapons like that.

At least the creature's claws didn't look as dangerous as his own. Although Jake had no doubt they could still do some serious damage if the guy got close.

Jake risked a quick glance toward the woods, catching sight of Jes about twenty feet in. She'd caught up to the third guy and had somehow gotten the Robinson kid out of his arms. As Jake watched, she put one shot after another into the guy, backing away with the boy at the same time. Knowing how ineffective bullets were against the creatures, Jake desperately wanted to help her, but at the flash of movement to his left, he knew he'd run out of time—again.

The man was even faster than Jake realized, closing the last few yards that had been between them before he could do more than take a breath. The guy slashed at him with both hands, claws whistling through the air. Jake was able to block most of the strikes, but no matter how fast he tried to counter, some got through. The sting of those jagged claws as they tore through his suit jacket and into his arms wasn't too bad, and Jake couldn't help but wonder why the guy wasn't aiming for a more vulnerable target. Then he sensed someone behind him and realized the guy he was fighting had been a distraction.

Cursing, Jake tried to spin around, only to feel a stabbing pain as Damien's claws dug into his lower back.

Shit, he'd been had.

Jake slammed an elbow into Damien's already-messed-up face even as he felt his legs go numb. For a moment, his heart froze solid, fearing Damien's claws had found his spine and that he was going to be momentarily paralyzed. But when his legs didn't collapse, he allowed himself a fraction of a second to breathe a sigh of relief before forcing his stubborn, pain-racked body back around to the man he'd been fighting with before.

His inner wolf shouted a warning, and Jake immediately jerked back, barely avoiding getting his face taken off as the guy's claws swept by mere millimeters from his nose. The man's momentum took him stumbling past, and Jake gave him a shove from behind.

Jake knew how lucky he was even as Damien came at him again, eyes glowing yellow.

This two-against-one crap was getting old, and Jake knew he couldn't keep it up much longer. Sooner or later, one of them would get in a shot that would slow him down long enough for them to gang up on him, then things would go downhill quickly. Worse, once he was out of the equation, there'd be nothing to keep them from going after Jes.

Jake couldn't let that happen.

A growl rumbling deep in his chest, he turned and quickly closed the distance between him and Damien, drawing back his leg before kicking the big man as hard as he could in the center of his chest.

Damien flew backward, slamming into the hood of the trashed SUV, then tumbling over the far side. Knowing that would only give him a few seconds' respite, Jake pulled his gun as he spun back the other way, to see that the second man had regained his balance and was coming at him again.

Jake put two quick shots through the man's chest. He already knew it wouldn't do much, but at least it slowed him down enough so when Jake raised the barrel of his weapon and aimed for the man's head, the guy never saw it coming. The .40 caliber round caught Damien's buddy right in the center of the forehead.

And bounced off.

The guy shook his head as if to clear it, a pissed-off scowl on his face, then came at Jake, claws out.

Jake started to aim for the man's chest again, knowing it wouldn't do much good but not having a better idea. But at the last second, he shifted his aim, unloading his weapon's entire magazine into the man's knees. The guy grunted in pain and stumbled to the grass.

Jake reloaded before the man slid to a stop, putting two more rounds into each of his shattered kneecaps. It was vicious, but there wasn't anything he wouldn't do to stop these things and keep them away from Jes and that little boy. Doing a number on the man's knees wouldn't kill him, but it would keep him out of commission for a while.

That was when he realized he hadn't heard the sound of Jes's weapon going off in a while. He looked up to see that she was still in the woods. She'd shoved the Robinson kid into the bushes behind her, leaving her hands free. She must have run out of ammo because she was fighting off the third man by hand. *Well, hand and foot actually*, Jake thought, watching her spin in a tight circle and landing a powerful back kick to her opponent's stomach, sending him stumbling back several feet, an expression of serious pain crossing his face.

But while the kick to the gut had obviously hurt, it didn't slow the man down for long, and within seconds, he was advancing on Jes again. This time, he blocked her shots aimed at his midsection, relentlessly pushing her back at the same time. Jes was fast and strong, and she knew what she was doing when it came to hand-to-hand combat, but the man she was facing was way faster and strong enough to kill her with a single blow from those claws at the tips of his fingers.

Jake was already around the SUV and into the woods before he realized he was moving, crashing through the bushes to get to Jes and the kid. When he got close enough, he put a round into the man intent on killing Jes. When the man turned to see who was shooting at him, Jake put his next shot through the man's left knee.

The moment the man went down, Jes scooped up the boy and ran toward Jake. She was still at least a dozen feet away when she suddenly froze, her eyes going wide in shock. Tingles of a warning raced up Jake's spine at the same time. In his haste to get to Jes and the kid, he'd completely forgotten about Damien.

Fuck.

Jake tried to dart to the side, but pain slammed through him before he could even move. He stumbled forward under the impact, something tearing inside him. His gun slipped out of his nerveless hand and he fell to his knees. What the hell had Damien stabbed him with?

Somewhere in the distance, Jes screamed. He jerked his head up, expecting to see Damien savagely attacking her and the boy. But instead, she stood there, a horrified look on her face as she stared at him—or more precisely at his chest.

Jake looked down in confusion to see a tree limb sticking out of his chest a few mere inches above and to the side of his heart. If Damien hadn't missed, that would have killed him as sure as a bullet to the head.

The pain hit full force then, and Jake collapsed to the ground, only to see Damien coming at him with a second tree limb. This one was long enough to qualify as a jousting lance and easily more than enough to kill him. And without a weapon, Jake had no way to protect himself—or Jes.

Then Jes was at his side, big Glock in her hand, firing round after round at Damien, slowly forcing him to back away from them until the slide locked back on an empty magazine. Damien stood there unfazed, blood running down his chest in freaking rivers, a smile slowly creeping across his ugly face to reveal his fangs as he strode toward them.

Suddenly, out of nowhere, the roar of an engine echoed in the night and Jake turned his head from where he lay on the ground in time to see a white van swerve off the road and into the park, smashing into Damien. The asshole—and the tree limb he'd been holding—flew through the air, disappearing into the darkness.

The driver of the van slammed on the brakes, sliding across the grass for at least thirty feet before coming to a halt.

Jake had no idea what was going on, since the pain was making it nearly impossible to think. He dragged himself across the ground, fighting to get closer to Jes and the Robinson boy, growling in his effort to protect them from whatever was about to happen. When the doors of the van burst open and Caleb jumped out, he finally remembered the van was one of their team's other rental vehicles. Misty followed close behind Caleb, a gun in her hands and looking distinctly out of place. Harley was there, too.

Jes was on her knees beside Jake. She wrapped her hands around the base of the tree limb protruding from his back and squeezed, like she was trying to keep his blood from pouring out.

"He's dying!" she shouted to their teammates. "Call an ambulance. We need to get him to a hospital."

Lying there on the grass, Jake decided he liked the idea of Jes being concerned about him. It would have made him feel all warm and fuzzy inside if it weren't for the sharp, pointy piece of wood in his chest making him feel all cranky and pincushion-y.

"He's not dying," Caleb said drily, walking over to stand on the other side of Jake. "And we're sure as hell not waiting around here for an ambulance. The Metro Police are already setting up a perimeter. This place is going to be ass deep with cops soon, and they won't be very understanding when they see all this."

Jes looked at Caleb like he was crazy. "But what about Jake? We have to do something for him."

"We're gonna do something."

Casually putting the heel of his boot into the center of Jake's back, he pushed down with his foot, and Jake had about a half second to think about how much this was going to suck at the same time Caleb yanked the tree limb out— hard and fast. Except it seemed to hurt a whole hell of a lot more this time.

Jake vaguely heard Jes screaming something about Caleb trying to kill him, then everything went dark.

He came to at some point later on, his back pressing against something harder than the leaves and grass he'd passed out on earlier. His chest felt like a thousand-pound pig was sitting on it, and breathing couldn't have been harder if he were trying to do it through a drinking straw.

Red and blue lights spun above him, and it took Jake a while to figure out he was seeing the lights of police and other emergency vehicles reflecting on the ceiling of the team's van. He tried to push himself up a little, wanting to see out one of the windows, but a gentle hand on his chest held him down.

"Don't move." Jes's voice was soft in his ear. "We're going through a police checkpoint and I doubt Caleb and Harley want to explain all the blood."

Jake relaxed, trusting Caleb and Harley to get them out of there. Besides, there wasn't anything he could do, not in this condition. So he closed his eyes and let the sound of Jes's heartbeat gently lull him to sleep, her hand over the wound in his chest, her breath warm on his face as she whispered over and over in his ear that he was going to be okay.

CHAPTER 9

"Put him on the bed," Jes said softly after she'd pulled the blankets back and placed several large bath towels down to protect the sheets from the blood and dirt. "Gently, so his wounds don't open up again."

Caleb—who'd carried Jake all the way from the rental van and upstairs to Jake's room—snorted, practically tossing him on the bed so roughly he actually bounced.

Jes glared at Caleb. "I said gently, you jerk."

She wanted to shout at him, but she didn't want to wake up Jake. Then again, if dropping him on the bed hadn't done it, she doubted raking Caleb over the coals would. Still, there wasn't any need for Caleb to be an asshat about it.

"Relax," Caleb said. "Jake's a werewolf. If getting skewered with a tree limb didn't kill him, he's fine."

She blinked. "Fine? You call having a hole the size of a baseball in his chest fine?"

"It'll heal up." Caleb regarded Jake, then shrugged. "It wouldn't hurt to clean him up and get the debris out of the wound, though. If any crap is left in there, it slows down the healing and hurts like hell when it finally closes up."

Jes opened her mouth to ask what he meant by *debris*, but before she had a chance, Caleb turned and walked out of the room, closing the door behind him.

Forgetting about Caleb and his crappy bedside manner, she turned her attention to Jake. She hoped Caleb was right about the wound healing on its own, because judging by Jake's ragged suit jacket and bloody dress shirt, he was a mess under there. She didn't know about the whole debris thing, but cleaning him up couldn't hurt.

Hoping it'd be safe to leave Jake on his own for a bit, Jes slipped out of the bedroom and down the hallway into one of the two bathrooms on the second floor. Taking a stack of washcloths out of the small linen closet, she ran a few of them under the faucet, then grabbed the first-aid kit. She wasn't sure what was in it, but there had to be antibiotic ointment and bandages, if nothing else.

As she made her way back to Jake's room, muted conversation drifted up from downstairs. It sounded like Misty was putting together the videoconference equipment. Harley and Caleb must have been helping, since Forrest wasn't back yet.

Forrest had been waiting for them when they got to the house, along with the Robinsons. Immediately after reuniting the couple with their son, he'd taken them to a safe house the support team had set up outside of London and probably wouldn't be back for a few hours.

When she got to Jake's room, Jes tried to close the door quietly behind her—and failed. She winced and could only hope it wasn't enough to wake him up.

"You can stop trying to be so quiet," a deep, husky voice murmured from behind her. "One, I'm already awake. And two, you suck at it."

Jes turned with a sigh to see Jake struggling to sit up and trying to work his shredded suit jacket over his shoulders. From the grimace on his face, it was obvious moving around hurt like hell.

She darted over to the bed, dumping the towels and first-aid kit on the nightstand. "Stop trying to sit up. You're going to make it worse. Let me help you."

When it looked like he wanted to argue, she grabbed one lapel of his jacket, using her free hand to ease it over his shoulder. Even though she did it slowly, she couldn't miss the grunts and groans of pain as his jacket came off—or the way her hands came away stained red.

"If you help me to the bathroom, I can shower off." He fumbled with the buttons of his dress shirt as he started to sit up again. "I'll be fine after a few hours of sleep."

Jes pushed him back down again. "Yeah right. You wouldn't make it two minutes in the shower before falling on your face. So why don't you skip the drama and let me clean you up? It's why I brought all that stuff in here in the first place."

She pushed his hands away from his shirt and undid the buttons. He scowled and looked like he wanted to protest, but then gave up, letting her gently peel his jacket and shirt off. She wasn't sure she even needed to bother with the buttons. It was so torn, it probably would have come off in pieces anyway.

Jes cringed when she saw his skin was just as damaged, especially along his forearms and biceps. But those lacerations were nothing compared to the gaping wound in the side of his chest. Even though it wasn't bleeding much now, it still looked god-awful. She'd never been particularly squeamish at the sight of blood, but now she found herself looking anyplace other than that hole.

Fortunately, it was easy to distract herself with the other parts of his body. Like his broad shoulders and the smooth, sculpted pec opposite the wound. To say Jake was well built would be a disservice to the definition of the term. He was an Adonis, with perfect muscles layered on top of other perfect muscles. Jacked enough to make Jes think he could bench-press a small car, but wiry at the same time. The combination of the two was breathtaking.

And those abs? If there'd been more men like him around back in the day, Maytag would have gone out of business before it even got started. She suddenly had visions of long lines of women standing around him with their laundry, waiting for a chance to put those washboard muscles to good use.

Forcing herself to stop thinking of things as distracting as that, she focused on the reason she'd helped him get his shirt off to start with. Picking up one of the wet washcloths, she sat down on the bed and gently cleaned the scratches on his forearm. The lacerations had almost completely sealed themselves with fresh pink scar tissue, which was rather amazing. Even so, there was a lot of blood to wash off, and her stomach twisted into multiple knots resembling balloon animals. Furry, wolf-shaped balloon animals.

The funny thing was, it wasn't the blood soaking into the washcloth that had her so bothered. It was the idea of Jake bleeding. Obviously, she never wanted to see a teammate get injured, but she was stunned when she realized it was much more than that. The thought of Jake being hurt made her ache somewhere deep inside.

It took three washcloths and one trip to the bathroom to rinse them out before she was done with his forearms and biceps. After that, she turned her attention to his chest. The wound still hadn't closed over. If anything, it looked worse than before. Like it was getting infected. There was no way in hell that tree limb had missed his lung and she wondered how he was still able to breathe.

"Why isn't it healing like the others?" she asked softly, carefully wiping the blood away without making the wound bleed more.

"I think there are pieces of that tree left in the wound," he said. "My healing abilities are slowing down to give me time to get the crap out."

So that's what Caleb had meant by *debris*. Jes blanched at the thought of how they were going to *get the crap out*. "What happens if it stays in there? Will it heal?"

"At some point, yeah," he admitted. "But it will take a few days, and I'll end up with reduced lung capability from the twisted scar tissue that will build up around the wood pieces."

Okay, that didn't sound good at all. "What do we need to do to get the pieces of wood out?"

"I'll need someone to root around in the wound with a pair of tweezers or forceps and pull the pieces out one by one."

She was afraid he was going to say that.

Jes bit her lip. "Should I get Caleb?"

Jake let out a half-hearted snort. "You don't seriously think I want a ham-handed brute like Caleb poking around inside me with a sharp implement, do you?"

Yeah, probably not. But that didn't leave a lot of options.

"I guess I could do it," she said, even though the idea made her queasy. "I don't have any medical training beyond basic first aid, but if you want me to try, I will."

His gaze locked on hers, the warmth in his deep brown eyes drawing her in. "I don't want to ask you to do something like that. I can do it myself."

Jes wasn't so sure of that. Even if he could manage it, there was no way he'd get all the wood chips out. And the thought of him having trouble breathing because pieces of wood were still in there was something she didn't want to think about.

"I'll do it." She dragged her gaze away from his and reached for the first-aid kit with hands that shook a little. She took a deep breath and forced herself to get a grip. "Tell me exactly what to do."

Giving her a nod, he rolled over onto his stomach, his hip brushing hers. It occurred to her for the first time that she was actually *in bed* with Jake. Although this was definitely not what she'd pictured when she imagined that scenario.

Where the heck had that come from?

Pushing that confusing thought aside, Jes focused on Jake's muscular back, cringing when she saw that the wound looked even worse from this side. She second-guessed herself about a dozen times as she dug through the first-aid kit and came out with a set of twelve-inch-long forceps wrapped in plastic. Maybe she was in over her head on this.

"Don't I need to sterilize these or something?" she asked, suddenly wanting to put off digging around inside Jake's body for as long as possible.

He chuckled, the raspy sound reminding her how difficult it must be for him to get his breath. "I'm pretty sure the tree limb wasn't sterile before it went in. I think the forceps are clean enough right out of the package."

She used one of the wet washcloths to wipe away as much of the blood from the wound as she could, then took a deep breath. "Okay, what do I do?"

"Slip the tip of the forceps into the wound and move them around slowly," Jake said, lifting his head from where it'd been resting on his hands and looking at her over his shoulder. "I can feel the pieces in there, so I should be able to guide you to where they are without too much trouble."

The thought of sticking the forceps in Jake and searching around made her a little light-headed. She really didn't want to do this. But she had to.

Pulling on a pair of rubber gloves from the first-aid kit—because it seemed like she should—she picked up the stainless-steel forceps and slipped them into the gooey mess that was the entry hole in Jake's back before she could change her mind.

"By the way," he added lightly, as if he didn't even feel what she was doing, "there might be a few bone chips floating around along with the wood chips. If so, you can go ahead and take them out, too."

The image of digging out pieces of Jake's bone with the forceps was more than she could handle right then, and she felt her stomach start to twitch.

"You need to start talking and distract me, so I can think of something other than what I'm doing right now, or I'm going to be sick," she said.

Jes expected him to ask what she wanted to talk about, but instead he flashed her a smile over his shoulder that almost calmed her frazzled nerves all by itself.

"I can do that," he said, turning back around. "Tell me about your family. Do they know that you work for STAT?"

"Um…" She paused, surprised at the question. She'd expected him to talk about the mission. Maybe he realized that subject really wouldn't take her mind off what she was doing. "Actually, I've never given them any reason to think I'm not still in the CIA." She let her hands function on autopilot while she concentrated on his question. "I don't think

I could ever tell them about STAT. My family is cool, but like yours, they aren't ready to know about what goes bump in the night. Fortunately, they aren't the kind to pry for a lot of information, which makes it easier."

"Tell me about them," he said before softly instructing her to move the forceps a little to the right.

She smiled a little. Her family was her favorite thing to talk about. "Dad just retired from the Army National Guard and Mom is a writer."

"Any brothers or sisters?"

"Three older brothers. Two of them are twins, which is kind of cool. They're all married, and the twins have kids of their own, which is fun. They think I rock, though to be honest, both of my nieces are barely a year old, so I'm not sure how much we can trust their opinion."

Jake chuckled again, throwing her another glance over his shoulder. "Oh, I don't know. From what I've seen over the past few days, I think your nieces might be onto something."

Jes knew Jake was messing with her, but she had to admit she liked it all the same. The way he was looking at her, his expression somewhere between amusement and smoldering, completely worked for her.

Forcing herself to think about something other than Jake's dark eyes—and what she was doing with her hands— Jes told him about her nieces and how adorable they were. She was so focused on talking about her family she didn't even notice the tree chunks piling up on the towel on the nightstand, along with a smaller stack of something sharp, white, and tinged with blood, which she refused to give a name to.

"I think you've gotten as much out of me from back there as you're going to," he said after she dropped another small piece of wood on the towel.

Jake started to roll onto his back, and Jes slid over on the bed a little, giving him more room. As he got settled, she realized cleaning out the wound was going to be much more difficult from this direction, since she'd be able to see every little flinch and grimace he made as she worked.

She braced herself, but when she slipped the bloody forceps into the wound to the side of his heart, he didn't react at all. Once again, it was like he didn't feel anything. She knew that couldn't possibly be true, but she kept going, following his softly spoken orders about what to do and where to move.

"When we were at Darby's place last night, you mentioned you took theater classes in college," he said as if somehow knowing she needed another distraction at that exact moment. "How did you end up in the CIA instead of Hollywood?"

Jes placed her left hand on the warm, smooth skin of his chest to steady herself as she pulled another piece of tree bark out of him. "I went to the University of Pittsburgh as a theater major and thought for sure I'd end up in movies or on TV, but then I started crushing on this hot guy my sophomore year."

Jake snorted. "There's always a guy, isn't there?"

She laughed. "I don't even remember his name now, but at the time I thought he was all that. He was a senior, from a wealthy family with connections on Wall Street, and didn't even know I existed. So in a desperate ploy to get his attention, I signed up for a class he was in, figuring I'd sit near him and ask him for help with my homework."

"That was devious of you," Jake pointed out, mouth twitching. "What class did you sign up for?"

"Some political science elective." She shrugged. "Honestly, I didn't know what the hell political science even was. I simply signed up for the class and bought the stupid textbook. Unfortunately, within a week, I figured out the guy I'd been chasing was an asshat. Of course, by then it was too late to drop the class. Turned out, it all worked in the end. Taking that class was the best mistake I ever made. I changed majors before the next semester started."

Jake rested his head on his forearm. "O-kay. Theater to political science. So where does the CIA come into the picture?"

Jes took a few moments to collect her thoughts, gliding the fingers of her free hand back and forth across Jake's muscular chest. He really had spectacular pecs, even with a hole currently in the middle of them. In fact, she could have happily sat here all night touching him like this. She could have done without the nasty wound and forceps part of the equation, of course, but as far as excuses went, it was certainly good justification to keep her hands on him.

Jake didn't seem to mind. If anything, the more she touched him, the more he seemed to relax on the bed.

"During one of his many deployments to Iraq, my dad worked at the U.S. Embassy in the Green Zone, where he met and ended up becoming good friends with a guy named Ken Alexander. Ken was supposedly working there as a liaison with the Iraqi government, but in reality, he was CIA."

"Ah, the plot thickens," Jake murmured. "So Ken Alexander's friendship with your dad was instead a thinly veiled plot to recruit you?"

"How'd you know?" She grinned. "Ken and the CIA tracked down my dad in Iraq and became friends with him while I was still in middle school because they knew they'd want to recruit me like fifteen years later."

His mouth quirked. "I wouldn't put it past them. Those spooks you used to work for are known to be tricky."

"True," she admitted, still working the forceps. "But in this case, it was merely random chance. Ken was visiting my mom and dad when I came home during spring break my senior year in college. During dinner, we started talking world politics, and he gave me insight into the stuff really going on in the world, a perspective I couldn't get in the classroom. Once he told me stories about some of the places he'd seen and the work he'd done, I was hooked, and after I graduated, the CIA was the one and only place I went looking for work. Ken helped me get an interview, and everything else is history."

Jake was silent as she continued pulling crud out of the wound in his chest. As she worked, those warm, dark eyes studied her so intently, Jes could almost feel the heat of his gaze against her skin.

The moment she got the last piece of tree bark out of the wound, the bleeding stopped completely, and the edges of the opening immediately began to close up. Even though Jes knew she was done, she found herself continuing to touch him after she placed the forceps on the nightstand, carefully gliding a moist towel across his skin, cleaning away every trace of blood and patting the edges of the slowly closing injury as if her fingers were the thing making it happen.

Jes didn't understand this crazy need to touch him. She'd been in relationships with men she thought might have long-term potential and had never felt this way. Right now, she had an almost uncontrollable urge to lean forward and press her lips to every single one of his cuts, scrapes, and bruises, and kiss it all better. Hell, she was already leaning over his chest a little, so bending to trace her lips over his skin wouldn't have taken much effort.

She resisted the urge—barely.

"It's not all history," he said suddenly, his hand coming up to cover one of hers where it rested on his chest. "You still haven't told me why you joined STAT."

No one knew the reason she'd joined STAT except McKay. She hadn't ever wanted to share the story. Until now.

"Two years ago, I was in Rome with a counterintelligence team doing a sting operation against a small group of former East German Stasi operatives who'd stolen a hard drive full of missile designs from the Department of Defense. Everything we had on these guys implied they were amateurs and that it should have been an easy recovery mission."

"But?" he prompted when she'd fallen silent, lost in her memories.

She sighed. "But everything went sideways when we discovered the group had somehow gained possession of a supernatural. I didn't know what the creature was back then, of course, because none of us knew about crap like that back then."

"What was it?" he asked.

Jes settled over onto one hip, leaning forward until she was resting her forearms on his chest, watching in awe as the wound on his chest continued to seal itself. She glanced at the lacerations on his arms and was stunned to see that they looked days old. *Incredible.*

She met his gaze again. "To this day I still don't know. When the thing showed up in the midst of the shoot-out, I thought it was a baboon or mandrill. It was nighttime and the warehouse where the exchange had been set up was dark, so it was hard to see anything."

Jake's hand moved up her forearm, then back down, causing little goose bumps to chase their way here and there.

"But it wasn't any animal like that," she added, amazed at how relaxing his touch was, especially in the midst of such a painful memory. "It was about three feet tall, though that was difficult to judge because it tended to stay hunched over as it moved, sometimes using its hands to help propel it, like a monkey."

Her breathing came quicker, and her heart began to race as she thought about the creature she'd fought in that warehouse. She'd spent a lot of sleepless nights battling the images that sometimes plagued her mind, and here she was recalling them on purpose.

"The thing was almost completely hairless except for a few wisps along its chest and belly and was very muscular, with fangs and claws that were longer even than yours." She reached up with her free hand to push her long hair behind her ear. "Before the creature got there, my team and I had nearly gained control of the situation, but that all changed when it attacked. It was so fast and vicious. I've never seen anything like it. One second, my teammates were there, and the next second, they were dead, torn apart by that thing right in front of me."

Jake slid both hands up to her shoulders, massaging lightly and relaxing the tense muscles there. "I'm sorry.

I didn't intend to make you have to relive something like that."

Jes crossed her arms over her chest and cupped his hands with hers, keeping them exactly where they were. She'd never experienced anything close to the warmth and comfort they gave her.

"It's okay," she said softly. "I still don't know how I survived. I was beat up, but I injured the thing badly enough for it to run away. The former Stasi operatives were all dead, and I somehow remembered to retrieve the hard drive. When my CIA backup arrived, they took one look at me and quarantined the entire site. They put me on a jet without a debrief and took me to a private hospital near Langley. I was put on total lockdown to give me time to recover."

"Is that when McKay came to talk to you?"

She nodded. "Yeah. He showed up one morning in my room and said he was putting together a special team to handle the kinds of things I'd just fought. He told me that if I worked for him, I might get a chance to find out what killed my teammates. I agreed on the spot and never regretted the decision, though I've never come close to finding the damn thing."

Jake's fingers caressed her shoulders through her blouse. "I think I understand now why you were so worried about working with us. After what happened in Rome, then here in London with Jaime and Neal, I don't blame you for not knowing whether to trust a pack of werewolves."

Jes was tempted to deny it, but that was difficult to do when it was true…at least to some degree. There was more to it than that though, and for some crazy reason, she wanted Jake to understand.

"I guess part of me was nervous about working with you, Harley, and Caleb, especially since I thought a werewolf had killed Jaime and Neal." She gave him a small half smile. "But if we're being honest, that wasn't the only reason."

Jake lifted a brow. "What was the other reason?"

She relaxed against him until her upper body was practically draped across his broad chest, her face close to his. "After Rome, I mostly worked on my own, only working with other agents when I absolutely had to. Losing my CIA team was hard, and I didn't want to go through that again. I know it's stupid, but when it happened again here, I thought that maybe I was cursed or something. I didn't want what happened to Jaime and Neal to happen to you guys. Like I said, it's stupid. All I can say is that I'm sorry."

Jake's arms slipped around her, pulling her tighter to his chest. This close, she could feel the warmth of his breath on her lips.

"It's not stupid and you don't have to apologize," he said huskily, his words vibrating through her whole body as he spoke. "As the only member of my SEAL team to make it off that mountain in Afghanistan, I understand what it's like to lose people you've fought alongside and care about. But I know for a fact that what happened in Rome and here in London isn't your fault. All you did was survive, and that's never something you have to apologize for."

Closing her eyes, she leaned forward until her forehead was resting against his, not sure why she was doing it, but knowing it felt right.

"But what if it happens again?" she whispered. "What if these creatures we fought tonight hurt you and everyone else?"

"They won't," he said firmly, his lips brushing hers. "We won't let it."

Jes stopped thinking about how foolish it was to be doing this and instead simply kissed him back. She'd kissed men before, of course, but it had never felt like this. She felt like she wanted to melt into Jake's arms and spend the rest of her life there.

His tongue teased against her lips until she opened up to grant him entry. He tasted so damn good that her tongue couldn't help chasing after his, reveling in the flavor. Tingles ran all over her body as she heard the low growl rumble through his chest. She liked knowing she could get to him like this.

Jake wrapped his big hands around her hips, dragging her up like she weighed no more than a feather until she was straddling his waist, planting her on top of the bulge in his dress pants. While she enjoyed grinding against his hard-on, Jes couldn't deny experiencing how strong he was definitely worked for her.

She hadn't realized she had a thing for strong guys.

Or maybe she simply had a thing for this one strong guy.

Jake kept one hand on her hip, holding her firmly in place, while the other slid up her back and found its way into her long hair. His fingers lightly massaged her scalp, creating a whole new set of tingling shivers across her body before he tightened his grip in her tresses and tugged her head this way and that as he deepened the kiss.

And yeah, the tugging worked for her, too.

The connection she felt with Jake was unreal, so it wasn't a surprise to feel heat pooling between her legs. She wanted Jake in the worst way right now.

Jes barely realized Jake's lips had left hers until she felt them wandering over her jaw, leaving a path of fire behind. As his hands found the buttons on her blouse, she thought about locking the door, but when he popped first one, then another, tracing along her collarbone with his tongue at the same time, she decided locking the door would have to wait.

She regretted that decision in the next breath as the door in question abruptly opened. Startled, she threw a look over her shoulder to see Caleb poking his head in.

"Sorry to interrupt, but McKay is on Skype and wants a full debriefing. As in five minutes ago," Caleb said. "I tried to tell him you were resting, but he insisted."

Jes steeled herself, waiting for Caleb to say something snarky, but instead he regarded them curiously for a moment, then ducked back into the hallway, closing the door behind him.

She turned around to look at Jake. His dark eyes swirled with heat, and it took everything she had to not kiss him again. Reluctantly pushing herself into a sitting position, she buttoned up her blouse.

"I guess we should go downstairs," she said, not looking at him.

She wasn't sure what else to say. Now that the moment had passed, she felt kind of flustered. She shouldn't have let things get out of control like that.

"I guess we should."

Swinging his legs off the bed, Jake stood and offered her a hand. Jes took it, letting him tug her to her feet. He didn't say anything else as he took another shirt out of the wardrobe and shrugged into it. She didn't, either.

What the hell were either of them supposed to say after what had just happened between them?

CHAPTER 10

"WHERE THE HELL DID ALL THESE FRIGGING POTS AND pans come from?" Caleb grumbled, dunking yet another saucepan in the sink filled with soapy water and swirling the sponge around inside it. "They must have multiplied when we weren't looking because I don't remember using this many to make dinner."

Jake chuckled as he finished drying one of the aforementioned pots and stowed it in the cabinet. Caleb was right—no one should need five pots, four frying pans, and three saucepans to make spaghetti and meatballs. Unless you were cooking for a pack of werewolves and used five pounds of ground beef, four boxes of pasta, and four jars of marinara sauce. That wasn't even counting the three loaves of garlic bread. And unfortunately, while the dishwasher could accommodate the plates and glasses, it wasn't big enough to fit all the cookware.

Maybe he and Caleb shouldn't have been so quick to turn down the help Jes, Harley, and Misty had offered. But after seeing how exhausted they all were, Jake didn't have the heart to take them up on it. Considering they'd spent over two hours briefing McKay on what had happened tonight with the Robinson kid, they probably should have gotten takeout and called it a day, but when Harley suggested making spaghetti and meatballs, everyone had been down with the idea, including Jake. Of course, if they *had* gotten takeout, he could be upstairs with Jes right now, instead of doing dishes.

And what? They'd pick up where they left off before Caleb had interrupted them?

"So, you and Jes, huh?" Caleb said, giving him a sidelong glance.

Jake took the saucepan Caleb held out with a barely suppressed growl. Could the guy read his frigging mind or something? He should have known Caleb hadn't offered to help clean up out of the goodness of his heart. He'd probably been waiting all evening to grill Jake about what he'd seen.

"There's nothing going on between Jes and me," Jake told him, focusing on drying. "We were talking, and it just happened."

That was a ton of crap. Something was definitely going on between them. He'd figured that out long before kissing her. Unfortunately, he had no idea what it was.

"That kiss didn't look like *nothing* to me," Caleb said, reaching for the sheet pan they'd made the garlic bread on and dipping it into the soapy water. "From where I was standing, it looked like a whole hell of a lot of *something*."

Jake bit back a snarl, the urge to go all alpha werewolf on the omega and tell Caleb to mind his own damn business hard to resist. But he ignored the impulse. Caleb was part of the pack he was putting together. So far, the guy seemed like he was making an effort to fit in. Ostracizing him would only jeopardize that. Still didn't mean he wanted to talk about his personal life with the guy.

"If you don't want to talk about it, dude, that's cool," Caleb said. "Even if I hadn't seen you and Jes kissing, it's obvious something's there. I'm sure I'm not the only one who's picked up on the lengths you went to in order to protect her tonight."

Jake scowled "What do you know about that? You weren't even there for most of it."

Caleb's shoulders lifted in a shrug. "Yeah, but Forrest mentioned how you reacted when Damien and his bros lit you up at the Robinsons' house. And I saw how Jes flipped when I tossed you in the back of the van. She just about lost it."

Jake hadn't known about that because he'd been unconscious at the time. As for what Forrest had seen, he hadn't thought his overwhelming need to protect Jes was so obvious. Apparently, he'd been wrong.

"I don't know what's going on," he finally admitted, sticking the saucepan in the cabinet. "I'm not really good at this kind of thing."

Caleb snorted. "And you think I am? You do realize omegas completely lack normal socialization skills, right?"

Jake shook his head with a laugh. As sounding boards went, he could probably do worse than Caleb, he supposed.

"Can we at least agree you're attracted to her?" Caleb asked.

"No shit, Sherlock." Jake took the sheet pan from Caleb, running the towel over it absently. "But it's complicated."

That was one word for it. *Perfect* was another. The tender way she'd cared for his wounds, how she'd opened up to him, revealing stuff she'd probably never told another soul, the kisses that had made his head spin. Yeah, *perfect* was a really good word to use.

Caleb drained the sink, giving him a confused look as he dried his hands. "What's so complicated about it? Jes is beautiful, smart, kick ass, and for some reason, thinks you're worth her time. What are you agonizing about?"

Jake put the sheet pan away and closed the cabinet with a sigh. "The very real possibility that if we act on this thing between us and it doesn't work out, it could rip the whole team apart."

"So make sure it works out," an exhausted-looking Forrest said from the doorway. "What, you think you're the first person to have a relationship with someone on their team?"

Crap, Jake hadn't even heard the guy let himself into the house. This thing with Jes had his inner wolf really screwed up. It was bad enough Caleb knew about him and Jes. Now, he had Forrest involved in his personal life, too.

"How much did you overhear?" Jake demanded.

Forrest shrugged. "Just the part about you having it bad for Jes but are worried getting involved with her would be bad for the team dynamics."

Jake glowered at him. "So, you pretty much heard everything then."

"At least he didn't hear that part about me catching you making out with Jes in bed," Caleb pointed out. "It'd be damn embarrassing if he heard that part."

Jake growled softly in Caleb's direction. The omega merely chuckled.

"Misty saved you a plate of spaghetti and meatballs," Jake told Forrest. "It's in the fridge."

Forrest grinned, eagerly taking the leftovers out and sticking them in the microwave to heat. Caleb grabbed three beers from the fridge, handing one to Jake and one to Forrest.

"How are the Robinsons doing?" Jake asked, changing the subject as he took a swallow of the British ale.

Forrest took his plate out of the microwave and carried it over to the table. "Better. The support team is with them at the safe house and will be guarding them around the clock until we figure out what the hell is going on. The boy is still a little freaked out, but he'll be okay. McKay was talking to Evie and her husband when I left, trying to figure out their connection to Darby and the other people on the list."

As he and Caleb joined Forrest at the table, Jake got him up to speed on their earlier conversation with McKay. There really wasn't much to tell, other than that their boss had people working around the clock trying to figure out what kind of supernatural creatures Darby and his crew were.

"I was listening to the local news on the way back to see if they said anything about you chasing Damien through Blackwall Tunnel and getting into a shoot-out with him," Forrest said, spearing a meatball. "Want to hear something crazy? The cops didn't make any arrests and they didn't find any bodies. After the way you guys described the amount of damage you did to those creatures in the park, it's hard to believe they're still alive."

Caleb cursed. "How is that even frigging possible? I hit Damien so hard with the van he sailed twenty feet through the air, then I drove over that other a-hole and crushed him to a pulp."

"Maybe Darby showed up and took them away before the cops moved in," Forrest suggested.

Jake was still considering that possibility when Forrest changed the subject.

"I know this might come as a surprise to you, Jake—and will probably piss you off when I tell you about it—but I think hearing it might help you and Jes figure out what to do," he said, wiping his mouth with a napkin and pushing his empty plate to the side.

Jake didn't say anything as he waited for Forrest to continue. He got the feeling he already knew where the former FBI agent was going with this. From the grin tugging at Caleb's mouth, he probably did, too.

Forrest took a deep breath, like he was working up the courage to reveal some big secret. "Misty and I started going out a few days after she began working at STAT. It was hard not seeing each other as much as we would have liked, since we rarely worked the same missions. When we heard McKay was putting a new team together, Misty got into the files and put us on the short list of volunteers."

On the other side of the table, Forrest looked like he was bracing himself in case Jake exploded at the news. When Jake didn't, he frowned.

"You aren't pissed?"

"No," Jake admitted, then added, "but that's because I already knew."

Forrest's eyes went wide. "You did? How?"

"I picked up your scents on each other the first morning we were here, when you and Misty were setting up the video teleconference equipment."

Forrest winced. "Shit. I didn't even think of that. So much for sneaking around when you're on a team with werewolves." His blue eyes darted to Caleb. "I guess you smelled our scents all over each other too, huh?"

Caleb shook his head. "Nah. Like I said at the embassy, my nose is crap compared to Jake's and Harley's. But my ears work great. Which means I heard you and Misty sneak into each other's rooms to have sex. Trust me, you're a lot louder than you think—to a werewolf anyway."

"You heard...?" Forrest's face turned red.

"Yeah, I heard everything." Caleb held up a hand. "But hey, I'm not judging here. You do you, that's what I always say. Although, if you could do it a little more quietly, that'd be cool."

Forrest had the grace to look a little chagrined for a second, but then he pinned Jake and Caleb with a pointed look. "Okay, we'll work on that, but when did this conversation become about me? The only reason I brought up Misty and me is so Jake can see it's possible to be teammates with someone and still have a relationship with them, too. You just have to be willing to make it work. And trust each other."

"Trust shouldn't be an issue," Caleb said, swigging his beer. "Since Jes is *The One* for you, I mean."

The words didn't register for a second, and when they finally did, Jake was sure he'd heard wrong. "What are you talking about? I never suggested she's *The One* for me. Why would you even say something like that?"

Caleb looked at him like he was a moron...again. But it was Forrest who spoke first.

"Am I missing something here? I thought you and Jes were already getting hot and heavy, but now it sounds like you're not sure if she's the one you want to be with? Are you just messing with her?"

Jake frowned. "I'm not messing with her. I'm sure Jes is the woman I want to be with. I'm just not sure if she's *The One*." He ran his hand through his hair. "Shit, this is even more complicated than I thought."

Forrest stared at Jake, clearly baffled AF. "Now, I'm really confused."

Caleb laughed. "It's not your fault, dude. It's a werewolf thing. When I suggested Jes is *The One* for him, I was talking about her being his soul mate. He's either terrified at the idea or too stupid to accept reality."

Forrest still looked perplexed. Jake couldn't blame him. He was a little rattled himself. While he might know what Caleb was talking about—there probably wasn't a werewolf out there in the world who didn't know the legend of *The One*—the thought that Jes might be his soul mate had never entered his mind. Seriously, how could she be? When it came to werewolves, soul mates were supposed to be a one-in-a-million thing. Hell, maybe even one in a billion.

"You've heard wolves mate for life, right?" Caleb asked Forrest. When the guy nodded, he continued, "Well, in some ways, werewolves do the same thing. There's supposed to be one perfect person out there for each of us who we're meant to be with forever. When a werewolf meets his or her soul mate, it's supposed to be like catching lightning in a bottle."

"Soul mates. Wow," Forrest breathed. "I mean, Misty and I are solid, but I made a lot of dumb-ass mistakes when we first started dating. Would have been nice to know we're soul mates the moment we met."

"You'd think so," Caleb agreed with a snort. "But for some reason, Jake is too busy swimming around in that river in Egypt to notice what's right in front of him."

Across from Jake, Forrest was regarding him with an expression that clearly suggested the guy thought he was an idiot. "Why don't you think Jes is your soul mate?"

Jake opened his mouth, then closed it again. "I don't know," he finally said. "It doesn't seem possible. I've literally known her only a few days."

"So what?" Caleb demanded. "Can you honestly tell me that Jes isn't the first thing you think about in the morning when you wake up and the last thing on your mind when you go to sleep? Hell, right now, you're probably thinking about the way her scent fills your nose almost all the time, the way her heartbeat seems to drown out nearly every other sound when she's near, and the way she tastes when you kiss her."

Jake stared at Caleb, stunned. He'd never pegged the big omega as the empathetic type, but seriously, the guy had nailed it when it came to describing the thoughts currently rolling through his mind. Jes had parked herself in his head-space, taking up permanent residency there.

"How do you know so much about soul mates?" Jake asked, wondering just how much he didn't know about the werewolf who was part of his pack. "Did you ever…?"

A short, harsh laugh from the big man cut him off. "No, I've never had a whiff of someone that might be *The One* for me. But I did see it happen once between two werewolves in Dallas. They weren't supposed to get together, either. They thought they were too different, kind of like you and Jes— well, except they were on opposite sides of the law at the time—but I saw it even when they couldn't. Just like I see it now and you don't. Because you don't want to see it for some stupid frigging reason."

Jake couldn't miss the way Caleb's heart thudded as he spoke. "Why is this so important to you?"

Caleb shrugged, gaze fixed on the label wrapped around

his beer bottle. "Because I'm an omega—a loner. Which means I'm always outside the pack looking in. If I had even half a chance to find my soul mate and not have to go this shit alone, I sure as fuck wouldn't turn my nose up at it like you're doing."

Before Jake could defend himself with a reply, Caleb pushed back his chair so hard he almost knocked it over, then strode out of the room, apparently done with the conversation.

Forrest nodded. "What he said."

Picking up his plate, Forrest put it in the dishwasher, then left, ditching his empty beer bottle in the trash on the way.

Jake sat there for a long time, nursing the rest of his ale and thinking about what Caleb had said. Finally getting to his feet, he tossed his beer bottle along with the one Caleb had left, then slowly climbed the steps. Upstairs, he stopped outside Jes's bedroom, listening to the sound of her breathing and the beat of her heart through the closed door. He had a sudden urge to walk into her room, wake her up, and ask her what she thought about the idea of being with a man who occasionally had fangs and claws.

But before he could give in to that desire, he continued down the hallway to his room and another long night without sleep.

Jes sipped her cappuccino, savoring the sweetly flavored drink as she covertly studied the Lanesborough Hotel directly across the street from the outdoor café where she,

Harley, and Misty were doing a recon of the place. Originally a hospital in the mid-1800s, the Duke of Westminster purchased the building in the late twentieth century and turned the four-floor Regency-style building into the poshest hotel in London. The outside was gorgeous for sure, but it was the inside with all the marble arched doorways and fancy furniture that was enough to take your breath away.

With Buckingham Palace, Big Ben, the London Eye, Hyde Park, and the Knightsbridge shopping district all within walking distance, it was easy to blend in with the other tourists grabbing a late-afternoon snack. Of course, if someone looked closely, they'd probably realize she and Harley were a little tense. That was because Misty was currently doing a deep dive into the virtual world through the laptop she appeared to be typing on. Thankfully, Misty was wearing sunglasses, so no one could tell her eyes were completely white.

"What do we do if she doesn't come out of there on her own?" Jes asked softly.

As she spoke, she kept one eye focused on the hotel across the street, sure Metro Police were going to show up any moment because the place had realized someone was hacking their computers. The Lanesborough was a five-star establishment that charged more per night for a room than her monthly rent on her apartment and her car payment combined. While the exterior facade might seem like something out of another century, the hotel's security system was obviously as modern and high-tech as could be, if the length of time Misty had been snooping around in there was any indication.

What if Misty had gotten trapped in the hotel's

convoluted IT system and was being held captive by an intelligent piece of antivirus software or locked behind a digital firewall?

She'd been in her trancelike state for almost two hours, so it was entirely possible.

"I don't think there's anything we *can* do," Harley said, her voice giving away how nervous she was even as she bit into her scone. "She almost died back at Darby's place when she got jerked out of his computer before she was ready. We'll have to wait and hope she knows what she's doing in there."

Jes nodded, sipping her coffee as the bustling London traffic went by. Harley was right. They had no choice but to sit there and wait for Misty to slip out of the hotel's computer system where she was currently surfing, hoping to learn whether tomorrow's meeting of select members of the secretive and exclusive Bilderberg Society was still a go. Because based on everything McKay had told Jes and the rest of the team at this morning's videoconference, that meeting was the reason behind everything Darby had been doing for the past several weeks.

Jake and the other guys were at the house working with the analysts back in DC to figure out where Olivia Phillips and the other kidnapping victims were being held while she, Harley, and Misty had offered to check out the Lanesborough. After looking around the hotel under the guise of tourists, Misty had suggested slipping into their security system to do some snooping. Jes hoped it didn't turn out to be a big mistake.

Sighing, Jes watched a big red double-decker bus go by, thinking how much Zoe and Chloe would love to visit the city, when she heard a sharp intake of breath. Startled, she looked across the table to see Misty grinning.

"The Bilderberg meeting is still scheduled for tomorrow," she said.

Reaching into the messenger bag slung over the back of her chair, Misty pulled out a pen and notepad. Flipping it open to a clean sheet of paper, she began scribbling like crazy.

"McKay was right about the attendees," Misty added as she kept writing. "It's not a meeting of the entire Bilderberg Society, but there will be twenty of the group's most powerful and influential members coming to it at noon tomorrow and staying until midnight. All of the members have been provided rooms near the meeting area, but it doesn't look like any are planning to spend the night. If Darby is going to make his move, it'll have to be during that twelve-hour window."

It was during their morning videoconference with McKay that everything had finally started making sense. It was Evie Robinson and her duties as concierge at the Lanesborough Hotel that finally put the STAT analysts on the right path. It turned out that one of Evie's jobs was overseeing accommodations for the hotel's more important guests, as well as anything they needed while on the property. When she'd mentioned to McKay that she'd recently been coordinating meeting spaces for a one-day get-together for select members of the Bilderberg Society, their boss at STAT knew it was too much of a coincidence for there not to be a connection.

The Bilderberg Society was made up of influential people from all around the world who got together several times a year to promote various humanitarian efforts. Of course, the conspiracy theorists claimed the society was actually a secret group ruling the world from behind the curtain. Jes had some serious doubts about that, but one thing she did know for sure was that every one of them was rich beyond belief. Seriously, if Darby and his men could get their hands on a few of them and hold them for ransom, he'd have more money than he'd ever be able to spend.

Of course, Darby already had more money than he could spend, but since it appeared his goal was kidnapping some or all of the Bilderberg Society people, he clearly wanted even more in his bank account.

Once they realized what Darby was after, everything with the missing kids had fallen into place. In one way or another, their parents were all involved with planning, security, or logistics for tomorrow's Bilderberg meeting. In addition to Evie being responsible for rooms and meeting spaces, Jack Phillips was in charge of the liaison between MI5, the local police, and the society's private security, while the other parents had been connected to hotel security, transportation routes, and catering.

Even without Evie's cooperation, Darby still had access to the meeting agenda, attendee list, security procedures, passwords, security badges, radio frequencies, floor plans, police response protocols, details on the society's security teams, and info on the exact routes the Bilderberg members would take into and out of the hotel. If Darby's intent was to give himself the best chance to slip in and grab a handful of the richest, most well-protected people in the world, he'd put together a damn good plan to pull it off.

"Did you run into problems with the hotel's security

system?" Harley asked Misty. "You were in there for a long time."

Misty looked up in surprise before glancing at the watch on her wrist. "Really? It felt like a few minutes for me. I guess I got wrapped up in all the information available in their system. And I do so love free Wi-Fi. Especially when you can access it from across the street."

Jes shook her head, still amazed Misty had been able to slip into the hotel's computer system through their own Wi-Fi modem from a coffee shop all the way over here. It made her glad Misty was on their side and had her wondering if there were other people in the world who could do what she did.

"Any indication hotel security is planning to change anything because Evie suddenly went on vacation?" Harley asked, spreading strawberry jam on her scone, apparently able to focus on the job and not Misty's bizarre abilities.

"No, nothing like that," Misty said. "No change in meeting locations or in the schedule. I'm not even sure they've noticed all that drama last night involved one of their employees."

"I still can't believe McKay wouldn't let us at least warn the hotel," Harley muttered, looking over at the Lanesborough like she was considering stomping in there to tell them herself. "Or the Bilderberg Society people. He has to know how risky it is using their members for bait like this."

Jes silently agreed. She'd been the first one to argue with their boss that they should push to cancel the Bilderberg meeting altogether, now that they knew Darby was going after them. But McKay—and the powers that be back in

DC—insisted it was worth the risk. They had faith in her and the team to stop Darby and the other creatures with him. They felt ambushing them at the Lanesborough would be the best way to do that since they'd most likely all be there together. While they were probably right, Jes still couldn't help but think they were being cavalier with people's lives.

"I was able to slip in and put you and Forrest into the employee database, Harley," Misty said, going back to her notepad. "I got Forrest a position with the maintenance staff, so he can roam around the corridors and the loading dock areas without raising suspicions. You'll be with the waitstaff, so you'll be able to slip in the meeting rooms with the Bilderberg people."

Jes didn't bother to ask about where the rest of them would be. Since they still hadn't figured out where Darby was hiding the missing kids, there was a lot of their planning left unfinished. There was a good chance they might have to hit both the hotel and the hostage site at the same time, which meant splitting the team was looking more and more likely. That idea worried her more than she cared to admit. While she trusted everyone on the team to do their jobs, she didn't like the thought of not being there to watch Jake's back.

Something she never would have given a second thought to before that kiss they'd shared last night.

Well, technically, it had been more than a kiss. There'd been a good bit of grinding involved as well and some groping. The scary part was that she could barely remember why she'd jumped him like that. Even scarier? She wanted to do it again.

"Have you known Jake long, Harley?" Jes asked, trying to sound casual.

Harley shook her head as she started in on her second scone, slathering it with more jam. "Not really. We met when McKay hired us."

Jes sipped her coffee, surprised by that answer. Yeah, it had almost been a throwaway question, but truthfully, she'd been curious about how a werewolf pack operated. "Oh. Since you're a pack, I naturally assumed you guys had been together a while."

Harley regarded her thoughtfully while she chewed. "Sometimes it feels that way since Jake and Caleb are easy to be around. But no, it's only been a few weeks. Why do you ask?"

Jes shrugged. "No reason. Just curious."

"Uh-huh." Harley said, a smile curving her lips. "And does this sudden curiosity with pack dynamics have anything to do with the fact that you and Jake are having sex?"

Jes felt her face heat. Her head snapped to the left and right, worried that everyone around them—and most of the people on the street—had heard what Harley said. "We are not having sex!" she whispered. "Why would you even think something like that?"

Harley's grin broadened and a quick glance at Misty revealed she was close to cracking up, too.

"Caleb said he saw you kissing," Harley said in a casual, matter-of-fact tone.

Jes gaped. "I can't believe he told you!"

"Of course, he did," Harley replied. "Like you said, we're a pack. Besides, it's not like he had to, since I could smell your scents all over each other this morning."

Across from Jes, Misty's eyes went wide. "Hold on! You can tell when two people have been sleeping together? Just from their scents?"

Harley nodded. "Yeah."

Misty went pale. "So you know about Forrest and me?"

Harley nodded again as Jes blinked in confusion.

"Wait," she said. "You and Forrest are a couple? Since when?"

Misty chewed on her lower lip for a moment before answering. "We've been together since I joined STAT, but no one knows. Especially not McKay. And you can't tell him. I know he takes care of his people, but I'm afraid he'll put us on different teams if he finds out."

"You don't have to worry about me. I won't say anything," Jes said.

How hadn't she known Misty and Forrest were seeing each other? So much for being observant.

"Me, either," Harley assured her. "Though I'm pretty sure Jake and Caleb already know. Jake would for sure, since his nose works as well as mine. And Caleb's room is right beside yours. To be honest, you and Forrest could stand to be a bit quieter at night when you're fooling around, if you know what I mean."

Misty blushed. "Point taken. As long as McKay doesn't find out, we can live with it. We always assumed everyone on the team would figure it out sooner or later." She looked at Jes. "Enough about Forrest and me. We were talking about you and Jake. Let's get back to the part where you tell us about what it's like sleeping with our hunky team leader."

Jes picked up her cup and took a sip. "I have no idea since kissing was all Jake and I did last night."

Harley and Misty gave her dubious looks.

"Yeah, but I bet you would have done more than that if Caleb hadn't interrupted you, am I right?" Harley said with a grin.

Jes considered denying it but then gave up. It was no use. "Maybe," she hedged. "Okay…yes. Just between us, I admit I almost certainly would have ended up sleeping with Jake if we hadn't gotten interrupted. Kissing him was…intense."

Misty took a sip of the tea she'd ordered, grimacing when she realized it was ice cold. "I somehow doubt there would have been a lot of sleeping going on in that bed."

Jes felt her face heat up again as she imagined Jake's naked body draped over hers, his muscles flexing as he pounded her into the mattress. Nope, there wouldn't have been much sleeping going on.

"Not that I blame you," Misty continued, completely oblivious to the X-rated moment Jes was having on her side of the table. "I might be totally in love with Forrest, but that doesn't mean I can't appreciate an attractive man when I see one. Don't blame you at all for wanting to jump him."

Jes forced her mind off the new image Misty had put in her head. Of Jes jumping into Jake's arms, him catching her and pinning her to a wall where he began to shred her clothes with his claws.

Claws? Okay, where the hell did that come from?

Truthfully, what did she know about sleeping with someone like Jake? Maybe claws were a valid concern. Maybe there were others.

"Harley, what's it like being with a man who's a werewolf?" she asked before she lost her nerve.

Jes made sure to lower her voice as she said the word,

afraid someone might overhear. No one nearby seemed to be eavesdropping, but still, they were talking about were-wolves for heaven's sake. They couldn't take even a small chance of someone overhearing them.

She held her breath as she waited for Harley to answer. She needed to understand what she was getting into if she decided to actually let this thing with Jake go any farther. Because yeah, they definitely had a thing between them.

"I'm probably not the person to be asking, since I've never been with a werewolf," Harley said.

Jes did a double take. "I thought you and Caleb…"

Harley made a face. "Caleb and me? Gross! That would be like sleeping with my brother."

Jes exchanged looks with Misty and realized she was as surprised by that bit of news as Jes was. That's what she got for assuming.

"But you must have been around other werewolves, right?" Misty prompted. "Ones you didn't think of like brothers?"

Brow furrowing, Harley looked down at her scone, slowly pulling a piece off and nibbling on it. "It's a long story that I really don't want to get into, but suffice to say, my life pretty much fell apart when I became a werewolf. For years I didn't know there was anyone else like me out there and even after I figured it out, I stayed on my own. If McKay hadn't found me and convinced me to join STAT, I never would have given this pack thing a shot." She lifted her head and met Jes's gaze. "While I know you have lots of questions about being with someone like Jake, I don't have a lot of answers. Sorry."

Even though Harley had left a lot unsaid, Jes was

beginning to understand why Harley kept to herself so much, especially when she'd first gotten to London.

"That's okay," Jes said. "A regular human woman like me can be with a werewolf though, right? Do I have to worry about getting bitten...or clawed up?"

That image she'd had a few minutes ago of Jake ripping her clothes off her body came rushing back and she felt her face heat a little. Part of her refused to think a man like Jake could even be so animalistic, but the fact was, Jake wasn't simply a man. He was a werewolf, too.

Harley sipped her latte. "Human women can definitely be with a werewolf, that much I do know. As far as biting and stuff, I've overheard other werewolves talking and they seemed to imply sex with a werewolf can get a little...wild. I wouldn't be worried about Jake clawing you or anything like that, but considering he's going to have his mouth on you, you might want to be prepared for a few love bites."

Okay, that didn't sound too crazy. "Do I need to worry about him losing control?"

"What do you mean?" Harley asked. "You don't honestly think Jake would ever hurt you?"

Jes shook her head quickly, looking down at her coffee cup. She'd never need to worry about that. She wasn't sure why she'd even asked. But every time she thought about being with Jake, her head started spinning like crazy and it was confusing the hell out of her.

"No, of course not! It's just..."

Harley reached out and covered Jes's hand with hers. "Are you okay? Your heart is beating like a drum right now. Did something happen between you and Jake that you're not telling us? You're not scared of him, are you?"

Jes lifted her gaze to see Harley and Misty regarding her worriedly. "No, nothing like that!"

"Then what is it?" Misty asked. "One second, you seem thrilled at the idea of sleeping with Jake, but the next you seem petrified at the thought. It's like you don't know what you want."

"Maybe because I don't." Jes sighed. "When I met him at the American Embassy, I was ready to hate him. It's complicated and stupid, and I've already apologized to him for it, but still, up until a few days ago, I had no intention of liking him at all."

"And now?" Harley prompted.

"And now, less than twenty-four hours after I kissed him, I can't get him out of my head. I close my eyes and there he is. I want to sleep with him so badly it hurts even though I'm a little worried he might bite me. Worse, I'm willing to risk messing up the whole team-chemistry thing we've got going on the off-chance this thing between us might work." She shook her head. "None of this makes sense. I'm not normally the kind of person who falls for a guy in a matter of days. That's not me. And it's freaking me out."

Jes held her breath, waiting for Harley and Misty to tell her she'd completely lost her marbles. Because seriously, who in their right mind would pass up the chance to be with a great guy like Jake?

"I think you're overthinking the hell out of this," Harley said. "Even though you just met Jake a few days ago, you're already into him. And even though Jake's a werewolf with claws and fangs and everything else that comes with it, you still want to sleep with him."

Even though it wasn't exactly a question, Jes nodded. Harley had nailed it.

"So, when we get back to the B&B, go sleep with him," Harley continued. "Stop thinking so much and worry about what comes next when you wake up in the morning. Even better, put off worrying about it until after we make it through the fight tomorrow against Darby and his buddies. Considering we still don't know how to even hurt those things, being concerned about a future with Jake might be a waste of time."

That wasn't a very cheery thought.

"Is that what you'd do if you were me?" Jes asked.

Harley took her hand away and sat back, sipping her latte again. "I'll never be you, but I can promise you if I ever found a person who looked at me the way Jake looks at you, I sure as hell wouldn't be sitting here drinking coffee. I'd be back at the B&B in bed with him."

On the other side of the table, Misty smiled. "Harley's right. You should go for it."

Jes laughed. They were right. She was overthinking things. Well, she was done with that. "Then what do you say we finish our drinks and head back to the house, so I can tell Jake exactly how I feel about him?"

CHAPTER 11

JES WAS SO PREOCCUPIED WITH WHAT SHE WAS GOING to say to Jake—not to mention excited about the prospect of finishing what they'd started the night before—she didn't give much thought about the rest of the team being in the house when they did it. Luckily, Harley and Misty did. The moment they walked into the B&B, Misty informed Forrest and Caleb they were going out to dinner with her and Harley.

"I just had a sandwich," Caleb said, coming out of the kitchen with a stack of shortbread cookies in his hand that were obviously dessert.

Harley grabbed his leather jacket off the coat rack in the entryway and tossed it to him. "What, you're telling me you couldn't eat again?"

Caleb shrugged, then stuck the cookies in his mouth for safekeeping while he slipped on his jacket.

"What about you and Jake?" Forrest asked Jes, looking confused as he got up from the couch where he'd been reading something on his phone. "Aren't you guys going, too?"

"We'll bring something back for them," Misty said quickly, giving Jes a wink as she took Forrest's arm and ushered him toward the door.

"Where is Jake, by the way?" Jes asked before they left, trying to make the question sound as casual as she could.

Forrest glanced at her over his shoulder. "Upstairs. He said something about grabbing a shower."

An image of Jake naked and wet, his perfectly chiseled

body covered in water droplets flashed into Jes's head and she stifled a moan.

As the door closed behind her four teammates, Jes tossed her purse on the couch and headed for the stairs, butterflies making her stomach quiver a little more with each step. Cornering Jake and telling him how she felt had seemed like a good idea over coffee with Harley and Misty. Now, she wasn't so sure. What if he thought that kiss last night had been a mistake and didn't feel the same way she did?

She reached the second floor just as Jake came out of the bathroom he and the other guys had laid claim to wearing nothing but a pair of running shorts and a towel draped around his neck. His jet-black hair was wet and tousled and glistening beads of water he had missed with the towel ran down the smooth skin of his chest.

Jes simply stood there and stared, not even bothering to hide the fact she was ogling him. Damn, he looked hot. It was all she could do not to run over and grab the towel from around his neck and help dry him off. Who the hell was she kidding? She didn't want to use the towel to dry him off. She wanted to shove him against the wall and lick those water droplets from his skin one by one.

Thank God for willpower.

"Did I just hear everyone leave?" he asked, reaching up with one end of the towel to dry his hair, making it stick up even more, which in turn only made him look sexier. The movement made his pecs and abs flex in the most hypnotic manner, and Jes decided she could watch him do that for days.

Breathing deeply, she forced herself to walk toward him.

The towel only partially obscured the wound in his chest, and she could see enough to know that while it was still slightly pink, it was completely sealed and healing fast. The wound looked like it was at least a week or two old.

"Yeah, Harley and Misty wanted to go out to dinner," she said. "Caleb and Forrest went with them."

Jake sauntered down the hall, meeting her halfway, the movements of the towel slowing as he regarded her curiously. "You didn't want to go, too? If you're hungry, I can put some clothes on, and we can catch up to them."

As a matter of fact, she was rather hungry. Starving even. But not for food.

She tucked her hair behind her ear. "They said they'd bring us something back. I thought since everyone was out, it might give us a chance to talk."

Jake studied her thoughtfully for a moment before nodding. "Yeah, that would probably be a good idea. I'll go get a shirt on."

She almost told him not to bother on her account, but then thought better of it. Talking about giving this thing between them a chance would be a smart thing to do. She didn't have to jump right into bed with him even if that was why Harley and Misty had practically dragged Caleb and Forrest out for the rest of the evening.

Jes fell into step beside Jake as he made his way to his bedroom. The sensible thing to do would have been to go back downstairs and wait for him, but she was rather fond of the memories they'd made in his room the last time she'd been there. There was no reason they couldn't talk there.

She stood in the doorway for a moment, stopping to watch the show as Jake pulled a T-shirt over his head. What was it about the way a guy did it that got to her? It was almost as much fun as watching a man take his shirt off.

Almost.

Jes moved over and sat in the chair by the desk, deciding it would be better if she sat there, rather than on the bed beside Jake. That would be too distracting.

She'd been too busy playing doctor last night to see what he'd done with the place, but now she took in the suitcase against the far wall, gun holster hanging on the peg beside the door, and handful of clothes in the wardrobe. There was a suit, a few dress shirts, jeans, and a stack of tees.

"We think we have a lead on where Darby might be holding Olivia Phillips and the other kids," Jake said, interrupting her perusal of his room.

"You do?"

"Yeah." He leaned back on his hands. "We spent most of the afternoon going over Darby's personal and business properties in London and the surrounding areas. Remember how we thought that since Olivia was the only one missing, we figured she could be anywhere? Well, now that we know Darby kidnapped multiple kids, we decided it made more sense for him to be holding them somewhere close by to get the most out of the hostages and dangle them in front of their parents if he had to."

She agreed. "Makes sense."

"Exactly. Which is why we helped the analysts in DC scrub through property records, utility bills, traffic cameras, anything we could think of that might narrow the possibilities down. We ended up with a long list, but the intel people hope to have something more manageable by tomorrow morning."

That was cutting it close, but it was better than nothing.

"Sooner would be better," she pointed out. "If we have to move on the Lanesborough target before we know where those kids are, it isn't going to end well for them."

"Tell me about it," Jake grumbled.

They both fell silent for a moment, and Jes was wondering how to bring up the thing she really wanted to talk about when Jake spoke again.

"Since Harley and Misty got Caleb and Forrest out of the house, can I assume they both know about us and what happened last night?"

Jes nodded, a little chagrined. "I hadn't really meant to say anything, but they already knew most of it because Caleb told them he caught us kissing." She couldn't help but smile when Jake rolled his eyes at that. "Anyway, I kind of needed someone to talk to about stuff."

"What kind of stuff?" He frowned. "Did what happen last night upset you?"

She shook her head. "No, definitely not! But the kiss and what we almost did afterward has me spinning a hundred miles an hour. It isn't the norm for me to make out with my teammates, then spend the whole night and next day replaying the moment over and over in my head." Before he could say anything, she hurried on. "I don't want you to think I regret anything that happened between us, because I don't. It's just that I needed someone to talk to about it, help me figure things out, you know?"

Jes held her breath, waiting to see how he'd react to her confession.

Jake's sensuous mouth curved. "I know the feeling. And in the interest of full disclosure, I had a similar conversation with Caleb and Forrest last night. I also spent a good part of the day thinking about that kiss we shared and how much I enjoyed it."

Her pulse skipped a beat at that. It was a relief to know she wasn't the only one who felt whatever this was between them.

"I'm not sure what comes next," she admitted. "Harley told me to stop thinking so much and just do what feels right, but I don't want to screw up the team we're building. I've been part of a lot of teams, and I really feel this group could be something special."

He considered that. "Agreed. But what if we—you and I—could be something special, too?" When she didn't say anything, he added, "I'm as worried as you are that this could all blow up in our faces, but I'm being honest when I say I've never met anyone like you. When it comes to being with you, I find myself wanting to take the risk."

At his words, goose bumps spread across her skin, and it was all she could do to keep herself from shivering. It was like he could read her mind.

She wet her lips. "So, how do we do this?"

He chuckled. "There's no rush. We could wait until we get back to DC and go out for dinner or something? You know, have a real date."

Jes liked that idea. It would be cool to meet Zoe and Chloe in person—after spending some time alone with Jake, of course. But then she remembered what Harley said about having no idea if they'd even get through tomorrow after going up against Darby and his crew.

Taking a deep breath, she got up and walked over to the bed. Though whether it was to climb on his lap or sit beside him, she wasn't sure because Jake stood as well. She didn't know which one of them moved into the other's arms first, but the next thing she knew, his lips were on hers.

The kiss last night had been enough to curl her toes, but when Jake's hands slid up her back and into her hair, and he locked her mouth against his, Jes realized she was going to need a new description for what she was feeling right now. Euphoric...drugged...orgasmic? That last one seemed the most apropos, since she was damn close to having a... lipgasm? She wasn't sure if that was even a thing, but with Jake kissing her like this, she thought she just might find out.

As his mouth explored hers, she could feel every inch of his body against her own. The shorts he wore did nothing to hide how aroused he was, his hard-on pressing insistently against her, making it hard to think about anything other than having him inside her.

Suddenly, Jes first felt his fangs scrape along the sides of her tongue. It was so jarring—and sharp—she couldn't help but pull away.

Jake looked confused for a moment, but that expression was quickly replaced with one of understanding...then disappointment. When his hands slid from her hair and he took a step back, it felt like Jes's heart and soul were being ripped out of her body. She stopped thinking then and threw herself into his arms again. Their lips came together, and she kissed him hard and fierce, trying to make up for what she'd just done.

He swung her up in his arms, crossing the room in two long strides, then setting her down on her feet and pressing her back against the wall. She kicked off her sandals and wrapped her legs around his waist, locking her ankles together behind his back. Groaning, he slid his hands down to cup her butt, holding her firm as his tongue got to know every inch of hers.

His thick, hard cock pressed against her softness, and it felt so glorious she wanted him to take her right there where they were standing. She felt his fangs against her tongue again...careful...tentative. She got a grip on his hair, yanking him close and kissing him harder, letting her tongue tease across those razor-sharp teeth, moaning as he trembled under her touch.

When the need for oxygen finally forced them apart for a second, Jes caught his scruff-covered jaw, locking eyes with him. "I didn't mean to pull away like that before. I would never do that to you. It's just that I've never kissed a guy with fangs and it kind of took me by surprise. You're going to have to give me a chance to figure this all out, okay?"

Jake grinned and nodded before going back to kissing her, still holding her against the wall like it was nothing. As their lips teased and tempted each other, Jes ran her hands down his shoulders to his triceps, loving the feel of the muscles tensing and flexing there.

"How long do you think everyone will be gone?" Jake whispered.

His lips moved teasingly across the curve of her ear, then glided lower, making tingles chase back and forth all over her skin. When she felt the tip of one sharp fang drag across the sensitive skin of her neck, she thought she might melt.

Was it weird to hope he might bite her...just a little?

"Long enough," she told him breathlessly. "Harley and Misty have a good idea what the deal is, so they'll keep Caleb and Forrest occupied for a few hours at least."

"Good."

Getting their clothes off was more complex than it should have been because Jake still had her pressed against the wall and Jes still had her legs wrapped tightly around his waist.

Jake got his T-shirt off first, ripping it over his head like he couldn't get it off fast enough. Jes was all ready to go to town on the parts of his chest she could reach with her mouth, but he took a step back to slide his hands under the hem of her top. His claws were peeking out, and she had no doubt the flower-print top with its fluttery sleeves was going to be totally ruined.

But she didn't care.

Instead, she clamped her legs around him tightly and held on for dear life, letting him work. She'd always liked watching people open their presents at Christmas and with the way Jake was removing her shirt, then her bra, it kind of felt the same way.

He pressed her back against the wall again, her legs around his hips and the friction of the wall the only thing holding her up, taking a few minutes to have his way with her breasts. Surprisingly, she was more okay with the idea of fangs near her nipples than she would have thought. Maybe deciding to be with a werewolf pushed her further along the wild-and-kinky scale than she probably would have ever traveled on her own.

Or maybe she simply trusted him.

The sensation of his warm mouth closing around one of her nipples had her moaning and squirming as he suckled and nibbled, his big hands coming up at the same time to cup and massage those parts of her breasts that his mouth couldn't cover. Wow, he had big hands.

After he teased and tantalized her nipples until she pretty much turned into a pleasured puddle of goo, Jake turned his attention to the buttons on her jeans, apparently planning to take them off while she was still wrapped around him like a tree sloth with dependency issues.

Jes lowered her feet to the floor—for safety's sake if nothing else—as Jake got the buttons undone and started working her jeans over her hips.

Everything stopped then as she stood there in front of Jake in nothing but her extremely practical cotton underwear. Bikini cut, they weren't exactly granny panties, but she felt a little mortified anyway. Maybe she should have looked around that pharmacy they'd stopped at for condoms after leaving the café for some sexy lingerie. Nah, they probably didn't sell stuff like that.

But then she caught the look of total awe on Jake's face and decided maybe her serviceable panties weren't as bad as she'd thought.

She eagerly waited for him to shove his black running shorts off and complete the big reveal, but instead he simply continued to stand there, his gaze roaming over her like he was trying to figure out which part to eat first. Seeing the hunger in those dark eyes heightened her arousal level, and it was all she could do to keep from squirming.

Just as she was about to give up and make the first move, Jake did. And damn, he was fast. One second he was a few feet away, the next she was in his arms, her back pressed firmly against the wall again. At this rate, she was going to need to autograph this particular section of the wallpaper since it spent so long in contact with her butt.

Jes expected Jake to pull her right back up against him,

so she was a bit surprised when he suddenly dropped to his knees in front of her and began to kiss and nibble his way down her stomach, pausing an extra-long time at her belly button. She'd never been kissed there before and realized she'd been missing out.

She was starting to squirm a little, praying he'd head a bit farther south, when she heard a tearing sound and opened her eyes in time to see her shredded cotton panties flying across the room. Wow, those had come apart easily. Then she caught a glimpse of claws and realized how he'd managed to rip her panties so effortlessly.

Why does that turn me on so much?

Jes didn't have long to ponder the question before Jake hitched one of her legs up and casually draped it over his strong, muscular shoulder. She had about half a second to let out a little squeak of alarm before she buried her fingers in his hair to help her maintain her balance. Then Jake's mouth was on her pussy, and she suddenly didn't care at all about having fangs near such a sensitive location.

Thankfully, Jake clamped his big hands around either side of her waist and held her steady as his tongue began to explore her wet folds, or she would have been on the floor for sure. He had an extremely talented tongue and seemed to somehow know exactly what she liked, touching her exactly where she wanted to be touched.

He started slowly, teasing the tip of his tongue up and down her wetness, carefully avoiding her clit for the moment. Over and over he went, teasing and denying at the same time, pushing her closer and closer to the edge. It was all she could do to hold in the screams threatening to burst out of her.

After what seemed like an incredibly short amount of time, her whole body began to tingle, ready to explode. If Jake moved his tongue a little higher, she'd be coming for sure.

But he refused to move higher, refused to trace that perfect tongue across her clit even once. And the hands on her hips, which had been there to hold her steady before, now held her pinned in place, refusing to let her wiggle herself into the position she so desperately needed. Jes twisted her fingers into his hair, trying to yank his head where she wanted it, but he resisted, and she simply wasn't strong enough to make him do anything he clearly didn't want to. He wasn't going to let her come until he was ready.

Surprisingly, it was her total surrender to his will that made the difference. The moment she relaxed and stopped fighting him, his mouth moved up and engulfed her clit, rapid-fire flicks of his tongue shoving her into orgasm so powerful it nearly hurt.

She could live with pain like that.

Jes cried out, endlessly grateful for what Harley and Misty had done for her by getting Caleb and Forrest out of the house. Not that she could spend a lot of mental energy at the moment thinking about how she'd pay them back. She was too focused on staying upright…and losing her mind to the pleasure.

When the final tremors of her climax finally faded, Jes found herself once again in Jake's arms, his mouth on hers, teasing her lips while her legs attempted to keep her upright. Then Jake was pulling toward his bed, and she knew the evening had just gotten started.

"Wait," she said, tugging at his hand. "I need to go downstairs and get my purse."

Jake stared at her, completely baffled. "Um...really? You need your purse right now?"

Jes laughed. "Yes...right now. Unless you happen to have condoms somewhere in the room?"

The expression on Jake's face went from confusion...to understanding...to urgency. A moment later, he was out the door and running for the stairs. Jes hoped their teammates didn't come back early or they were in for a hell of a show.

"I think I left it on the couch in the living room!" she called out. "Maybe the kitchen counter!"

Jes knew Jake was werewolf fast, but when it came to getting condoms, he showed her she had no idea what fast really meant. Fifteen seconds later, Jake came through the door, running so fast he slid halfway across the room when he tried to stop. He practically threw her purse at her.

She opened it and pulled out the box of condoms Harley and Misty insisted she buy, refusing to leave the pharmacy until she did. Jes had thought it was a bit optimistic at the time, but right then, she was thrilled at their foresight.

Tossing Jake the box, Jes languidly crawled on the bed as he tore into the package. She'd barely had a chance to turn over and get comfortable before he had his shorts off and was moving toward her, foil wrapper in hand.

As he walked, she took a moment to lean back and appreciate Jake's totally naked form.

Broad shoulders, long legs, powerful muscles across his chest and arms, ripped abs with a sexy happy trail leading down to a shaft that made her mouth water it was so perfect. He must have a serious workout regimen.

Sitting up, she rested her hands on Jake's hips, stopping him before he could climb into the bed with her. He looked ready to complain until she slid one hand down and wrapped her fingers around him. He groaned as she caressed him. He was so hard with arousal, she could feel his heartbeat with every pulse. It was...mesmerizing.

Jake's breath hitched when her fingers glided all the way up to the head of his erection, her thumb sliding through the glistening droplet there. She leaned forward, her mouth coming down to take in as much of him as she could, which wasn't nearly enough in her mind. But the exquisite flavor made up for that, and this time, she groaned right along with him.

Part of her wanted to keep licking him, teasing and toying with him exactly as he had with her, but her body wanted him too badly. Though she promised she wouldn't make herself wait too long before trying that particular treat.

She pulled back slowly, making sure Jake would be as eager for the next time as she was. Then she reached out and took the foil condom packet from his hand. She ripped it open and they rolled it on him together. Even something so practical was still sexy when Jake was involved.

When they were done, Jes wiggled back on the bed, never taking her gaze from Jake's. She was already more excited than she thought she'd ever been in her life, but when she saw the hunger in his eyes, she swore she could feel the heat rolling through her body.

Jake climbed on the bed, moving over her with the stealth and grace of a pure predator, yet she'd never felt more protected in her life. Her legs fell open of their own accord as her arms came up to drape around his strong neck and shoulders.

He paused, his shaft hot against her inner thigh, eyes locked with hers. "Are you sure?"

He gazed down at her with a longing and intensity that would have scared her if she hadn't been feeling the exact same thing—not just a need to be with him, but to have him…possess him…like he was something she needed to live.

Jes didn't answer with words, instead dragging him down for a kiss at the same time her legs wrapped around his waist, pulling him closer.

They came together like two pieces of a puzzle. No fumbling or hesitancy. Just pure perfection as the head of his cock found her opening, then slid in deep, making her gasp as he filled her.

She dragged her mouth away from him so she could cry out his name, knowing it would never be like this with anyone else and terrified she didn't understand why that was.

Jake stayed buried deep and unmoving for a few moments before slowly pulling out until only the very tip was inside her. Jes expected him to thrust back in harder, but instead he slid in as slowly as before. The results this time were much like the first—lightning crackled through her body as he filled her, a gasp ripping from her as he found places never touched before.

Eyes never leaving hers, Jake set a steady pace, pulling all the way out, then shoving back in deep. At first his movements were almost gentle, but within moments, the thrusts became harder, the sound of their skin slapping together audible over their moans and groans. She tightened her legs around him, urging him on.

Every time he pounded into her, he sent delightful tingles through her, and Jes knew she wasn't going to last very long before orgasming. She could already feel the heat building up in her middle, spreading outward like a fast-building fire.

Then, when Jes was sure this night couldn't get any better, Jake pressed his face to her neck, burying himself in her hair as his mouth moved over her skin, whispering smoldering words into her ear.

"You're so damn hot and perfect," he murmured, his lips teasing her ear, tracing down to that point along her neck where her pulse pounded in time with her heartbeat. "Like you were made just for me."

She'd thought she was on fire before, but those words, whispered in that deep, rumbling voice of his? When he told her that he wanted her to come for him, it made her wonder if she might burst into flames.

Then she felt the sharp tips of his fangs trailing along her neck, scraping her tender flesh, not enough pressure to break the skin, but enough for her to feel it.

Wow, did she feel it.

The scary part was that there was something inside of her that wanted him to bite her harder, to feel those fangs breaking skin.

He didn't. But she exploded into orgasm all the same. Not a gentle, relaxing release, either, but a violent spasm of pleasure that ripped a long scream from her throat and made her feel like there was no way she'd ever survive the moment.

Her climax came in one long, hard wave, then continued with dozens of lighter ripples that left her weak and shaking. At some point in the mind-blowing process, Jes heard Jake let loose a sexy growl as he came. As he pulsed inside her, he bit down a little bit harder, which resulted in several more delicious spasms of her own. Then he was flipping them over, bringing her trembling body to rest on top of him, her cheek on his sweat-slick chest, her ear treated to the thumping of his rapid heartbeat.

She'd done that to him.

She'd made his heart lose control like that.

They lay there for a long time, their breathing and heart rate slowly returning to something approaching normal. Jes knew hers wouldn't go all the way back to baseline, not when she was draped so casually across Jake's perfect naked body. But she calmed down enough to at least think straight.

Enough to know that nothing would ever be the same again in her life. Whatever it was between her and Jake, everything had changed drastically. She couldn't put a word to what it was now, but she knew it was something she'd never experienced before.

As she lay there thinking, Jes realized her fingers had gone exploring, working with a will of their own as they moved back and forth across the warm skin of his chest, one fingertip lightly tracing the circular scar there. Was it her imagination, or was it even smaller than before they'd started making out tonight?

She played there for a bit, letting her thoughts roam freely, replaying their lovemaking, the primal nature of her attraction to him.

"They haven't come back yet, if you were wondering," Jake said softly, pulling her out of the moment she'd been lost in and reminding her there was a real world out there.

She sighed. "They probably will soon. Should we get dressed and go downstairs so they won't know?"

Jake's strong arm tightened around her, his fingers trailing across her skin as he pressed a kiss to the top of her head. "They already know."

He was right of course.

"We can still get dressed and go downstairs if you want, though," he said, his tone careful and a little uncertain.

Jes pushed herself up off his chest to look down at him. His face was carefully composed, his expression neutral. She ran her fingers gently along his jaw, giving him a smile. "What I want is to stay right here with you. Unless it turns out you're more the hit-it-and-quit-it type of guy?"

"No, I'm not that type." He smoothed her hair back, the corners of his mouth edging up. "I'd love for you to sleep here tonight. As for the team, we won't rub it in anyone's face, but we won't hide it, either. That work for you?"

She smiled. "That works for me."

Resting her head on his chest again, she resumed her exploration of his muscles. Slowly. Like she was cataloging each and every dip and swell.

They lay there in silence, enjoying each other's company. When Jake finally spoke again, she jumped a little, not realizing until then that she'd been falling asleep.

"I'm worried about tomorrow," he murmured, the softly spoken words waking her right back up. "We don't know how many of those things we're going to be facing and we still don't know how to stop them."

She pushed herself up to look at him. "What are you worried about? Beyond the obvious of not knowing how we'll deal with Darby and his crew?"

Jake gazed at her for a long time before answering. "I'm scared you're going to get hurt tomorrow," he finally said, and the pain in his voice took her breath away. "The thought of anything happening to you—"

Jes didn't let him finish. Instead, she climbed on top of him, kissing her way up his chest to his jawline and then across to his lips. "I'm just as worried about you getting hurt. So why don't we make a promise to each other? I won't let anything happen to me, and you won't let anything happen to you, okay?"

He slid a hand up her back until he weaved his fingers into her hair, holding her tight. "Okay. I promise."

Jes knew it was a promise neither one of them could really make, but they made it nonetheless. Then they focused on kissing as she felt the heat building up once more between her thighs. She stopped thinking about tomorrow and focused on the man under her, praying the rest of the team didn't come back for a while.

CHAPTER 12

"I FOUND AN OUT-OF-THE-WAY CORNER NEAR THE REAR loading dock area," Forrest announced in Jake's earpiece over the main radio frequency they were using.

In the background, Jake could hear a rustle as the guy pulled a shortbread cookie from the package he'd brought with him. Because, according to Forrest, he'd been on enough stakeouts to know they could run longer than you usually thought, and he didn't want to deal with an empty stomach. Not that this was exactly a stakeout, but Jake could see his point.

"There's no one here yet," Forrest added, "but from the way all the security types are moving around, the Bilderberg guests should be arriving soon."

"Copy that," Jake said.

To say he was relieved was an understatement. Misty might not have found anything in the Lanesborough Hotel's computers to indicate the meeting had been changed in any way, but he'd still been worried something would come up at the last minute to screw up their plan. So far, it looked like their luck was holding.

He and Misty had been hiding in one of the hotel's unoccupied guest rooms for the past hour. While she'd been wandering around the Lanesborough's computers yesterday, she'd reserved what the hotel called a junior suite. In addition to the bed, nightstands, and dresser, there was a sitting area with a love seat and an antique desk and chair. Floral draperies that matched the pastel-green walls hung from the windows as well as framed the bed. Jake had to admit, the place was money. Even better, the room was a thirty-second sprint from the conference rooms where the Bilderberg Society was meeting.

Well, a thirty-second sprint for him. Probably closer to a three-minute run for Misty. Still, close as far as he was concerned.

"Harley, everything good with you?" he asked into his mic.

"Good here," Harley said softly. "We're already putting the salad out on the tables, which means Forrest is right about the Bilderberg people getting here soon."

No one had questioned Harley when she'd shown up for work that morning dressed as one of the hotel waitstaff. Either her new coworkers thought she was a recent hire or were simply too busy getting everything ready for their VIP guests. Jake still wasn't sure how Misty got into people's computers, but he had to commend McKay for assigning her to the team because she was invaluable. Having Harley inside the meeting room with the Bilderberg members when Darby and his buddies attacked would be critical.

On the downside, having Harley in that room came with no small amount of risk, too. Flat out, they had no idea if Darby and his crew possessed an enhanced sense of smell or not. It was possible they'd ID Harley as a werewolf the moment they walked in. If that happened, she was as good as dead.

Jake had told Harley as much back at the B&B this morning, but Harley agreed to go through with the dangerous assignment anyway. As far as she was concerned, stopping Darby and rescuing those kids outweighed the risk. While Jake could appreciate that, he was already kicking himself for putting her in that room on her own.

"Caleb just radioed in. They're almost in position and waiting for your signal to move," Misty murmured from where she sat at the desk, part of her attention on the conversation coming into her earpiece, the other part focused on the laptop screen she'd been staring at intently for the past fifteen minutes.

The computer allowed her to tap into the hotel's security cameras, flipping from view to view, giving them eyes into nearly every part of the building while the earpiece let her monitor the team's backup radio channel Jes and Caleb were using for the other part of today's operation—the one they were trying to pull off completely on their own.

McKay had come through with a location on the hostages a little over two hours ago thanks to a random delivery receipt for nine cheap twin-sized mattresses Misty had found while searching Darby's computers the other night. At first, no one had thought much about it because up until then, they thought Olivia had been the only kidnapping victim. But after realizing Darby had abducted more children, the intel analysts had dug deeper and tracked the mattress delivery to a big farmhouse located twenty miles northwest of London just outside the town of St Albans. The home had been rented about two weeks earlier by a shell corporation indirectly connected to the Darby empire and the utilities had been turned on several days later. Since then, there'd been a steady stream of takeout delivered to the place—pizza, ham and cheese sandwiches, donuts, cookies, cereal, and lots and lots of milk. It wasn't much to pin their hopes on, but it was enough to make McKay believe they'd found where the kids were being held.

Of course, finding where the hostages were hopefully located meant their team would have to hit two targets at the same time—the farmhouse on the outskirts of St Albans and the Lanesborough Hotel in the center of London. Any other option put either the kids or the Bilderberg people at risk. While the support team McKay had sent over would help as much as they could, it'd be on Jake, Harley, Misty, and Forrest to take care of Darby and his crew while Jes and Caleb handled the hostage rescue.

It twisted Jake's gut into knots being separated from Jes like this, but there was nothing else they could do. Ultimately, this plan gave them the best chance to take down Darby and rescue the kids at the same time. Hell, it was the *only* chance.

He ran his hand through his hair, cursing silently.

"They're going to be okay," Misty said, looking at him as if she could read his mind as easily as she did a piece of computer tech. "Jes is highly experienced and Caleb is a werewolf. If anyone can pull this off, it's the two of them."

Jake nodded, knowing Misty was right. Jes was good at her job, and Caleb was the most capable werewolf he'd ever worked with. Even so, it was difficult trusting the guy to protect someone so important to him, but he had no choice.

This was what it meant for him and Jes to work together on the same team, though. There would be times when he couldn't be right there beside her, when he would have to let her take risks and trust she'd be okay. If he wanted them to be more than teammates, he was going to have to learn to deal with the stress this kind of situation provoked.

But damn, it was hard.

"Look alive, people," Forrest called over the radio.

"Vehicles are arriving at the loading dock now, and the Bilderberg Society people are on-site."

"Roger that." Jake glanced at Misty. "Give Jes and Caleb a heads-up. Darby could hit at any minute, and they need to be ready to move."

Misty nodded and relayed the information into her radio.

Jake felt his heart speeding up more than it ever had during his days back in the SEALs, and he paced back and forth in front of the coffee table, his boots soundless on the plush green carpet. He'd gone on more missions than he could remember when he was a SEAL, and he'd never been this tense about any of them, even when he probably should have been.

His fingertips and gums tingled so much it was almost painful. Shit, he was on the edge of shifting. Not because he was worried about walking into a gunfight himself but because he was terrified about Jes walking into one. The thought made his inner wolf want to howl.

That's when it hit him. Caleb was right. Jes truly was *The One* for him...his soul mate.

He only wished he'd told her last night after they'd made love. Or this morning when he'd woken up with her in his arms. But instead of talking about something important like that, or even spending a few extra minutes kissing, they'd been too focused on sneaking her out of his room and back into her own before anyone saw. Like they were embarrassed to get caught.

Jake prayed he didn't regret that stupid crap.

"The Bilderberg contingent has arrived," Misty announced over the radio. "Be ready to move the moment Darby and his people attack."

Knowing Caleb wouldn't bother, Jes paused to answer Misty. She was good at multitasking, but low crawling through knee-high grass while talking on a radio at the same time simply didn't go together.

"We'll be ready," she murmured to her teammate back in London. "Tell everyone to be careful."

"Don't worry, Jes," Misty replied. "I'll keep an eye on everyone, especially Jake."

Jes opened her mouth to point out she was worried about Misty, Forrest, and Harley just as much as Jake, but then decided not to bother. It was obvious Misty knew what she'd meant.

Sighing, she continued moving carefully toward the quaint two-story Tudor-style farmhouse ahead, parting the grass slowly so no one looking out a window would notice anything unusual.

This stretch between St Albans and Harpenden was full of trees, fields, and farms. While the area had a distinctly English flavor, it reminded her a lot of where she'd grown up in Pennsylvania. It had been so much simpler back then. Before she discovered creatures like whatever Darby was were out there terrorizing people.

When she finally caught up with Caleb, it was to find him sitting against the wall of a weathered wooden tool-shed a few yards away from the back door of the house. The omega werewolf looked positively casual as he leaned against the building. If she didn't know better, she'd think he was hanging out at a family barbecue.

Jes gave him a nod, repositioning the small messenger bag slung over her shoulder and peeking around the side of the shed, then continuing toward the back of the house, Caleb silent as a ghost behind her. The grass closer to the house was shorter, and their trek across the yard left them completely exposed to whoever was inside, but it wasn't like they could wait until tonight to do this. So broad daylight it was.

She and Caleb took their time, slowly working their way along the back and around to the side of the house, carefully peeking in the windows they passed. The kitchen with its brick oven was empty, as was the small mudroom and small study. None of the areas looked like they'd seen people in years. But Jes knew that couldn't be true because they'd seen the two vans parked out front.

As she and Caleb rounded the front to sneak to the other side of the house, they finally found the occupants of those vehicles in the living room, along with the kids Darby had kidnapped. Jes quickly ducked, then slowly peeked over the windowsill again. Beside her, Caleb did the same.

The room had little in the way of furniture, unless you counted the two uncomfortable-looking wood chairs near the arched opening that led to the back of the house. Empty takeout containers and soda cans littered the floor, along with piles of used paper napkins.

Two big, surly-looking men sat in the chairs, handguns casually resting in their laps, their attention locked intently on the hostages.

There were eight kids in all—five girls and three boys, ranging in age from about five to seventeen—sitting on four bare mattresses positioned by the far wall of the living room.

Olivia Phillips sat shoulder to shoulder with the oldest boy on the mattress in the front, like they were trying to protect the younger kids who crowded behind them, clearly terrified. Olivia was obviously scared, too, but determined at the same time.

To a child, every one of them sported bruises and scrapes of some kind. The boy beside Olivia looked like he'd been punched in the face hard enough to break his nose. Both his eyes were blackened and blood stained his T-shirt, but the fierce expression on his face showed just how brave he was.

Jes's heart went out to each and every kid in there, and she wanted nothing more than to storm into the house and kill the men who'd abused and terrorized them. But she couldn't do that. Not yet.

Caleb must have sensed her anger because he touched her arm and pointed at the back of the house. She nodded, knowing they needed to check out the rest of the place.

Jes covered the first floor while Caleb climbed the rock exterior to peek into the upstairs windows. They met up a few minutes later behind the shed to radio Misty and tell her the kids were okay, then compared notes, so they could come up with a plan. Because up until now, they hadn't even known if the kids were still alive. She'd honestly thought when they got here, they'd find nothing but bodies. She'd never been so happy to be wrong.

"There are four more men sitting around the table in the dining room," Jes told Caleb softly as she settled down on the ground beside him.

"Two more are upstairs in the bedrooms getting some shut-eye," Caleb said.

"Crap," she muttered. "When we go in, we're going to be heavily outnumbered."

Caleb considered that. "We'll have the element of surprise. That should help balance out the odds a little bit."

Jes didn't comment on the part of that observation he'd left unsaid. That trying to arrest these men wasn't an option. With the kids in there, it wasn't something they could even consider. They'd have to storm in shooting and wouldn't be able to stop until they'd taken out every last bad guy. Or the bad guys took them out.

She didn't even want to think about that possibility.

A backup team of four STAT agents was positioned half a mile away waiting to take care of the kids after she and Caleb rescued them, but they wouldn't be able to assist. That wasn't their area of expertise.

"Can you tell whether any of the bad guys are creatures like Darby?" she asked, praying they weren't.

Caleb kept his attention focused on the house as he answered. "My nose isn't good enough to tell the difference from outside the house. We're gonna have to assume at least some of them are like Darby. If so, shoot them in the gut, just like we talked about."

Jes nodded.

After spending a good part of the morning discussing how they were supposed to go up against creatures that were seemingly indestructible, she'd mentioned the creature she'd fought in the park when they'd been saving the Robinson boy had stumbled back in what looked like serious pain when she'd kicked it in the stomach.

But would shooting them in the gut even slow the things down?

Jake had put a magazine's worth of large-caliber bullets in the knees of one of those creatures in the park. Caleb had hit another so hard the vehicle's front bumper had been completely destroyed, then run over his buddy, crushing him flat. After all that, the three creatures had still walked away. Probably without a scratch. And their big plan was to shoot them in the gut and hope for the best.

We are so screwed.

"I was thinking I'd go in through the back door and deal with the ones in the kitchen, while you go through the front door and worry about the kids," Caleb said casually as he pulled his Colt .45 automatic and slowly chambered a round.

Jes started to agree, but then stopped, feeling the need to point out the obvious. "You know you just volunteered for the most dangerous part of this operation, right? One against four aren't good odds."

"Somebody's got to do it. Might as well be me." Caleb shrugged. "Besides, Jake would be pissed if I let anything happen to you."

Caleb must have picked up on her confusion, because he grinned. "Jake pulled me aside this morning before we all split up and asked me to watch out for you. Not that I wouldn't have done that already, but...you know..."

"Know what?" she asked sharply. "Does he think I can't watch out for myself? Or do my job?"

She didn't want to think Jake was the kind of guy who thought she wasn't as good in the field because she was a woman, but...

"It isn't like that," Caleb insisted. "Jake knows what you can do and that you're good at it, but you're important to him. He worries about you. Of course, he's gonna be over-protective. He doesn't have a choice."

All she could do was stare at Caleb in confusion. *He doesn't have a choice?* What the hell was that supposed to mean?

But before she could ask, she was interrupted by the radio squawking in her earpiece.

"The bad guys have just arrived," Misty announced. "Get ready. We'll give you the signal to move as soon as the shooting starts."

Jes almost groaned in frustration, realizing this conversation would have to wait. But she sure as hell would get back to it—soon.

"Okay, we go with your plan." Getting to her feet, she pulled her Sig from its holster, racking a round in the chamber, then clicking off the safety. "You go in the back, through the kitchen, and I'll go in the front. Watch out for the ones coming down the stairs."

She glanced at the house, then looked at Caleb. He was on his feet now, his fangs elongated and protruding over his lower lip. His claws were partially extended and the muscles of his neck and shoulders visibly twitched. She'd never seen Jake look this jacked up. Maybe it was an omega thing. Crap, she hoped she could trust him in there. There were a bunch of frightened kids depending on them.

"You ready?" she asked.

Caleb jerked his head violently to the side, cracking his neck first one way, then the other. Rolling his shoulders, he grinned at her, revealing a lot more of his fangs than she ever wanted to see.

"Oh, hell yeah," he growled. "I am so ready."

CHAPTER 13

IT WAS OBVIOUS WHEN DARBY AND HIS CREW ARRIVED because Misty immediately lost video feeds all over the hotel. To anyone on the hotel staff watching, it probably seemed like random static, but if you followed the patterns of the outages, you could trace the path as the bad guys made their way through the Lanesborough Hotel's service corridors.

Jake kept his eyes glued to Misty's laptop over her shoulder, hoping to catch sight of something that might tell him how many people they were dealing with even as she told Jes and Caleb over the radio to be ready to move. They needed to move fast on the farmhouse once Darby arrived at the hotel. Ruthless efficiency dictated he'd almost certainly order the hostages executed the moment he got access to the Bilderberg people. Once he had that, he no longer needed anything from the children's parents.

"I heard someone heading down to the floor below the loading dock," Forrest said. "I'm going to check it out."

"Stay alert," Jake told him.

"Copy that," Forrest replied.

Jake frowned as another video camera cut in and out. "What's your status, Harley?"

"The guests are having lunch, blissfully unaware of any threat."

He knew Harley didn't like the idea of using the Bilderberg people as bait. For the record, neither did Jake.

It was now clear why Darby had gone to such great

lengths with his convoluted scheme to kidnap all those kids. With the information they had, his crew was slipping through the hotel like the place didn't have any security at all. No camera caught sight of them, no locked door slowed them down, no security guard even saw them.

"Dammit, Misty," Jake muttered when the outages of the hotel's security camera system approached the meeting room, a sure sign Darby was about to make his move. "Can't you do something to give me eyes on these people? I need to know what we're up against."

"I'm trying."

Misty rested her hand on the laptop again, her eyes going completely white. A few seconds later, the video feeds began to clear. Not completely, but at least enough to see shapes moving down hallways and through dimly lit rooms as the view on the monitor changed rapidly from camera to camera.

There was no sign of Darby, but Jake cursed when he saw Damien and at least twenty other men with him. Some had stopped to form a security perimeter at each entrance to the areas where the conference rooms were to keep people from wandering into the action, but most were heading straight for the room the Bilderberg Society was using. And weapons were already coming out.

"Shit," Jake said. "Misty, whenever you're done in there, we're going to need your help."

Hoping she not only heard him but would slip out of the computer in time to lend an assist, he headed for the door, flipping channels on his radio on the way.

"Jes. Caleb. Damien is here and he has an army of assholes with him. It's going down now."

Jake paused with his hand on the doorknob, wanting

to say more. But there wasn't time. Besides, the things he wanted to say were for Jes's ears alone.

"Be careful," he finally said, hoping Jes understood everything he couldn't say.

Jerking open the door, he raced down the brightly lit hallway, through one arch then the next as he headed for the stairwell. The moment he flipped back to the main team's radio frequency, it was to hear Harley's soft voice saying she could smell the creatures—lots of them.

"I'm picking up at least ten distinct scents outside the room," she added. "They're surrounding us."

That announcement was followed by Forrest's low whisper letting them know there were three people in the basement.

"I think they're going to cut the power to the hotel," he said.

The words were barely out before the deed was done and the hallway Jake was in pitched into darkness. It was broad daylight outside, but without windows in the corridors, it could just as well have been midnight. He expected emergency lighting to come on immediately—maybe even an alarm of some kind—but neither happened. Darby's people had disabled everything. If he didn't hate the fucker so much, he would have been impressed.

Luckily, Jake didn't need light to see where he was going. Werewolves could see just fine in the dark. His ears picked up the sounds of confused murmurs from all around the hotel, people wondering what had happened to the power, why the back-up generator wasn't coming up, and why the hell they were paying two thousand dollars a night for a place that didn't have one.

All at once, the shooting started and the general babble

of confusion he could hear around him turned to shouts and screams of outright panic, accompanied by the thud and crash as people running for their lives, no doubt smashing into each other and everything in their path.

Jake made the last turn down the hall toward the conference rooms and found four men waiting for him. He wasn't sure if he was disappointed or relieved when his nose told him none of the men were like Darby. They were just normal everyday men—wearing night vision goggles and armed with H&K MP7 submachine guns.

It took them a few seconds to catch sight of Jake running at them in the dark hallway, but when they did, they didn't hesitate to light him up. Four weapons with extended magazines firing at full auto put a lot of metal in the air, and he felt several of the armor-piercing high-velocity rounds slice right through him.

If Jake hadn't been so close before they noticed him, it could have gone badly for him. Fortunately, he was able to get into their personal space before one of them put a bullet through his head. Or heart.

Jake didn't realize until then that he'd yet to draw his Glock. It had been sitting heavy in its holster the entire time he'd been running. And now that he was within grappling distance of four men trying their best to kill him, it was too late to bother. But his claws and fangs had come out at some point during the run, which were just as good if not better.

When one of the men aimed the insanely short submachine gun at him, Jake instinctively grabbed it and shoved it aside as it rattled out a short burst of rounds. The trigger puller had intended to put the bullets through Jake's chest, but instead ended up shooting one of his buddies in the face. Jake was glad it was dark and that his enhanced vision lacked the same color clarity at night as it did in the daylight. The vision of the man's head coming apart and the resulting splatter against the back wall wasn't something he needed to see.

One down…three to go.

Jerking the small submachine gun out of the man's hands, Jake swung it around to smash it into the face of the closest guy on the left before he could get a shot off. A quick slash with his right hand took out the first shooter's throat while a vicious kick sent the guy stumbling back into the other attackers.

Two down…two to go.

Jake spun the MP7 around in his hand and slipped his index finger into the trigger guard. That was a little tricky with his claws fully extended, but he managed it just as the man he'd smacked in the face with the weapon's butt recovered enough to come at him.

The MP7 burped in Jake's hand, the rate of fire insane but recoil hardly noticeable. The bolt locked back on an empty magazine and the man he'd been aiming at went down with half a dozen holes in his chest even though he'd been wearing some kind of body armor. But that's what the MP7's armor-piercing ammo was meant to do—kill people wearing Kevlar.

Three down…one to go.

The last one almost got Jake because he was willing to do anything after seeing three of his buddies go down within the span of a couple seconds. He lunged forward still holding on to the body of the first shooter, using the man's corpse as a shield and blazing through an entire 40 round magazine of ammo in an attempt to make Jake dead.

One of the bullets punched through Jake's shoulder, but it wasn't enough to slow him down. Slipping to the side out of the man's shot line, he closed the distance between them and threw himself on the a-hole with an ear-splitting growl that froze the man solid for a moment.

Jake used the distraction to drop his empty weapon, then drive his target to the floor, the corpse with its throat torn out still wedged between them. Once he'd batted the other man's weapon aside, all it took was a second or two to reach out and get his clawed hands on the guy's head, snapping his neck with an audible crack.

He scooped up one of the MP7s lying on the floor but didn't bother wasting the time searching the bodies looking for spare magazines. The entire time he'd been fighting the four men in the hallway, the sounds of the melee in the conference rooms had gotten louder. The scariest part was that he hadn't heard a peep out of Harley the whole time. He needed to get in there.

Now.

There was another one of Darby's armed men standing outside the doorway to the conference room, the bodies of several other men lying scattered around him. Based on the quality of their suits and the expensive handguns still held loosely in their dead hands, no doubt they were the security guys the Bilderberg Society people had brought with them.

Jake shot the man guarding the door without slowing down, leaping over the body even as it fell to get into the room beyond. He had to stop then just to make sense of the complete and utter chaos taking place within the large conference space.

The room was pitch-dark, lit only by the sporadic muzzle flashes of the various weapons being fired around him. Tables had been arranged in a loose V shape, but most had now been overturned or crushed flat. Plates, utensils, food, and bodies lay everywhere, hotel waitstaff, security guards, and Bilderberg members among the fallen.

The stench of smokeless powder, blood, and those muddle-scented creatures was everywhere. There were small clusters of fighting going on all around the room, people hunkered down behind overturned tables trying to defend themselves against the creatures who seemed nearly invincible in the face of the weapons being used against them.

Nearly invincible, but not completely.

Several of the creatures lay facedown on the floor, unmoving. It was impossible to know exactly where they'd been hit, but from the way the bodies were curled into a fetal position, he was willing to bet they'd been shot in the gut.

Jes's idea had worked.

Jake followed his nose to Harley. She'd herded a group of people to one corner of the room, tables, chairs, and a speaker's podium piled up to give them some level of protection. There were maybe a dozen of the Bilderberg members crouched down behind the makeshift barricade, along with four or five of their security guards, and a bunch of the hotel's waitstaff.

Since Jake had first met her, Harley had always struck him as the most reserved and unassuming alpha he'd ever met. To the degree that sometimes he wondered if she really was an alpha. But that moment, seeing her standing tall,

9mm in her hand, keeping the band of survivors together and directing their attention to one threat after the next, made him forget any doubt he'd ever had.

Jake looked around the room, trying to find Damien, but the big man was nowhere to be seen. Oddly enough, Darby's crew and the humans with them weren't making any attempt to kidnap anyone. They were flat-out aiming to kill anyone they could reach, Bilderberg Society member or not.

Obviously, trying to grab these people for money wasn't the plan.

Harley caught sight of him and pointed toward the large group of men attacking her position. Jake nodded and waded into the fight, the MP7 chattering in his hands. A few of Darby's human goons and another one of the creatures went down before they even realized Jake was there. But when they finally figured it out, the counterattack was immediate and vicious.

Without any cover to hide behind, Jake had no choice but to fall back. He was thinking he might have to retreat all the way out the door when Misty's voice in his ear caught his attention.

"Jake, Damien and a handful of his men are slipping away through the service corridors with three hostages. Their hands are tied behind their backs and they have bags over their heads, so I can't tell exactly who they are, but the clothing tells me they're members of the Bilderberg Society. They're moving toward the front of the hotel. What do you want me to do?"

As if the remaining member of Darby's assault team had been listening in on the radio traffic, the shooting suddenly dropped off sharply as the heavily armed men began to back out of the conference room. They fired enough to keep people ducking, but mostly they focused on getting away. A few of the creatures even paused long enough to reach down and scoop up their dead. Just the creatures, though. Apparently, human goons didn't rate.

"Jake, Damien is almost at the front lobby of the hotel," Misty announced urgently. "What do you want me to do?"

Jake growled in frustration, torn between letting the bad guys get away out the back or Damien and his hostages out the front. In the end, the answer was obvious.

"Harley and I will go after Damien," he shouted, gesturing for her to follow him even as he ran for the door. "Find Forrest, then get to the conference room. Try and help the wounded, then deal with the police when they arrive."

Then he was off and running, hitting the hallway outside the conference room at a full sprint. As he ran through the hotel toward the bedlam he could already hear from the direction of the lobby, he prayed Jes's part of the mission was going better than his.

Because so far, this was a frigging clusterfuck.

Jes and Caleb were on the move before Jake even finished telling them Damien was starting his raid on the hotel. But the angst in his voice when he'd hesitated, then told them to be careful, had been enough to almost make her heart freeze in her chest. It took everything in her to not flip on her mic and tell him to watch himself and not do anything that might harm a single hair on his head. But she had a job to do, and an open channel was no place to tell Jake she was worried about his safety.

Low growls rumbled from Caleb's throat as he disappeared around one side of the farmhouse, heading for the door to the kitchen and the overwhelming number of bad guys waiting for him inside. Based on the visible spring in his step, Jes got the feeling he was looking forward to the murder and mayhem.

It was entirely possible the omega werewolf was slightly deranged. Then again, maybe *omega werewolf* and *deranged* were synonymous.

Jes ducked under the window on the front porch, slipping up quietly to stand beside the door. Caleb had told her earlier he planned to kick in the door leading into the kitchen, but that approach wouldn't work for her. She simply didn't have enough body weight to do it. Fortunately, there was another way.

Pulling the small explosive breeching charge out of her messenger bag, she attached it to the door in between the knob and the frame. Then she applied the electric initiator and flipped the arming key on the handheld trigger unit.

"Ready when you are, Caleb," she whispered, moving to the side of the door a little so she could peek in the window.

"Ready," he replied. "On three. One…two…"

"Three!" Jes shouted, pushing the red button on the trigger unit as she saw the men who'd been sitting on the far side of the living room stand up and advance on the kids, their guns down at their sides, fingers on the triggers. The guy on the right had his cell phone to his ear and while she couldn't hear what he was saying, she got the gist of the conversation. And he wasn't calling for takeout.

Darby was giving them the go-ahead to kill the hostages.

The kids must have realized the same thing. They started screaming, knowing they were as good as dead.

The blast of the front door blowing in sent the kids scrambling for the floor. While one of the men turned toward Jes, the guy who'd been talking on the phone kept his attention locked on the kids, aiming his weapon at Olivia as she threw herself over two of the smaller kids.

Jes momentarily ignored the guy bringing up his weapon and pointing it in her direction, focusing on the guy going after Olivia. Praying these guys weren't like Darby, she stepped inside and put a bullet through his head. Without waiting to see if it took him down, Jes half spun and did the same to the other man. She held her breath for half a second before both men dropped to the floor with solid thuds...and didn't get up. She was still holding her weapon on them when the sound of growling and automatic weapon fire came from the kitchen, shattering the momentary silence.

The kids scrambled backward across the mattresses, screaming bloody murder when they saw Jes coming their way. Keeping her gun low, she motioned for them to sit down.

"Stay on the floor," Jes told them firmly as she edged toward the kitchen.

Caleb expected her to get the children out of there, but she couldn't leave him on his own, regardless if he was a werewolf or not. Besides, if any of the bad guys who were left were supernatural creatures and came after them, this would turn into the shortest rescue in history. It was better to face the creatures head-on, not with her back turned, trying to herd a bunch of kids across the front yard.

Jes had only taken a few steps toward the mayhem going on in the kitchen when she heard the sound of boots on the stairs.

She and the men caught sight of each other at the same time, all three of their weapons coming up. Jes swore she could feel the bullets zipping past her so closely they heated her skin and plucked at her clothes. Ignoring how close she was to dying at that moment, she focused on returning fire.

When she successfully put three rounds through the center of the first guy's chest, she thought dropping him would expose his buddy behind him. Instead, the guy in back latched an arm around the dead man, hiding behind the body like it was a freaking shield.

Jes kept shooting, trying to nail the guy in the legs or the arm he had around the body, but she ran out of time—and ammo—when the man stumbled down the last few steps with his dead buddy and crashed right into her, knocking her weapon from her hand.

The combined weight of both men landing on top of her sent the air exploding out of her lungs. Her vision went a little dark and she would have probably passed out if it wasn't for the gun coming toward her face.

Jes reached around the dead man on her chest, trying to shove the other guy's weapon away. She'd barely managed to nudge the pistol a few inches to the side before it went off, burying a bullet into the floor so close to her face she felt wood chips nick her skin, never mind what it did to her ears. They were going to be ringing for days.

She struggled at the dead weight on her chest, knowing if she didn't get the corpse off soon, the living goon would put a bullet through her within seconds—if he didn't suffocate her first. So she took a chance and shoved one hand between her and the body, getting it on the corpse's chest and trying to push it to the side.

Unfortunately, that move didn't achieve a damn thing. But on the upside, it did put her in contact with the extra magazine for the dead guy's weapon. Fully loaded, it was big and heavy.

The man above her was already moving his weapon back into position to turn her head into a bloody mess, and she didn't stop to think. She simply grabbed hold of the magazine filled with bullets and swung as hard as she could.

She'd been aiming for the man's temple. While she missed his head, she did get him in the throat.

The guy tumbled to the side, rolling onto the floor, coughing and choking. He wrapped his free hand around his crushed throat while swinging his pistol around wildly with the other, pulling the trigger over and over again in a mad attempt to kill her.

The dead body that was still on top of Jes saved her life, absorbing every bullet that came her way.

As soon as the guy ran out of bullets, Jes shoved the corpse off her and went on the offensive. He was still choking and half-blind from tears and lack of oxygen, so Jes threw herself on him and started beating the crap out of him with the base of the magazine in her hand, finally ending it with that temple shot she'd been going for earlier.

Jes climbed to her feet, gasping for air and OD'ing on adrenaline. Out of the corner of her eye, she caught a glimpse of the kids over by the wall, staring at her in shock. Ignoring them, she looked around wildly for her weapon, finding it a few feet away, at the bottom of the stairs. Quickly reloading the Sig, she spun around, heading for the kitchen, abruptly realizing it was now deathly silent in there.

Oh crap.

She cautiously entered the room, ready for anything, only to conclude she needed to get a new definition of the word *anything*.

The kitchen was completely demolished, the trestle table smashed to smithereens, the brick around the wood-fired oven broken and lying on the floor in pieces, blood covering the walls. Caleb was in the middle of it all, the jacket he'd been wearing when she'd last seen him nowhere to be found. His T-shirt was shredded from the multiple bullets he'd been hit with, blood staining the fabric an even darker hue. If she hadn't seen how much damage a werewolf could sustain and keep going, she would have assumed he was a dead man standing.

Four bodies—some no longer possessing all their limbs—were scattered around the kitchen, one hanging from the opening of the oven, throat torn out. Caleb's long claws were extended, covered in blood and bits of stuff Jes didn't want to think about. Even more disconcerting was the fact that his fangs had blood on them, too. Glistening red droplets ran onto his shirt as he stood there holding the body of a man he'd killed mere moments earlier.

At the sound her footsteps on the kitchen's tile floor, Caleb let loose a savage snarl, his eyes glowing vivid blue. Jes was pretty sure the man she'd come to know over the past few days wasn't home at the moment. Jake had said something about omegas having control issues. This must be what losing control looked like for a werewolf.

She took a deep breath, wondering how to handle this

situation. She didn't think Caleb would actually attack her, but she wasn't sure.

Jes took a cautious step toward him when she heard Misty's urgent voice in her earpiece.

"I hope everything is okay on your end, guys, because we could seriously use your help back in London. Damien has three members of the Bilderberg Society and is trying to get them out of the hotel now. I have no idea where he's taking them."

Jes cursed, earning her another snarl from Caleb. He hunched down over the last man he'd killed, dragging the body closer to him like it was his favorite blanket she was going to try to steal from him. He seemed ready to kill anyone who got close to it. Either that or jump out the window with it.

"We're on the way, Misty," Jes said softly.

Moving carefully, so she wouldn't spook Caleb, she took out her cell and called the support team, telling them they could come get the kids. Jes would have preferred to stay, to make sure all the children were indeed as okay as they appeared, but that wasn't an option. Unfortunately, neither was waiting around for Caleb to snap out of omega mode.

Holstering her gun and hoping for the best, Jes marched straight up to him and smacked him across the face. When he growled at her, she did it again—harder.

"Snap out of it," she said. "Our teammates are in trouble and we need to help. Let's go!"

Caleb growled again, softer this time, the blue slowly fading from his eyes. Frowning, he looked down at the body he was still holding before letting it fall to the floor.

"I'm not even going to ask what I was doing with that," he murmured. "But I'm gonna need a new shirt before we go unless you want people staring at us all the way back to London."

CHAPTER 14

THE PEOPLE IN THE LOBBY SCREAMED AND SCRAMBLED out of the way as Jake and Harley raced through the crowd that had formed there after Damien and his men stormed through only seconds earlier. Several men lay on the floor bleeding heavily from the wounds they'd sustained from either getting in the way or trying to stop them. Jake wanted to help the wounded, but he couldn't—not if it meant letting Damien and his crew get away. So he shoved his way to the automatic glass doors and headed outside, careful to make sure his claws and fangs were safely stowed, Harley on his heels.

Once on the sidewalk, he slowed long enough to see four large SUVs squealing out of the hotel's parking lot and onto Grosvenor Place, heading south. Damien and the three men from the Bilderberg Society he'd kidnapped were in the first vehicle, which was the only one Jake cared about.

Knowing it was probably insane, he took off running down the sidewalk with a growl, refusing to let Damien get away that easily.

Keeping his claws and fangs hidden from people was easy, but no way were they going to miss how fast he was running as he cut across the major intersection south of the hotel, darting around moving cars and leaping over the ones that stopped right in his path. Hopefully, no one had their cell phones out or this was going to be difficult to explain.

The traffic was fairly heavy, which slowed down the four SUVs a little, but they drove like psychos, not stopping for lights, and slamming into any vehicle that had the nerve to get in their way.

Jake was only fifteen feet behind the last vehicle in the escape convoy at the intersection of Grosvenor and A3214. He thought for sure he was going to catch up when the back window of the SUV exploded.

Even though he knew what was coming, Jake barely avoided the bullets as they slammed into the asphalt around him. Cars squealed and jumped up onto the sidewalk to get away, pedestrians screaming as they threw themselves down behind anything that would protect them.

Still ducking bullets, Jake pulled his Glock, waiting for the right moment to surge ahead and get close enough to put a bullet in one of the vehicle's back tires, not to mention one of the shooters. He could tell from the stench coming out of the broken rear window that the guys with the MP7s weren't normal humans, but shooting them in the stomach wasn't an option from this angle.

Jake was less than half a dozen feet away when Damien's vehicle suddenly turned down a side street near the post office just as a woman with a tiny toddler in her arms was crossing the street. Eyes wide with panic, she quickly back-pedaled, only to nearly get hit by the second SUV. She stumbled forward to avoid it, her arms wrapping desperately around her child as she fell. The third vehicle missed her by inches and the fourth clipped her just enough to send one of her shoes flying.

The woman had somehow avoided getting run over, but when the two men in the last SUV started shooting at him again, Jake knew the woman's luck wouldn't hold.

Taking the turn at a sprint that would make an Olympic

runner seem slow, Jake ducked down to scoop up the woman and kid even as bullets kicked up fragments where she'd just been. The woman and her little boy weren't much in the weight department, but when you're trying to take a turn at thirty-five miles an hour, it was still enough to throw him off balance.

Jake went down hard, protecting the woman and her kid as he took the impact on his shoulder, then rolled violently, trying to stop his momentum. And after running as fast as he'd been, there was a lot of momentum to lose.

He ended up slamming into the side of a parked van, hard enough to leave a deep dent, but when he finally stopped and rolled onto his back, the woman and her little boy were fine. Well, maybe they were a little scuffed up and rattled, but they were mostly undamaged. Out of the corner of his eye, Jake caught sight of several Metro foot patrol officers coming his way, staring at him intently as they spoke urgently into their radios.

"Sorry," he muttered, setting the woman on the ground as gently as he could as she stared up at him in disbelief. "I gotta go."

Then he was up and running again, the Metro Police yelling at him even as the row of dark SUVs disappeared out of sight around a corner three blocks up.

Shit.

He was going to lose them.

Jake was damn close to stealing the first vehicle he came to when he heard the roar of an engine behind him. He threw a look over his right shoulder, expecting to see a cop car full of pissed-off Metro Police officers. Instead, it was a familiar silver Audi, Harley behind the wheel.

"Get in!" she shouted out the open passenger window as she drove. "We can still catch them!"

Jake didn't pause to wonder how the hell she'd thought to get the car when it hadn't even occurred to him. He simply veered to the left, grabbed the edge of the window, and vaulted inside. The moment he did, Harley punched the accelerator.

Two blocks down, Harley took the same right turn Damien and his crew had—at sixty miles an hour. Jake grabbed the overhead handle, pretty sure the tires on her side of the vehicle actually left the ground. Oncoming cars swerved wildly, honking horns and running up onto the curb.

"You're on the wrong side of the road!" he yelled.

"No, I'm not," she shouted back. "They are!"

Jake didn't bother to point out the obvious: *Their country…their rules.* Instead, he grabbed his seat belt and prayed they survived long enough for him to get it on.

Harley caught up with the SUV convoy in an amazingly short period of time. Probably because she was driving like a frigging lunatic. But he guessed he couldn't argue with the results.

The men in the vehicle with the broken rear window didn't see them coming until Harley slammed the front of the car into the back of the SUV. When one of the men flew out, landing on the hood of the Audi, Harley tapped the brakes hard enough for the creature to roll off, then punched the gas and drove over the top of him as if stuff like that happened to her all the time.

The thud and subsequent crunch as the thing passed under the car sounded bad, but when Jake took a quick glance out the back window, he was stunned to see the man already scrambling to his feet, arms held out to his side at weird angles.

Shit.

Harley was just approaching the last vehicle again, a little more carefully now, when the second and third vehicles suddenly turned left, splitting from the others.

"Which ones do we follow?" Harley demanded, hands gripping the wheel as if ready to spin the car into another crazy turn at Jake's word.

"Stay with the lead SUV," he said without hesitation. "Damien is in there with the Bilderberg hostages. We can't lose them."

Harley nodded and kept with the two vehicles going straight, weaving as the lone man left in the backseat of the one in the rear tried to get a bead on them with his MP7.

How much frigging ammo are these people carrying?

Just then, two Metro Police cars pulled across the intersection ahead of the first SUV, probably thinking it would stop. Instead, it smashed right through both vehicles, sending the smaller cop cars spinning away into traffic.

"Jake, where are you?" Jes's beautiful voice suddenly asked through his radio earpiece. "Misty said you need our help. What's the situation?"

Relief like he couldn't believe flooded through Jake's body, and it was all he could do to keep from asking if Jes was okay, if she'd gotten hurt in any way.

"We're heading west on Redesdale Street," Harley answered for him. "Just past the Royal Hospital Chelsea, running parallel to the Thames, following two SUVs."

"Damien has three of the Bilderberg people in the front

vehicle with him," Jake added. "The bad guys are heavily armed."

There was a moment of silence over the radio, then Jes was back. "Okay, got ya. We're coming toward you from the west, only a couple minutes away. We'll try and cut them off. Let us know if they change direction."

Jake wanted to ask how the hell they'd gotten down from St Albans so fast, but with Harley still trying to avoid the bullets coming at them from the SUV in front of them, he knew the questions would have to wait. Instead, he focused on continuing to provide position updates to Jes, leading her and Caleb closer to them with every passing second.

Less than a minute later, Jake spotted Jes and Caleb coming toward them in their rented SUV. Damien must have seen them, too, because his SUV abruptly turned left on a much smaller road heading straight for the river. The other vehicle went with them.

"According to the map on my phone, this road is going to dead end at the river in a few hundred feet," Jes called out as she and Caleb followed him and Harley. "There's nowhere for them to go."

The side street weaved in and out of several big industrial-looking buildings, Dumpsters, and haphazard piles of boxes and pallets. But at least there wasn't any traffic or people around. If this was going to turn into a shoot-out, an abandoned dead-end street was the best place for it to happen.

"Remember there are three hostages in the lead vehicle," Jake said. "Check behind your targets before you pull the trigger. Assume they may try to use them as human shields."

The slow-moving water of the Thames came into sight

as the rearmost SUV slammed on their brakes, kicking up loose chunks of the pavement as the vehicle slid to a stop sideways on the narrow road, completely blocking the way ahead. Damien's vehicle kept going, racing for the river's edge.

Harley immediately slammed on the brakes, and Jake tensed, waiting for impact when Caleb smashed into their rear bumper. Thankfully, that didn't happen because Caleb was able to stop in time.

Jake jumped out of the car along with Harley to confront the three men who'd taken up defensive positions behind their SUV. His nose told him all three of them were creatures like Darby and Damien, their muddled scent heavily camouflaged by the acrid stench of smokeless powder from all the shooting they'd done.

The automatic weapon fire from their guns shredded the Audi's exterior like it was tissue paper. Jake rolled to the left, finding cover behind a heavy-duty Dumpster full of construction debris, while the men—creatures—continued to rip both the Audi and Caleb's SUV to pieces. Out of the corner of his eye, Jake saw Harley scramble away to safety. He prayed Jes and Caleb found something to hide behind as well.

As he, Jes, Harley, and Caleb returned fire, Jake quickly realized the men with the submachine guns were going out of their way to make a mess out of the two rental vehicles while doing little more than making him and the rest of his team duck and cover.

A sinking feeling in his gut, Jake risked standing up behind the Dumpster, peeking around the back side to get a view of the river. What he saw confirmed his worst fears.

"Dammit," he growled. Now, he knew why the a-holes had been willing to drive down a dead-end street. "Damien had a boat waiting for him. They're getting away!"

Moving out from behind the safety of the Dumpster, Jake ran toward the SUV, ignoring the hail of bullets that came his way. Out of the corner of his eye, he caught a glimpse of Harley and Caleb sprinting to catch up to him. Hopefully, Jes wasn't foolish—or brave—enough to follow. He didn't want her anywhere near those effing creatures.

A round tagged Jake in the left calf, then the right thigh, and then another one sliced through his left upper arm. He ignored all of them, running faster, then throwing himself down and into a slide across the broken asphalt in front of the SUV.

The move momentarily took him out of the line of fire of the three creatures on the other side of the vehicle, and before his slide had even come to a stop, Jake fired under the vehicle, aiming for the only part of the three creatures he could see—their lower legs and ankles. The screams of pain told him he'd hit what he was aiming for.

Jake was up and running a split second later, slipping around the back of the SUV as Harley and Caleb went over the top of it. He slowed only long enough to put a couple rounds in the gut of the nearest creature, then he hauled ass for the river, leaving the creatures for his teammates. He heard the rapid thump of lighter shoes behind him and knew without looking it was Jes. She was ignoring the risk of the creatures putting a bullet in her back so she could chase after him. He let out a growl, fighting the urge to spin around and tell her she needed to be more careful. But there wasn't time for that. Not that she'd listen to him if he tried.

Jake heard the dull thrum of boat engines before he reached the dock and the abandoned SUV parked there. There were several larger, commercial-looking vessels lined up at the concrete pier, so it took him several seconds to find the one Damien had taken.

It was a fancy yacht, all gleaming white and chrome, already in the middle of the river. A good seventy-five or hundred feet out, it was moving upstream quickly. The three hostages were lined up on their knees in the back of the boat, a creature behind each of them, claws digging deep into the men's necks. Damien stood to the side, a smirk on his face that Jake could see all the way from the dock.

One by one, the creatures jerked the black bags off their captives' heads. The men blinked rapidly in the sudden bright sunlight, pain etched on each of their faces. A dark-skinned man with a heavy black beard, a white man with gray-flecked hair and a matching beard, and a dark-haired man with olive skin, they all shook their heads as if to clear them.

As Jes came to a stop beside Jake, he raised his weapon to get a shot lined up on Damien, but then hesitated. At this distance, aiming at a moving boat, he'd be just as likely to hit the hostages as that bastard. And unfortunately, getting out to that yacht wasn't an option. None of the commercial vessels were going to have keys in them, and trying to race along the shore to keep up with the boat as it moved upstream would be impossible with all the buildings and fences along the river. And while he was a damn good swimmer, he wasn't nearly fast enough to catch up to a boat.

"Jake, look," Jes said softly, pointing.

He turned his attention back to the yacht to see Darby

step out from the cabin. As if knowing Jake and Jes were there, he looked their way for a long moment, then walked up to stand behind the three men kneeling on the deck. Taking a handgun from inside his jacket, Darby shot each hostage in the back of the head in quick succession, then turned and walked back into the cabin without a backward glance.

"Shit," Jake muttered.

Lifting his weapon, Jake pulled the trigger while Jes did the same. They hit the rear of the craft several times but didn't do any damage, and all either of them could do was stand and watch the vessel disappear from sight around the next bend in the river.

"Why the hell did he go to all that trouble to kidnap them and drag them halfway across the city only to effing shoot them after he got away?" Jake growled, fangs and claws extending in frustration as much as anger. "It doesn't make sense."

Jes rested a gentle hand on his arm. "I don't know why he did it, but at least we saved all of those poor kids he kidnapped as well as the other members of the Bilderberg Society and countless other people at the hotel. That has to count for something."

As Jake stared at the dark blue water of the Thames, listening to the drone of Darby's yacht fading away, he wasn't sure he believed that. They'd lost the three men Darby had grabbed and some people at the hotel, too. On top of that, there was the insane number of crashed vehicles as a result of their chase through the city. It would be stupid to think no one had gotten hurt—or worse—during all that mayhem.

He doubted anyone would call this a win.

"Jake. Jes," Harley called from behind them. "I think you two are going to want to see this."

He clenched his jaw. What the hell else could go wrong today?

Sirens filled the air as he and Jes headed back to where Harley and Caleb were standing, staring down at something on the ground by the bad guys' SUV. Luckily, the police hadn't realized they'd come down this side street, but sooner or later, the cops would figure it out. Somebody had heard the gunshots for sure.

Jake stopped cold when he saw what Harley and Caleb were looking at. Although, he wasn't exactly sure what the hell he *was* looking at.

What the...?

He thought they were the bodies of the three men Harley and Caleb had tussled with and killed, but they didn't look like men. In fact, they didn't look human. Which made sense, since they were supernatural creatures.

They reminded him of mannequins you'd find in a department store. Pale, almost translucent skin was stretched tightly over androgynous, nearly featureless faces. The mouths were evident and filled with what had to be a hundred tiny, needlelike teeth, but beyond that, there was almost nothing else recognizable. A vertical ridge divided the top portion of their faces in place of a nose, and two sunken patches of skin were where eyes should be. The things had no ears or hair of any kind.

Seriously, it was the creepiest thing Jake had ever seen, made even worse by the fact that all three of these things had looked like completely normal humans a few minutes ago. Humans that could have walked down any street in the world without attracting attention.

The sounds of rapidly approaching sirens shook Jake out of his musings. He lifted his head and listened closely. The cops were getting closer. They'd deployed a helicopter, too, if the droning sound of a propeller was any indication.

"We need to get these bodies, and ourselves, out of here," he announced. "We can't get caught up in trying to explain all of this, and we have to get these things back to McKay to be examined. We need to figure out what the hell we're dealing with and what they're up to. We keep coming out on the short end of this deal because we don't understand the script these things are following. That changes now."

Jake turned his attention back to the three creatures on the ground, taking in their disturbing faces again as Jes called in the support team, telling them they needed an immediate extraction and a priority airlift back to the States for three supernatural bodies.

CHAPTER 15

JES STARED AT THE REMAINS OF FLUFFY SCRAMBLED eggs and buttered toast on her plate. She should eat the rest, but she was simply too damn tired to do it. She'd gotten an hour's worth of quality sleep last night and the lack of rest was taking its toll. If it wasn't for the gallon of coffee she'd consumed already, she wouldn't even be capable of functioning as a human being right now.

Picking up her fork, she pushed a few more bites of egg into her mouth, chewing mechanically. A few forkfuls and another bite of toast later, she finally gave up, scraped what was left on her plate into the trash and poured more coffee into her mug. After adding cream and sugar, she walked into the living room to sit down on the couch. Taking a sip, she tucked her legs under her, then wrapped her long cardigan around her and allowed herself to enjoy the early morning quiet as the sun streamed through the big bay window, warming the whole room.

Directly across from the couch, the videoconference monitor was still hooked up and ready to go, currently in standby mode until it was needed again. Even though it was barely after three o'clock in the morning back in DC, McKay wanted the channel left open, so they wouldn't have to wait to establish an Internet connection if anything critical came up.

Fortunately, it hadn't.

Yesterday and last night had been crazy to say the least. The support team had barely gotten her, Jake, Harley, and

Caleb out of the alley before the cops had arrived. In fact, if it wasn't for the EMS-style vehicles they'd used to pick them up, they probably wouldn't have made it out of there at all. That was one of the things she loved about STAT—they had a plan for everything.

After dropping them off at the house, the support team had immediately headed back out to pick up Forrest and Misty from the crap storm at the hotel. That hadn't been as complicated as Jes thought it might be, mostly because the Lanesborough had been an absolute madhouse, with every law enforcement agency in London showing up and attempting to take control of the situation, including MI5.

Misty had made it through the melee at the Lanesborough Hotel with little more than a few scrapes and bruises. Forrest, on the other hand, had come back looking half-dead. In fact, when Jes had first seen him covered in blood from head to toe, his hotel maintenance shirt shredded by claws, she was sure there was no way he'd make it. And yeah, Misty had been freaking out. Jes didn't blame her.

Luckily, very little of the blood had been his. Apparently, he'd tangled with two of the creatures down in the basement after they'd cut the hotel power. While Jes really didn't want to think too much about what it would be like to fight those things in a pitch-black room with no windows, it squicked her out even more to imagine being trapped under one of them after gutting them and having gallons of their blood gushing all over her.

Okay, gallons might be an exaggeration. But if how much blood had been on Forrest's clothes was any indication, those creatures had a lot more of it than regular humans. It was thicker and darker in color, too.

Jes heard footsteps on the stairs and turned her head to see Jake standing in the doorway. Dressed in jeans and a T-shirt, his hair stuck up in a few places, like he'd just run his fingers through it. He looked as exhausted as she felt. Actually, he looked worse than she felt. Her heart ached a little at the sight of him. He might be a werewolf, but he'd still gotten shot a hell of a lot of times yesterday. It had taken Jes more than an hour to tend to his wounds when they got back to the B&B. Getting the bullets out hadn't been fun, but thankfully, there hadn't been any debris in the openings, so they'd healed over quickly.

Of course, Jake had been far more concerned with the few scrapes she'd gotten during her wrestling match at the house in St Albans, personally tending to every boo-boo she had on her body. Truthfully, she hadn't minded the attention. While all that TLC hadn't led to sex—mostly because they'd had to spend endless hours briefing McKay on what was going on— simply having Jake's hands on her was an amazing experience. It was hard to put into words, but in some ways, the care he'd taken last night was as intimate as when they'd made love.

"Any coffee left?" he asked hopefully.

Jes nodded, wincing as he walked slowly into the kitchen. She had no doubt the gunshot wound through his calf was bothering him more than he'd let on last night. Then again, he was a guy as well as an alpha werewolf, so he was clearly trying to hide it from her. Still, the urge to jump up and run into the kitchen to see if he was okay was difficult to ignore. But she resisted the impulse. He wouldn't appreciate her hovering over him.

So instead, she sat on the couch sipping her coffee and listening to Jake moving around the kitchen, wondering if they might be able to grab a few precious moments alone together before the craziness started all over again and they'd be on the move to try to track down Darby.

Jake returned to the living room a few minutes later, a gigantic mug of coffee in one hand and a package of chocolate chip cookies in the other. He sat down beside her, so close that his thigh rested against hers, and little tingles raced up her leg.

Damn, she had it crazy bad for him.

Or she was losing her marbles.

One or the other.

He held out the package, offering her a cookie. "Anything else from McKay?"

Jes took a cookie, dunked it in her coffee, then nibbled on it. Although smaller than the chocolate chip cookies she was used to in the States, the British version was still sweet, crunchy, and had loads of chips. "Not yet."

Jake nodded and sipped his coffee, his brow furrowing.

While Jake hadn't said it in so many words, Jes knew he blamed himself for every life that had been lost yesterday, both at the hotel and on Darby's yacht, even though there wasn't anything they could have done differently to change any of it.

The upper level desk jockeys back at STAT headquarters hadn't helped the situation any. Their 20/20 hindsight allowed them to nitpick every single decision she, Jake, and the rest of the team had made. While they'd saved a lot of people, including the kids who'd been kidnapped, and recovered the bodies of a type of supernatural that no one had ever seen before, at the end of the day, that didn't seem to be enough. They couldn't understand why Darby had killed those three men he'd abducted and weren't above implying she, Jake, and their teammates had gotten them killed because they'd screwed up. McKay, the only supervisor with any field time in this century, was the only one to stand up for them.

That said, McKay wasn't thrilled with what had happened yesterday. The UK press was all over the supposed terrorist attack on the hotel, as well as the high-speed chase through the city. Since the incident was not only high-profile but also involved the Bilderberg Society, their boss had been forced to contact British intelligence and give them a heads-up. The press hadn't revealed the identity of the three men Darby had murdered yet, but they would soon.

Biting into a cookie, Jake leaned forward and flipped open the magenta file folder on the coffee table to once again pore over everything they knew about the three men Darby had killed. Unfortunately, there wasn't much. Like all members of the Bilderberg Society, the men had been intensely private about their personal lives and had the money to keep it that way.

"Ryo Arsenault," Jake murmured, reading the bio of the olive-skinned man Darby had shot last. "A billionaire from South America, he made his money in the space industry and was currently involved with the space center in French Guiana."

Jes frowned as Jake stared at the man's photo, reviewing notes about Arsenault's family and business dealings. He'd already read everything in there last night—more than once. Reading it again would only make him feel even more responsible for what had happened to the men, but Jes knew Jake didn't want to hear that, so she didn't say anything.

"Lais Khan from the Arab Emirates," Jake continued, turning to the photo of a dark-skinned man with black hair and a full beard. "He owned a number of chemical manufacturing facilities throughout the Middle East, Africa, and India."

Jake flipped the page, but before he could say anything, Jes interrupted him, repeated the man's bio from memory.

"Laurent Marconi, born and raised outside of Paris. He was a philanthropist and major shareholder in Airbus Defense and Space, Europe's leading defense company."

Jake nodded but kept reading the file in front of him anyway.

Jes reached out and flipped the folder closed. "You've read those files a hundred times already and you can read them a hundred more," she said gently. "But it isn't going to tell you why Darby kidnapped those men or why he murdered them. All we know is that he did and that we're going to hunt him down and make him pay for it."

"Damn straight we will," Caleb said gruffly as he walked into the living room, a mug of coffee in one hand and a jar of peanut butter in the other.

Misty, Forrest, and Harley trailed slowly behind Caleb like a pack of overworked and undercaffeinated zombies, each with their own cup of coffee.

Jes sat back on the couch with a sigh. She'd been hoping to have a little time to talk to Jake privately, but it would have to wait.

"You forgot to put cream and sugar in your coffee," Misty said, glancing at Forrest over the rim of her mug as he sat down on the arm of the wingback chair she'd curled up in.

He looked down at his mug with a frown, then shrugged.

"I need caffeine too much to worry about what it tastes like. I'll add cream and sugar later—after I wake up."

Caleb snorted in obvious amusement at that as he sat on the floor beside the coffee table. Taking the lid off the jar of peanut butter, he took out a generous spoonful and shoved it in his mouth. Jes didn't realize she was staring as he shoved the freshly licked spoon into the container again until he paused with the next serving of peanut butter halfway to his mouth and stared back.

"What?" he demanded.

Jes shook her head. She didn't know why she thought she could expect any better from him. "What if someone else wanted to eat some of that?"

Caleb considered the question as he ate what was on the spoon, then went back for another helping of peanut-buttery goodness. Okay, double-dipping was bad enough, but this was taking it to extremes.

"I was going to put it back when I was done," he pointed out.

The expression on his face made Jes think he clearly didn't see what the big deal was, and she didn't feel like explaining it to him.

"Speaking of disgusting," Jake said. "Did you decide to skip that shower we all talked about, Forrest? Because you still reek."

Forrest dropped his head back with an audible sigh.

"You've got to be kidding me," Misty said. "He still smells like those creatures? How is that possible? He took two showers last night and another one this morning."

This was one of those times Jes was glad she didn't have a werewolf's nose. Apparently, after getting doused with the blood from those creatures, Forrest had absorbed their scent. According to Jake and Harley, it was really bad.

"Even I can smell it," Caleb said around a mouthful of peanut butter.

"Those things have blood like motor oil," Forrest said morosely. "No matter how much I scrub, it still feels like there's a film of grease on my skin."

"Have you tried using dish soap?" Harley suggested from the other wingback chair. "You know, like they do with birds who get stuck in oil spills?"

Forrest gave Misty a questioning look. "What do you think?"

"It's worth a try," she replied, then, as if on impulse, grabbed his hand and squeezed it. "I don't care what you smell like. I'm just glad you're okay."

Amen to that, Jes thought.

"Do you think the creatures' bodies are back in DC yet?" Caleb asked, taking a break from shoving peanut butter in his face to swig his coffee.

Jes glanced at her watch, calculating how long it would have taken a military cargo plane to get back to the states. "Definitely. Although I have no idea who they're going to get to do the autopsies. I'm pretty sure STAT doesn't have a lot of experts on supernatural anatomy on call."

"Actually, McKay might," Jake said. "There's a woman named Davina DeMirci who runs a nightclub out in Los Angeles that caters to supernaturals. She's not a medical examiner, but if anyone can tell us what these things are, it would be her."

Before Jes could ask how the woman knew so much about supernatural creatures, Misty's cell phone rang. Picking it up from where it rested on her lap, she glanced at the screen.

"It's McKay," she said, thumbing the button and answering it. After a quick conversation, she hung up and grabbed the TV remote from the coffee table, handing it to Forrest. "There's something on BBC he wants us to see. He didn't say what, but whatever it is, it's serious."

While Forrest flipped through the channels looking for the right one, Misty quickly got McKay on Skype. Behind his glasses, his eyes were red and tired looking, and his usual neatly tied tie was loose, the top two buttons of his dress shirt undone. Crap, their boss looked wiped out. That was saying a lot since McKay operated on little to no sleep on a regular basis.

"Do you have BBC on yet?" he asked without preamble.

Jes wanted to ask what was so important on TV but forced herself to wait patiently while Forrest figured out which channel was BBC. When he finally did, Jes gaped at what she saw. Around the room, everyone else looked equally stunned.

Standing behind a big podium with large projector screens to either side of them, were the three men Darby had murdered, only they looked a lot less dead than they had yesterday.

"What the hell?" Caleb murmured softly, eyes locked on the TV.

Jes stared as Ryo Arsenault, the South American billionaire, stepped up to the cluster of microphones on the podium. The crowd of eager journalists in front of the men immediately began to quiet down, the cacophony of noise diminishing until there was nothing left but the occasional rapid-fire clicking of cameras.

"For those who do not know me, my name is Ryo

Arsenault, and this is Lais Khan and Laurent Marconi," the man said in a rich, deep voice. "As I'm sure most of you are aware, yesterday afternoon, the Lanesborough Hotel was attacked by a group of unidentified terrorists. Many people were injured in the attack, and unfortunately, some were killed. What has not been released to the public is that the three of us were kidnapped. If we had not escaped our captors earlier this morning, we would all almost certainly be dead by now."

Cameras clicked away even louder, and reporters shoved their handheld recorders a little bit closer. Jes could almost feel the anticipation building in the room. This guy had the group of reporters eating out of his hands.

"The target of yesterday's attack at the Lanesborough was a special meeting of the Bilderberg Society, an organization that these other men and I are proud to be associated with. While there were several topics on our agenda yesterday, there was only one project that would provoke these anarchists to such extreme action: the ACE program."

As he spoke, the projector screens to either side lit up. The one on the left depicted a long-range view of a huge rocket standing on a launch platform, while the one on the right displayed what appeared to be some kind of satellite.

"Our planet is running out of fresh water in those parts of the world least able to manage it—the Middle East, India, North Africa, and Central Asia." Arsenault motioned toward the image to the right of the screen. "This is the Aquifer Climate Experiment satellite. The ACE was developed by the Bilderberg Society in conjunction with NASA and the University of California, Irvine. When placed into a low earth orbit and connected with others like it, ACE will allow us to locate new water sources at depths never before possible. This technology will help us save billions of people around the globe."

As if they had practiced the speech a dozen times, Arsenault immediately moved away from the microphones to be replaced by Lais Khan. "The three of us attended the meeting at the Lanesborough to finalize plans for the launch of the first ACE satellite at the end of the month. That is the reason we were the ones kidnapped and selected to be executed by people who care little whether people in these parts of the world live or die—people who thrive on misery and death."

"But we will not be deterred from our efforts," Laurent Marconi stepped forward to say. "If anything, this attack has convinced us that we are moving too slowly. That is why we're going to accelerate our plans and accomplish something never attempted before—the launch and delivery of three satellites into orbit all at the same time."

The screen on the right changed, showing a lush green landscape with multiple large buildings positioned at well-spaced distances from each other.

"This is the Guiana Space Centre outside of Kourou in French Guiana, South America," Arsenault said. "Three ACE satellites are on their way there as we speak, where they will be mounted onto three Ariane 5 rockets and prepared for immediate launch in three days."

The press seemed to realize how huge this whole thing was and eagerly asked their questions all at once.

"Why are you rushing the launch?"

"Is it possible to do something like this so quickly?"

"Why launch three satellites at once?"

"Do you expect another attack?"

But rather than answer any of their questions, Arsenault continued. "The space center will be supported with the most extensive security forces available. Nothing and no one will be allowed to stop these launches. We will not be swayed from our course. Not by threats. Not by actions."

And with that, the news conference ended as all three men walked off the stage. Right before the men disappeared through a side door, a familiar face was briefly visible standing in the shadows waiting for them.

"Did you see that? There, just inside that door." Jes pointed at the man just before he disappeared. "What the hell is Arran Darby doing there?"

"That's what you're worried about?" Caleb grumbled. "How about the part where three dead guys just gave a press conference?"

"I'm with Caleb on this one," McKay said, drawing their attention back to the computer screen. "Jake, would you and Jes care to explain to me how three men you said you personally watched Arran Darby execute were live on television a few seconds ago?"

Jake shook his head. "I can't explain it. I watched those men die. Darby shot them in the head."

Jes shuddered at the image Jake's words provoked. "There was no way they faked it. Blood was everywhere. Jake and I both saw it."

McKay regarded them for several moments before finally nodding. "Okay, I believe you. Truthfully though, I'm probably the only one in STAT who will. British intelligence is already on the phone wanting to know what the hell we were smoking. It won't be long before people upstairs start questioning whether this mixed-supernatural-human-team concept was a good idea. Which means we've got forty-eight hours before this whole thing blows up in our faces. We need answers—fast."

On each of her teammates' faces, Jes saw the worry she felt at the possibility of the brass at STAT headquarters breaking up the team. Even Caleb, despite the laissez-faire attitude he seemed to have about everything, looked concerned.

"Understood," Jake said.

Jes echoed that sentiment, along with everyone else.

"Good," McKay said, and Jes was pretty sure she caught a smile tugging at the corner of his mouth before he hid it. "I want you packed up and on your way to Heathrow within the hour. Tickets will be waiting for you at the British Airways check-in counter for a flight to Cayenne, French Guiana. If Darby and those three men are planning to put something into space, I want to know what it is and be ready to stop it if necessary because I sincerely doubt they're going to all this effort and expense to find water. I'll have details on the space center and the bodies of the creatures you sent back before your team arrives in South America. Stay safe."

McKay didn't wait for them to respond before logging off.

Jake looked around the room, his gaze lingering on Jes, the determination in those dark eyes letting her and everyone else know he wasn't going to allow STAT to break up the team. That this time, they were going to stop Darby from whatever heinous thing he was planning.

"Okay, you heard McKay," Jake said. "Let's do this."

CHAPTER 16

Kourou

"THAT'S OUR WAY IN," JAKE SAID, POINTING AT THE video footage of the space center their STAT drone had filmed early this morning that was currently playing on Misty's laptop. "When the guards change shifts in the morning, there's a five-minute period when no one is covering the eastern side of the facility. The helicopters are grounded for refueling then, too. That's our window."

"We get video on one morning's shift change, and you're willing to risk all our lives on the assumption that tomorrow they'll do the same thing?" Caleb snorted. "I'm not sure if that's ballsy or just plain stupid."

Leaning back against the wall in Jake's hotel room, Caleb frowned at the mile-long stretch of golden sand, rough scrub brush, and lush trees between the shoreline and the Ariane launch complex. Jake knew without asking that Caleb was doing the calculations in his head, trying to figure out how long it would take the team to run from the beach to the perimeter fence in the early morning darkness. If it were only Jake, Harley, and Caleb, the sprint wouldn't be a problem. But with Jes, Misty, and Forrest in tow? Caleb was right. It would be risky as hell.

Jake leaned back in the leather desk chair, soft music and the sweet scent of the Victorian lilies drifting in from the pool area outside the window, as he studied the other members of the team sitting wherever they could find space in the room, be it the floor, bed, or even on top of the low dresser. Not only was the hotel where they were staying one of the nicest in Kourou, it was also less than two miles from the front gate of the space center. The rooms weren't intended to accommodate this many people, though. Or all the equipment cases that had somehow ended up in here. Even though it was crowded, it was still nice having the team all together. Especially since there was no way of knowing how many of them would make it through tomorrow's mission.

Jake bit back a growl.

Shit.

He needed to stop thinking like that.

But seeing the doubt on their faces and knowing they were all as uncomfortable with the whole thing as Caleb made it difficult to think anything else. He wasn't thrilled with the plan either, but it was the best they'd been able to come up with.

Jake threw an extra-long look in Jes's direction, where she was sitting on the bed, doing his best to not stare. That was easier said than done. Since they were trying to blend in with the other tourists at the hotel, they were all dressed like they were on vacation. Today, she wore a pretty flower-print sundress that left her shoulders bare except for two thin spaghetti straps and showed off her shapely legs. Even though they'd only been there two days, her perfect skin had a golden glow to it. And damn, did it make him want to lick her all over.

The thought immediately brought back memories of the night they'd shared in London. Unfortunately, they'd been going nonstop since they'd gotten here. When they hadn't been doing recon on the space center, they'd been giving status updates to McKay or going over drone surveillance footage the support team had recorded for them. As much as he'd wanted to, Jake hadn't been able to find time to be alone with Jes even for a minute. Besides the obvious desire to sleep with her again, he had this urgent need to hold her in his arms and tell her how he felt about her.

Because sometime between when they'd made love at that B&B in London and arriving in South America, he'd finally figured it out.

But now wasn't the time to think about that.

"I agree that the plan isn't ideal, but we're going to have to make it work," he said in reply to Caleb's earlier comment. "The launch of those satellites is scheduled for sunrise tomorrow and we need to get inside that facility before they take off."

Ryo Arsenault hadn't been kidding at the news conference when he'd said the space center would have the most extensive security forces available. The huge launch facility was currently protected by a frigging army of paramilitary security forces, while members of the Guiana military patrolled the coastline and inland perimeter. There was also at least one armed helicopter in the air above the complex at all times. It didn't help that Darby had replaced the aforementioned security forces with his own people. Jake recognized them from the party at Darby's manor.

No one even tried to argue with Jake—not even Caleb. They all knew this mission was going to be suicidal. Then again, that was quickly becoming their specialty.

"So, just to make sure I have this right," Forrest said from where he was sitting on the floor. "We take the boat along the coastline until we're due east of the main launch complex, then wait until the guards change shifts, which is when we run a mile to the perimeter fence and hope no one sees us. Then, when we get inside the facility, we figure out what Darby and the Bilderberg people are up to, so we can somehow stop it. But that's the part of the plan that we haven't come up with yet. Am I getting this all right?"

"Well, when you put it that way, the plan doesn't sound nearly as bad as I thought it did," Jes said wryly. "Hell, we should be back before breakfast."

Everyone laughed at that, Jake included. He would have made a quip, but Misty's phone rang, interrupting him.

"It's McKay," she said, sliding off the dresser where she'd been sitting beside Harley to flip on the video teleconference computer on the desk beside the laptop.

McKay looked more rested than during their previous Skype call, but not by much. It helped that French Guiana was only an hour ahead of DC, so at least it wasn't the middle of the night there. "Tell me you've found a way into the facility."

"We did," Jake said. "We go in just before dawn."

He didn't bother to mention the part about the plan being absolutely certifiable with a minuscule chance of success. Luckily, McKay didn't ask for details.

"Good," their boss said. "I know you probably still have a lot of planning to do, so I won't take up a lot of your time. I've only got two things for you anyway. First off, and most importantly, we finally have something on those bodies you sent back. The autopsies are done and Davina has looked at the photos I sent her, as well as the medical examiner's report. There's not a lot more we can tell you from a tactical perspective, since you already know how to kill them, but at least we think we know what we're up against."

"You *think*?" Jake repeated.

McKay nodded. "Davina believes we're dealing with an underground dwelling creature known as *natum*. I said I *think* we know what we're up against because these creatures have been nothing more than folktales, even in the supernatural world. Davina said no one knows much about them, other than that they're supposed to live deep in the earth near geothermal hot spots and areas of intense volcanic activity. When they have been seen on the surface—which hasn't been confirmed for hundreds of years—it's only in places that are extremely hot. Think the Sahara or the equator."

"If they haven't been aboveground in hundreds of years, it must be something big to make them resurface after all that time," Jake said.

"Exactly," McKay replied.

Jes frowned. "What's the deal with their stomach area being so vulnerable?"

"Ah, that." McKay picked up a coffee mug from his desk and took a sip. "Turns out, their hearts are directly in front of their stomachs. According to the doctor who did the autopsies, the heart is located there, so it can absorb heat better, to keep them warm. The creatures also have essentially no eyes, ears, or nose, at least not as we think of them. They see the world through taste sensors on their tongues and have a complex sonar mechanism in place of eyes."

Huh. That explained why their faces looked like they did.

"What about the shape-shifting thing?" Caleb asked.

"How do they do it? Can they just look like anyone they want? Is there a way to tell if those three Bilderberg guys are really the real deal or natum?"

McKay shrugged to the only damn question that mattered. "It's difficult to say. There's so much we don't know about these creatures. Obviously, they can take on a human appearance, but as for how they do it, or if there are limitations, we have no idea. But since Jake and Jes saw the creatures dig their claws into those men on the yacht, that might have something to do with the process. And since Jake and Jes watched Darby execute Arsenault, Khan, and Marconi, it's safe to assume the natum have taken on their forms."

Crap.

It occurred to Jake then that the man they'd been thinking of as Arran Darby might not be Darby at all, but could instead be a natum. If that was the case, where was the real Darby? Lying dead in a ditch somewhere? More likely, the natum had incinerated the body, so no one would accidentally expose the fact that the thing walking around in Darby's expensive suits and driving his expensive cars wasn't really him.

"You said you had two things for us," Jake said, prompting their boss. "What's the second?"

"We got information from one of the people involved in the transportation of those satellites Arsenault mentioned at the press conference," McKay said. "Four large cargo planes flew out of Abu Dhabi two days ago. While the entire operation was conducted under high security, our informant was able to get close enough to confirm that at least one of the aircrafts was carrying a large amount of a flammable gas called chlorodifluoromethane.

Interestingly enough, our informant didn't catch sight of the satellites."

Jake wondered what that meant, if anything.

"What's that chemical used for?" Misty asked. "*Methane* was in the name somewhere. Does that mean it's some kind of fuel?"

"Maybe," McKay said. "I've been told it could be some kind of coolant, too. But there seemed to be a lot more than you would expect for a satellite, even an experimental one."

As far as what they could do with this new information, the short answer was *not much*. Other than the obvious: lighting matches around the satellite probably wouldn't be a very good idea with a bunch of chlorodifluoromethane lying around. McKay logged off a little while later, telling them to stay safe and report back as soon as the mission was completed.

Everyone went their separate ways after that, with Harley and Caleb going to grab dinner at the hotel restaurant while Misty and Forrest said something about hanging out by the pool.

"You want to go get something to eat?" Jes asked after everyone left, taking Jake's hand and lacing her fingers with his.

He took her other hand with a sigh. "I do, but I told the twins I'd Skype with them tonight, and I'm already twenty minutes late. I don't want them worrying any more than they probably already are."

Jes nodded, understanding but also clearly disappointed. "How about I grab takeout from the restaurant and bring it back here? We can eat after you talk to the girls."

Jake resisted the nearly overwhelming urge to pull

Jes into his arms and kiss her until neither of them could breathe and had to come up for air—barely. But he did give in a little, bending his head to lightly press his mouth to hers. Even that little taste made his heart thump like mad. He had it so bad for her.

"That'd be great," he said. "I'll only be a little while."

"Take as long as you want. And let Zoe and Chloe know I've been thinking about them and can't wait to meet them."

Smiling, Jes went up on tiptoe to kiss him again, then left, closing the door with a soft click. Jake stood where he was, focusing on her scent. It was funny what it could do to him.

Giving himself a mental shake, Jake got his head screwed back on, took his laptop out of the safe where he'd left it, then set it on the desk and opened Skype. As soon as it connected, Zoe and Chloe were both on the screen, their expressions a mix of eagerness and worry.

"You were supposed to call half an hour ago," Zoe said.

"Yeah," Chloe said. "Don't scare us like that!"

He chuckled, both at the twins' obvious concern and the two puppies, Sam and Dean, who were wandering around the kitchen behind the girls, licking the floor and shoving their noses into every corner. "Sorry about that. I told you that sometimes I wouldn't be able to call you on time if I was busy with something."

Zoe sighed with resignation. "We know. We know."

Chloe, on the other hand, immediately tensed. "You'd tell us if you were doing something dangerous, right?"

Jake bit back a curse. Sometimes he thought Chloe was psychic. She definitely had a habit of making scary good guesses when it came to what he was up to.

"I'll always tell you as much as I can," he said, hating

there were things he couldn't be open and honest about with them. "But you know there are parts about what I do that I can't talk about. You both knew that when I took the job. You have to trust that my teammates will keep me safe and that I'll keep them safe."

Neither girl looked very happy, but they both nodded. He didn't mention the part where he and his teammates were currently in South America about to go on a dangerous-ass mission.

"Speaking of Jes," Zoe said casually as she reached out to grab some M&M's from the bowl on the counter, "have you and she been keeping each other safe...and warm?"

Jake's eyes went wide. "I cannot believe you went there. I'm not having this conversation with you. Not going to happen."

"I'll take that as a yes," Zoe said with a satisfied smirk. "So you and Jes went out on another date, huh? Where'd you go?"

Jake thought about telling them that he'd taken Jes on a romantic motorcycle ride through the city, but then his mind immediately jumped to visions of him and Jes together in his bed at the B&B in London, followed by the golden glow of her skin exposed by the sundress she'd had on earlier. He was so lost in the fantasy he didn't realize he was sitting there with what had to be a ridiculous grin on his face until Zoe laughed.

"Wow," she said. "You really like her, don't you?"

"When did that happen?" Chloe asked. "A few days ago, you were insisting your date wasn't even a date."

Jake hesitated, trying to figure out how to explain it when his head was still kind of spinning over all of this.

On the other side of the laptop, Chloe was staring at him like he had Christmas tree lights wrapped around his head.

"What?" he demanded.

"You're in love with her already, aren't you?" Chloe asked, her eyes getting wider by the second. "Oh. My. God. She's *The One*. You found her...your soul mate!"

Zoe looked back and forth between her sister and Jake, as if she expected one of them to jump up and scream *psyche!*

"Is that true?" Zoe finally asked, as amazed now as her twin. "You and Jes? How is any of this possible?"

He opened his mouth, then closed it again. He shook his head. "I'm not really sure. It's complicated. I tried to convince myself this didn't have anything to do with her being *The One,* but it's getting harder to keep telling myself that. When I'm around her, I feel more alive than I've ever felt."

Jake expected to see as much confusion in their eyes as he felt in his head, but instead, Zoe and Chloe were looking at him with the most godawful sappy expressions he'd ever seen. Like they were holding a basket full of puppies while watching a *Twilight* marathon. He should have known it was a bad idea to spill his heart out to a pair of teenage girls.

"What did Jes say when you told her about the legend of *The One*?" Chloe asked excitedly.

He sat back in the seat, running his hand through his hair. "I haven't told her. There hasn't been a good opportunity to get her alone long enough to do it right. And like I said, I only recently started believing it myself."

Chloe studied him curiously. "How recently?"

He shrugged. "I don't know. Maybe within the past ten minutes?"

The girls turned to look at each other for a while, doing

that silent communication thing the twins did all the time, which freaked some people out a little. After a long moment, Zoe turned back to regard him seriously.

"You have to tell Jes how you feel," Zoe said. "If she's *The One* for you, she has a right to know everything because she's probably feeling as confused as you do."

Jake knew Zoe was right, but that didn't make telling Jes any easier. "Well, as it turns out, Jes went to get takeout for dinner. She should be here any minute."

"Great!" Chloe grinned. "You two can sit down and have a quiet dinner together while you talk about being soul mates and your future together."

Jake almost laughed at how romantic Chloe made it all sound when the reality was that Jes would probably think he'd lost his frigging mind. He was about to tell the twins that when he heard Jes approaching his room. A few moments later, she knocked on the door.

"You guys want to talk to her for a bit?" he asked, partly because he knew Jes would love it and partly because he'd be able to delay the conversation about *The One* he was trying to figure out how to have with her.

"Good try, but you aren't getting out of it that easy," Chloe said with a soft laugh. "Just be honest and talk to her. It's easier than you think. And be careful with whatever you're doing there, okay?"

Jake promised both of them that he'd be careful and that he'd let them know how it went with Jes. Sighing, he closed the laptop and opened the door.

"I didn't mean to interrupt your call with Zoe and Chloe, but it didn't take nearly as long to pick up the food as I thought it would," she said, holding up two bags that were putting out some awesome aromas. "You want me to give you a little more time? I can come back in a little while."

He shook his head and motioned her inside. "No need. In fact, your timing is absolutely perfect. I just finished up the call with the girls. I'm glad you're back. There's some stuff we need to talk about."

She gave him a wary look as she set the food on the tiny table in the room's kitchenette, her heart suddenly beating faster. "That sounds a little serious."

Jake chuckled. "It is serious, but in a good way. It might be a bit freaky for you to hear, but it's all good—if you're open to the impossible."

Jes chewed her lip as she opened the paper bags and started setting everything out on the table. Out of the corner of her eye, she watched Jake open the small bottle of wine the maître d' had insisted would go perfectly with the dinner she'd ordered. There was no way to miss how tense Jake was. He'd said there was some *stuff* they needed to talk about, and while he'd insisted it was all good, that part about being *open to the impossible* had her a little freaked out.

What the hell does that even mean?

"Dinner smells amazing," Jake said, pouring the chenin blanc into the two plastic wineglasses the restaurant had included. "What's on the menu?"

She popped the takeout containers open and slid his dish in front of him with a flourish as she sat down across from him, trying to remember what she'd ordered. "Wild peccary fricassee with rice and kidney beans, and for dessert, we have doku, which is a creamy mashed corn with cinnamon and brown sugar."

"I don't know what wild peccary is, but it sounds good." Flashing her a smile, Jake picked up his wineglass, tipping it toward her in a toast. "To being open to the impossible."

Jes tapped her plastic wineglass against his, wanting to ask what he meant by that, deciding to simply go with it instead. Trusting Jake hadn't failed her yet.

"To the impossible," she murmured, having no idea where this was going.

For the next few minutes, it didn't go anywhere in regard to the impossible. Instead, they ate dinner—which was delicious—and talked about the subtle blend of French, Creole, and Caribbean seasonings in the dish. They'd both eaten a lot of different food from around the world, and it was fun to talk about how the spicy peccary fricassee compared to other things they'd eaten. The peccary tasted like pork to both of them, so they concluded that peccary must be a type of pig. Within minutes, Jes stopped worrying about whatever bombshell Jake intended to drop and relaxed like she would on a date with a man she was completely into.

Then again, it was difficult to be anything but relaxed when she was with Jake. His mere presence was enough to calm her nerves, even with the prospect of tomorrow morning's dangerous mission looming large in the back of her mind.

But it was more than him making her feel relaxed. And yeah, more than the fact that she wanted to jump on him like he was a jungle gym and stay in a bed with him for days on end. The truth was, Jake made her think about things she'd never given much thought to. Like the future and sharing it with someone special. Like having something more than work to make her get out of bed in the morning. Like letting herself get close to someone.

After what had happened to her previous teammates, she didn't think she had it in her to do that again. And she hadn't even been romantically involved with any of them. That's what made falling for Jake even crazier.

She couldn't believe she was contemplating something like this, especially within a week of meeting a guy. But Jake was different. Special. What she felt for him was exhilarating. And also a little terrifying.

While the sweet dessert was definitely delicious, Jes couldn't nurse it for the rest of the night. The bowl wasn't that big. Jake said they needed to talk, and she was done waiting for him to start the conversation. So, after finishing her dessert, she pushed the empty bowl aside and went for it.

"How are the girls?" she asked, figuring that was a good segue, not to mention a safe topic. "I'm bummed I didn't get a chance to talk to them."

Jake smiled. "Yeah, they wanted to talk to you, too. But when I told them you were back with the takeout, they said they'd rather I spend the time talking to you about us instead."

The nerves she'd felt earlier came back with a vengeance, her shoulders tightening and her heart racing. Jake reached across the small table and took her hand in his, tracing soothing circles over her skin with his thumb.

"Jes, relax," he murmured in that deep, sexy voice of his. "It isn't anything bad. At least, it doesn't have to be."

She took a deep breath, wetting her lips. "You keep saying that, but all you're doing is confusing me. So why don't we stop tiptoeing around the subject you obviously want to talk about and get on with it?"

Maybe this was his way of letting her down gently and telling her he didn't want to be in a relationship with her. If so, his timing sucked. Couldn't he have waited until after tomorrow's mission? She needed to be focused one hundred percent on what they were doing, not moping around in a funk.

Crap. They'd slept together once and her heart was already breaking a little at the idea of not being with Jake.

Taking his hand away from hers, Jake went back to eating his dessert. Yes, she'd gotten him four servings of everything, but this procrastination of his was ridiculous. Even if watching his sensuous mouth move while he ate the creamy confection was extremely enjoyable, never mind distracting as hell.

"Does it feel like this thing between us happened really fast?" he asked suddenly, gaze focused on what was left of his dessert. "That we went from zero to sixty at warp speed?"

She didn't answer, mostly because she was too busy trying to figure out where he was going with that. Was he saying he wanted to take things more slowly? While that was better than breaking up with her, it still made her feel uneasy.

When she didn't reply, he stopped eating to look at her. "Then again, maybe that's just me. I mean, every time I get close to you, my heart beats so fast I feel dizzy and all I want is to be with you. And when I'm not with you, I can't seem to breathe, and all I can think of is being with you. And the idea of you coming on that mission tomorrow scares me more than anything because the idea of anything happening to you makes me lose my mind."

Jes blinked, still at a loss for words. She wasn't sure if she was more stunned Jake felt that way about her or that he'd admitted it so early in their relationship. But then, relief quickly replaced shock. She wasn't the only one who felt those same things.

She took a deep breath and plunged into the deep end of the pool. Opening up like this was easier now that Jake had been brave enough to do it first.

"It's not just you," she said softly. "Sometimes, I find my heart thumping out of control when you get close. Other times, when you aren't in the room with me, it's like I can't breathe, either. And when I even think about you getting hurt on the mission tomorrow, something inside me wants to crawl into a little ball and hide in the corner."

There, she'd said it. She'd admitted how she felt about him.

On the other side of the table, Jake pushed his empty bowl away, his dark eyes holding hers captive as he rested his forearms on the table and leaned in a little closer. "I know you probably think it's insane to feel like this over someone you met a week ago. Especially someone you work with—a werewolf no less."

She laughed softly. "I won't argue with that. Insane is a good word for it. Weird would work, too. Confusing, as well. I might even go so far as to say a little distressing."

Jake chuckled, the husky sound making her feel warm all over. "Yeah, that pretty much covers it. But as odd as all this might seem, there *is* an explanation."

Jes wasn't sure how anything could explain whatever was going on between the two of them. "There is?"

"Uh-huh. There's a legend among werewolves about *The*

One that I admit I thought was completely made up because I couldn't imagine how it could ever be true. Until I witnessed it firsthand back when I was in Dallas." He paused, suddenly introspective. She was just about to prompt him when he continued. "It's a story about there being one— and only one—person out there in the world a werewolf is supposed to be with for their entire life because that person is the only person who can accept a werewolf for what he—or she—is."

Jes held her breath, waiting for him to say more.

"It's supposed to be rare for a werewolf to find *The One*—their soul mate—but when it does happen, it's impossible to miss." He looked at her again, his dark eyes glinting with a hint of gold. "That person has a scent so unique and perfect, it's all that werewolf can smell. She has a taste that's so intoxicating, it makes it difficult to think. When a werewolf is with *The One*, he wants to be with that person forever and protect them with his life."

The idea that she was Jake's soul mate and he was hers was so incredible she should have laughed at the pure insanity of it all. But she didn't laugh because it all felt…right. The realization that they were soul mates explained everything. She'd worked hard keeping everyone outside her family at a distance for so long it had become second nature. But for the first time in what felt like forever, it was okay to let someone else in. To let Jake in.

They were supposed to be together.

Meant to be together.

She was so wrapped up in that epiphany she didn't realize Jake was saying something about being *The One* didn't mean a person lost their free will. He was talking fast, like he wanted to make sure she understood that all the magic did was bring together people who were meant to be together.

Jes was on her feet and around the table before she even knew what she was doing. Then she was sitting on Jake's lap, kissing him.

That taste thing he'd mentioned seemed to go both ways because she felt like she could get drunk off him. He tasted like wine and brown sugar and cinnamon and something else she couldn't put a name to, but she knew it was all him. And damn, did he taste delicious.

"You can stop talking now," she murmured when she pulled back to get a breath of air. "We're soul mates. I get it. And I'm okay with it. So stop talking and take me to bed. We have to leave for the mission soon, and I don't want to waste the rest of the time talking."

Jake stared at her like what she said had completely blown him away. Eyes flashing gold, he picked her up in his arms and carried her to his bed, where they slowly undressed each other.

When they'd made love for the first time back in London, it had been crazy and out of control. This time was completely different. They kissed and caressed each other for what felt like hours. And when he rolled a condom on and slid deep inside her, there was no headlong race to the finish line. Instead, it was a slow, relaxing ride as his shaft made her body tremble and his mouth made her believe her neck was her most sensitive erogenous zone ever.

There were no fangs this time, though his eyes glowed that vivid yellow gold. She found herself loving the way he looked at her with his inner wolf. It was like she was the most precious thing in the world to him, and it wasn't difficult to believe they were meant to be together forever.

Jake was right there with her when she toppled over the edge. She bit down on his shoulder to keep from alerting the entire hotel she was coming and rode him through what had to be the longest, most intense orgasm of her life. Then she collapsed against his chest, breathless.

They lay there together under the blankets, their bodies intertwined as they talked about what it meant to be soul mates and sharing secrets with each other that they'd kept from the rest of the world.

All too soon, there was a knock at the door as Caleb announced the boat was at the dock and it was time to head out. Jake told him they'd be out in a minute, then kissed her gently on the mouth.

"Be careful today," he told her softly. "You've got someone else to live for now, okay?"

Jes smiled. "Yes, I do. And so do you. Remember that."

o

CHAPTER 17

JAKE MIGHT HAVE BEEN A NAVY SEAL, BUT THAT didn't mean he liked doing anything in wet clothes. But when it was obvious the engine on the boat the support team had rented was way too noisy to take them all the way up onto the beach, he'd resigned himself to the misery of spending the next few hours in a soaking wet tactical uniform. They'd considered wearing wet suits for the swim to shore, but with how fast they had to get from the beach to the launch complex, there wasn't time to strip off the gear and put on fresh clothes. That meant getting wet.

The motorboat coasted to a crawl about a hundred feet offshore just as the two helicopters that had been patrolling the area turned and headed back toward the main building. That was what they'd been waiting for.

"That's it," he said, grabbing his gear and heading toward the back of the boat. "Shift change is starting and we don't have time to waste, so let's move."

Jake, Jes, and the rest of the team slipped over the side of the boat as one, using their waterproof backpacks to help them stay afloat as they swam to shore. Behind them the two members of the STAT support team began silently paddling the boat back to deeper water. The plan was for the boat to hang around about a half mile out, beyond the farthest distance they'd seen the helicopters roam. If the raid went to hell in a handbag, the support team would try to extract them.

Jake secretly didn't hold any more hope for that part of

the plan than he did the rest of it. If they were forced to bail in the middle of the operation, that boat would survive for all of two seconds once the helicopter caught sight of it. A few rounds from the .50 caliber machine guns on those birds, and their extraction plan would be toast.

He and his teammates moved quickly through the water, the sound of their feet kicking covered by the pounding of the waves on the shore. Well, most of them moved quickly. Surprisingly, Forrest floundered like a drunk goat, bringing up the back of the pack. The guy was fit, so he should have been more graceful in the water. It was something Jake could worry about later though...if they all survived this mission. Until then, Jake reached out and got a hand on the other man's backpack, hauling him to shore.

They moved quickly once they hit the sand, taking tactical vests and weapons from their backpacks, then stowing what they didn't need near the rocks. They split into teams of two to make their way across the mile-wide strip of beach and vegetation that stood between them and the closest section of the perimeter fencing. Moving in pairs, instead of all at once, was risky because the team could get separated, but it reduced the chances of anyone seeing them.

Before they left the hotel, they'd all agreed it'd be best to pair each human with a werewolf—him with Jes, Caleb with Forrest, Harley and Misty. If the shit hit the fan, that arrangement improved their individual chances of survival, though Jake had gone to great lengths to make sure Jes was on his team. No way in hell was he letting her farther out of his sight than necessary.

Jes darted across the sand and scrub ahead of him, making good time considering the soft footing. The black tactical uniform she was wearing to match his and the rest of the team—exactly like the ones the local security personnel wore—helped her blend into the dark shadows cast by the taller brush and trees.

Jake and everyone else were breathing hard by the time they made the fence line. The watch on his wrist told him it had taken them eight and a half minutes to get there. Not a world record by any means, but across soft sand and rolling terrain, carrying the M4 carbines and all the extra gear and ammo they had, it wasn't horrible. And with the helicopters and roaming guards nowhere to be seen, he'd definitely take it.

Caleb and Harley slipped behind a cluster of brush hugging one particular section of the fence and started to cut through it with handheld snips. It was time-consuming, but easier than trying to climb over the razor wire atop the fence, especially for Jes, Misty, and Forrest. Besides, if they had to run to get out of here, having a hanging flap might just be a lifesaver.

The two werewolves worked fast, and in less than two minutes, they had a four-foot wide section of the chain link they'd lifted away like a garage door. When they let it go after they were all on the other side of the fence, it hung so naturally no one would see it if they weren't looking for it.

Straight ahead of them, about a quarter mile away, were a group of buildings, collectively called "mission control." They housed most of the systems and personnel who managed the space center and controlled the launches. The front side of the complex was lit up like a small city, but fortunately, the back side wasn't, which was why they'd chosen this section of the fence line to make their entrance. It was the only route that gave them any chance to approach the buildings without being seen.

The launchpads were farther to the south, each with its gigantic Ariane 5 rocket already standing there tall and proud. The rockets and their gantries were lit up even better than the mission control building. Darkness covered everything outside these four parts of the complex, since the space center was way too big to keep every square inch of it illuminated. But sunrise was getting closer by the minute. Then, the whole place would be lit up.

"Damn, those things are frigging huge," Caleb whispered in awe as he knelt down inside the fence line alongside everyone else. "I hope we can figure out an easy way to stop whatever Darby has going on because if we don't, I'm not sure what we're supposed to do with those things."

"True that." Jake agreed. "Which is why figuring out what the hell is going on is our first goal. So the primary plan is just that—we split up into our teams and go sniffing, starting with the mission control building, then the launchpads. The moment one of us finds something, we radio the other teams. Then we regroup and go from there. Harley, plan B is all you and Misty. If everything else goes to shit, get her to a computer, then cover her while she goes in and wipes out everything she can on the mission computers. It's not a long-term answer, but it will keep them from launching those damn satellites today at least."

They did a quick comms check to make sure the time in the water hadn't screwed up their radios, then got to their feet. As they made their way across the lawn toward the back of the mission control building, Jake glanced at his watch again. They still had another couple minutes before the helicopters came back around, even more until the ground patrols moved through this area.

A few steps later, Jake felt a tingle run up his spine.

Shit.

"Incoming!" he shouted.

The words had barely left his mouth before both helicopters appeared over the top of the building, turned sideways so their door gunners had a wide-open shot at their whole team.

Large .50 caliber rounds ripped up the ground around them at the same time Jake heard the roar of large diesel engines. Tactical vehicles sped around both sides of the building ahead of them, headlights and spotlights illuminating the entire area as roof-mounted machine guns slewed their way.

It was a perfect fucking ambush—like security had known exactly where and when they'd be coming in. And Jake had led his team right into it.

"Spread out and get to the mission control building!" he shouted as he lifted his M4 and started firing rounds at the closest helicopter. "It's the only chance we got!"

His teammates immediately moved forward, Harley taking on the second helicopter while everyone else split up and returned fire against the oncoming tactical vehicles.

Jake had barely moved ten feet before a .50 caliber round from the helicopter slammed into his right thigh, putting him on the ground. Cursing, he rolled over and looked down, terrified he'd find a shattered mess where his leg used to be. He breathed a sigh of relief when he saw the damage wasn't nearly as bad as he thought. It was a bloody wound to be sure, but he'd survive.

A flash of movement on the right caught his eye, and he looked up to see Jes hurrying over to him. He shoved himself to his feet, waving her off.

"Keep going! I'm okay!"

She hesitated for a moment but did as he instructed.

Stumbling forward, he lifted his M4 again, growling as he steadied himself and put half a magazine's worth of rounds through the open door of the helicopter hovering over them. There was a startled cry barely audible above the rotor noise, then the gunner was falling out of the bird, only to be pulled up short after a few feet drop by the straps that were designed to keep him from plummeting to the ground.

Useless without its gunner, the helicopter peeled away. Jake kept moving forward, gritting through the pain as he turned to see if the rest of his people were okay.

Jes, Misty, and Forrest had made it to the door of the nearest mission control building, but only because Harley and Caleb were standing twenty feet away from them, laying down a wall of bullets to give them time to get away.

Jake joined his werewolf pack mates, spinning around to face the oncoming threat. Several of the guard vehicles had crashed, flames and smoke coming out of them. But more were coming—a lot more. His gut tightened as he saw how bad things were. And it was getting worse by the minute. Knowing he was going to hate himself for saying it, but not having a choice, he turned to find Jes, catching her eye.

"It's plan B time!" he shouted. "Take Misty and Forrest and get them out of here!"

Jake saw the hesitation in her eyes, knowing she didn't want to go. Hell, he didn't want her to go. They weren't supposed to get separated. But they both knew Misty and Forrest would need help if they were going to do what had to be done.

With a frustrated curse, Jes spun and shoved Misty and Forrest through the door.

Jake's heart seized in his chest as Jes disappeared into the building after them, but he couldn't let himself focus on that. He had other issues to deal with first.

"Caleb! Harley!" he called loudly as he avoided the incoming rounds and reloaded his M4. "We need to give Jes, Misty, and Forrest time to get to the computers!"

Harley murmured her agreement, but Caleb didn't reply. Jake glanced at him to see Caleb's eyes glowing vivid blue. A moment later, Caleb dropped his weapon and took off running, a loud growl echoing in the darkness. The sound quickly turned into a rage-filled snarl as Caleb sprinted headlong toward the nearest approaching truck.

Cursing, Jake ran after him, Harley right beside him. But there was no way they could catch up to Caleb. A split-second later, the omega threw himself at the truck coming at him. Glass shattered, then Caleb was inside the cab of the truck. The roars and shouts coming from the vehicle were horrendous, but not nearly as bad as seeing the remaining windows splashed red with dark blood.

Caleb was out of the truck and running for the second one before the first rolled to a silent stop. Jake and Harley didn't bother to try stopping their pack mate this time. Instead, they started shooting at the bad guys, covering the out-of-control Caleb as best they could.

Every step Jes took down the darkened corridor of the mission control building was a battle. All she wanted to do was turn around and run back to Jake. To save him and get him to safety. The thought of him out there facing danger without her was enough to make her almost pass out.

But she kept going, because Jake was trusting her to get the three of them to a computer so Misty could implement plan B.

The hallway they were moving down was eerily quiet, with nothing to be heard except the sounds of the battle going on outside. Jes had expected to find the building crawling with scientists and Darby's security guards, especially considering this place was supposed to be launching three rockets in barely over an hour. But after going a few hundred feet and crossing several main intersections, they still hadn't seen anyone.

Something was seriously wrong here.

Jes threw a glance over her shoulder, catching Forrest's eyes. "Watch our six and cover Misty no matter what. We could be walking into another ambush, and if something happens to her, this whole plan falls apart."

Forrest regarded Misty with an expression that told Jes she never had to worry about him keeping an eye on her. He obviously had reasons of his own for thinking how valuable she was.

Jes continued to lead them through the complex, half her attention focused on the sounds of the fighting outside filtering through her earpiece. From the growls and snarls, it sounded like Caleb had lost control of his inner omega again. Jake and Harley seemed to be okay, too. They were still shooting and scooting at least.

She was beginning to think the entire building was empty when they rounded a corner and came across four middle-aged men in dress pants and short-sleeved white shirts. Jes had barely raised her weapon before the nerd herd took off running in the other direction. Curious, she followed them, Misty and Forrest trailing behind. Within a few seconds, they were in a huge open room full of desks, computers, and lots of big TV screens on the wall. But very few of the computers were turned on and none of the TV screens, which made no sense. Wasn't this the place where they launched the rockets from?

Jes didn't have a chance to voice her thoughts before Misty raced over to one of the few computers that was powered up, dropping her butt into the chair there and reaching for the mouse.

"Cover me," she said before her eyes went completely white.

While Forrest watched Misty like a hawk, Jes turned her attention to all the different entrances into the control center. If security hit them now, coming in from multiple directions at once, they'd be screwed.

She heard a gasp behind her and turned in time to see Misty's eyes turning lavender again. Forrest stood close to her, holding his M4 in a firm grip.

"We're in deep crap," Misty said. "The computers in this building normally control the launch sequence for all missions, but they're not online right now. That's because someone purposely shut down most of the system. They're going to handle the rocket launches from the backup control systems located at each launchpad. And before you ask, those systems are completely stand-alone, which means I can't access them from here. We'll have to stop each one separately, from each launchpad system. If that isn't bad enough, the launch countdown has already started. We're inside thirty minutes. It looks like they're planning to go the moment the sun starts to rise."

Jes cursed while Forrest stood there looking freaked out as hell. This mission could literally not get any worse.

"Jake," she called out over her radio, praying he could hear her. "This might not be a good time, but plan B hit a major snag."

There was a long burst of automatic gunfire that almost had Jes snatching her earpiece out, followed by an animalistic snarl, then a pain-filled scream. Only then did an amazingly calm voice answer her back.

"I'm a little busy right now, Jes," Jake said. "Caleb is having a moment and we're trying to keep him from eating someone. Is this snag something you can handle yourself?"

"Nope, afraid not," she told him, thrilled beyond reason to hear his voice and know that not only was he alive, but generally calm and snarky as well. That had to be a good sign. "Darby or one of his goons has locked out the primary launch computer in this building and is planning to use the stand-alone backup systems located at each pad. We'll have to go to each location and deal with them one by one. And by the way, the launches have been moved up. We've got less than thirty minutes before they start lighting the matches on these things."

Jake growled and let out a string of angry curses, most of which she'd never heard before, which was saying a lot. Maybe it was his navy background. Finally, after a lot more gunfire, Jake was back, calm as ever.

"Take Misty and Forrest and head for pad one, the west-ernmost rocket," he told her. "Harley, Caleb, and I will deal with the other two. And move fast. We don't have much time. Do whatever you have to do to stop those launches."

Jes wanted to ask him if he was okay, but like he'd said, they didn't have much time. She, Misty, and Forrest had to stop the first launch and pray Jake, Harley, and Caleb fig-ured out how to stop the second and third launches without Misty there to help them.

"Come on," she said to Misty and Forrest.

Hurrying out of the room, they headed toward what Jes hoped was the front of the building. With the fighting going on along the back side, they sure as hell didn't want to go that way. She had no idea how they were going to get to pad one, since it was at least a mile away. Sprinting there was a lousy option.

A few minutes later, they reached the front door only to run into a three-man security team. She, Misty, and Forrest ended up getting pinned down for much longer than Jes would have liked before taking them out. But on the bright side, the security team no longer had any use for the armored Land Rover they'd arrived in, while she and her teammates did.

It took Jes a few seconds to figure out how to get the vehicle started, but luckily, she'd played around in the Hummers in her dad's unit enough times when she was a kid to understand the basics of driving a tactical truck. The best part was that there wasn't any key to worry about, just a starter switch that got the big thing rumbling.

Jes sped the truck toward pad one, mostly sticking to the narrow facility roads, but cutting cross-country when it seemed faster. Misty and Forrest obviously weren't thrilled with the way they got bounced around inside the big metal truck when she did that, but they didn't complain too much.

Within minutes, the launchpad and its ginormous Ariane 5 rocket was in sight, looming high over them—so tall that even in its gantry, it looked ready to topple over any second.

"Jes, we've got company coming," Misty said.

Before Jes could ask what kind of company Misty meant, a hail of bullets tore up the ground in front of them as a helicopter roared over their heads.

Jes involuntarily flinched. They might be riding around in an armored vehicle, but she wasn't sure it could take many hits from the large gun the helicopter was using. Especially not when it could hit the lightly protected upper side of the truck.

"Forrest, get on that roof-mounted machine gun!" she shouted, swerving the heavy vehicle side to side to make them a harder target for the door gunner on the bird flying above them. "And keep that helicopter away from us long enough for me to get us to the launchpad!"

In the backseat, Forrest scrambled to open the roof hatch and push it out of the way. He was barely able to keep his footing as he stood to lean through the opening and cycle a round into the chamber of the machine gun.

The helicopter continued shooting at them, but Forrest was able to keep it far enough away so the shots the gunner took at them weren't all that accurate. It was enough, and a few minutes later, they were at the launchpad.

Jes practically bounced Misty off the seat and almost pitched poor Forrest off the top of the roof when she slammed the brakes, sliding the truck to a stop only inches away from the earth-covered bunker that served as the backup control center for pad one. Forrest tumbled to the ground from the top of the vehicle, unsteady. Misty immediately jumped out of the vehicle and lay down a steady rate of fire at the approaching helicopter, giving Jes and Forrest time to deal with the guards trying to keep them from getting into the building.

Judging by how many rounds Jes had to put in two of the guards to knock them off their feet, they were almost certainly natum. She was worried Forrest had a concussion or something because his aim was complete crap. As a result, she was forced to deal with them on her own, putting several rounds in their stomach while Forrest aimed everywhere but. Her assumption that they were natum was confirmed the moment they hit the floor and turned into the creepy-looking creatures.

"Misty, let's go!" Jes shouted, ducking her head in to take a peek inside the facility. The place was similar to the main control room they'd been in earlier, but a lot smaller. There were maybe twenty computer stations and only two large TV screens, along with a big digital clock in between them that was currently counting down from twenty minutes. "Forget the damn helicopter and get in here and stop the launch!"

There were a whole group of unarmed scientists—both men and women—cowering against the back wall, eyes wide with fear. Jes considered keeping them around to help stop the launch, but between the language barrier and the terror on their faces, she decided it would be a waste of time. Instead, she motioned them toward the door with the barrel of her M4 and waved them out. They ran, no questions asked. One thing about engineer types—they were good at problem solving. And this situation was definitely not their problem.

Misty ran into the room a moment later, purple ponytail bouncing behind her. "The helicopter gave up and bailed toward the east."

Hurrying over to one of the computer stations, Misty sat down and immediately did her thing, her lavender eyes going milky white within seconds. As before, Jes left Forrest to watch over his girlfriend while she guarded the door. But at least there was only one way in this time.

"You know, I never really thought you people would make it this far," Forrest suddenly said.

The tone in his voice combined with the odd word choice sent a shiver up Jes's spine, and she turned around to see Forrest standing beside Misty, the barrel of his M4 pressed against her temple.

What the hell?

"You were supposed to all die on that open stretch of ground between the fence line and the mission control building," he continued, his eyes locked on Jes. "I didn't honestly know what to do when that didn't happen. And then this freak started surfing around in that computer, and I have to admit, I panicked a little. I wasn't sure if it would be better to kill you there or see what you would do next. I never in a million years thought you'd have a chance of stopping the launches. I can't let that happen."

Jes didn't think. She brought her weapon up and squeezed the trigger, popping off a three-round burst at Forrest—or the thing that looked like Forrest—without even aiming.

A stomach shot was out of the question with Misty sitting in front of him, so the rounds ended up hitting the creature in the upper left chest and shoulder. It wasn't fatal for a natum, but it was enough to flip him over the nearest computer desk and send his weapon flying.

Jes quickly moved forward, M4 raised to her shoulder and ready to fire. If the natum was still on the ground, she'd put whatever was left in her magazine in his stomach and end this.

But when she looked over the top of the computer table and saw the creature looking like the Forrest she knew and liked lying there, dark, oily blood pouring out of his shoulder, she hesitated for a split second.

That hesitation cost her.

The natum was off the ground and coming at her in a blur that rivaled the way she'd seen Jake and his fellow werewolves move. It hit her so hard she saw stars as she flew backward through the air and hit the ground with two hundred pounds of creature on her chest.

Air exploded out of her lungs and everything went fuzzy, but Jes kept fighting, one hand coming up to try and shove him away while the other reached for the Sig holstered low on her right hip. But Forrest—the thing that looked like Forrest, dammit!—was so freaking strong. She got her weapon out, but he simply grabbed her wrist and pinned it to the floor, then wrapped his hand around her throat.

Jes felt the tips of its claws digging in and her vision got even darker. She punched and clawed at his face with her free hand, but then she remembered natum didn't have eyes like humans, so her scratching out the ones that were there probably wasn't doing much.

The darkness around the edges of her vision got worse, no matter how much she kneed the thing and twisted side to side. Jes knew she wasn't going to survive much longer, but the only thing she could think right then was that the damn creature was going to kill Misty next. Jake would fall apart when he found out, almost certainly blaming himself for their deaths.

"First you, then the other fucking bitch," the creature above her hissed.

Jes kept struggling, refusing to give in no matter how hopeless it was.

Then, somewhere, a gun went off. The natum arched his back and cried out in pain, his hand falling away from Jes's throat. Gasping, she grabbed her Sig and put half a dozen rounds in its midsection.

There was a lot of dark, thick blood, then the creature was falling forward. Jes shoved it to the side, and it landed in a heap on the floor next to her. Misty still stood there, holding her sidearm out in front of her, face pale.

"Forrest's dad is a minster," she whispered brokenly. "He'd never use that word. Never."

On the floor, Forrest's features slowly morphed into the faceless creature that was the natum.

As if suddenly realizing what happened to the real Forrest, Misty dropped to her knees on the floor, sobs racking her body. Tears welling in her own eyes, both for Forrest and for Misty, Jes pulled her into her arms, holding her tightly. Jes's heart broke for her.

"Shh," she said softly. "It's going to be okay."

That was a lie. For Misty, things would never be okay again.

Over the radio, Jes heard Jake tell Harley and Caleb to hurry, that there wasn't much time before the launch. Still holding on to Misty, Jes glanced at the clock on the wall to see fifteen minutes left on the countdown.

She tried to tell Jake what happened, but her microphone wasn't working. It must have gotten damaged when the natum tried to choke her to death.

"Misty, honey," Jes said, gently pulling away to look at her. "We're going to find our Forrest and we're going to bring him home, I promise. But right now, we need to stop the launch of the rocket at this pad."

Misty wiped the tears from her face with a trembling hand. "I already did."

Jes caught a fresh tear with her thumb as it rolled down Misty's cheek. "That's good. But now we need to help the others, okay? I'm going to help Jake at pad three. I need you to head to pad two to help Harley and Caleb. Can you do that for me?"

Misty looked over at the body of the natum on the floor, then back at Jes. "Yeah, I can do that. Let's go stop these creatures, then go find Forrest."

Giving her a tearful smile, Jes helped Misty to her feet, then they both ran for the door. Jes only prayed they weren't too late.

CHAPTER 18

JAKE RAN AS FAST AS HE COULD, IGNORING THE PAIN in his thigh and ribs as he raced for launchpad three and the bunker, which he hoped wasn't too difficult to find. He would have preferred to take the Land Rover the security guards had been driving during the ambush, but between the shoot-out and Caleb, that hadn't worked. The damn omega had ripped a tire off the truck and used it to beat a natum to death. Jake was starting to think there was something seriously wrong with that werewolf.

But at least there was no one left to chase him in his dash across the space center. And since the helicopter had disappeared a while ago, it was almost a leisurely run.

He tried his radio again, but all he'd gotten was static since getting hit by that Land Rover a few minutes ago. He'd ended up with nothing more than a couple broken ribs, but the radio hadn't been so lucky. He wasn't sure if he'd lost both transmitting and receiving capability. All he knew was that he hadn't heard from Jes or anyone else in a while.

He prayed they were all okay. He'd sent Harley and Caleb to pad two a while ago, and the last he'd heard from Jes was that she, Misty, and Forrest were heading for pad one. The idea that Jes might be out there right now, in some kind of trouble, scared the hell out of him.

Jake was still envisioning all kinds of horrible scenarios involving Jes when he realized he'd reached the control building for the launchpad. A long, low building, it had multiple doors and windows on the side facing him. The entire front, which faced the launchpad, was covered with a huge mound of grass-covered earth. There were half a dozen vehicles parked along the back, and the helicopter that had been shooting at him earlier—the one with the dead gunner—was sitting off to one side, rotor blades thumping quietly through the air. Clearly, the thing was ready to take off at a moment's notice.

He glanced around but didn't see anyone except the pilot of the helicopter in one of the front seats, apparently checking the gauges. Jake looked down at his watch to see he had maybe eight minutes left on the countdown—if he was lucky. He needed to move.

Ignoring the helicopter pilot—the guy couldn't see him from where he was seated anyway—Jake sprinted toward the control building. He was still twenty feet away when he picked up the scent of multiple creatures inside, as well as one that shouldn't have been there—jasmine and fresh laundry.

At first, Jake thought he was picking up her scent because he did it all the time, even when she wasn't around, but it was too strong for that.

Jes was in the building.

Jake's claws and fangs were out before he took another breath, and it was all he could do to not charge into the building. He fought down the animal instinct. He had to be smarter than the beast inside him that only wanted to attack and kill at that moment.

Moving slowly and carefully, he headed for the farthest door on the left. Opening it a crack, he took a sniff. As he suspected, there were several natum in there as well as humans. But it didn't seem like any were close to the door, which was all he cared about. He pulled the door open all the way and slipped inside as silently as a ghost.

Somewhere down the hall, Jake heard voices. One of them was Darby. The other was Jes, her tone anxious and tense.

Thank God she was okay.

Inner wolf pacing restlessly, Jake followed the sound of their voices down the dimly lit hallway and took a quick peek into what turned out to be the control room. Jes was on the far side, Ryo Arsenault and Lais Khan—or rather the natum wearing their forms—each holding one of her arms. Her attention was fixed firmly on Darby and Damien, who stood a few feet away. Darby had a smug smile on his face, while Damien was focused on the digital countdown clock attached to the wall, which was fast approaching seven minutes.

Laurent Marconi and three other natum were spread around the room, their weapons pointed at a group of scientists sitting at a row of computer screens. Jake could smell the fear rolling off of the men and women in waves.

"Why the convoluted scheme with the Bilderberg Society?" Jes asked, jerking at her arms, trying to get the natum to let her go. It didn't work. "If you wanted to launch a few rockets, why not simply buy your way in? Darby probably had enough money to do it. Hell, the man had more money than you could ever spend."

The natum wearing Darby's form laughed harshly. "You think money has anything to do with this?"

"If not money, then what?" she demanded.

Jake stifled a growl. What the hell was she doing, antagonizing these things?

Jaw clenched, he quietly slipped a fresh magazine in his M4, ready to attack the second they went for her.

But Darby merely laughed again, clearly amused. All at once, the sound became a high-pitched screech, and Darby's features melted away to reveal his true form, the same one Jake had seen on the three dead natum on the riverbank in London, complete with gray skin, a ridge where a nose should be, and what seemed like hundreds of needle-like teeth on display when he grinned at Jes.

The scientists at the computers immediately lost their frigging minds, crying out in terror and trying to run. The natum viciously shoved the men and women back in their chairs, refusing to let them escape.

"Humans are so predictable and stupid," the creature who'd worn Darby's face spit out, the voice completely different now, more like the scratch of steel over stone. "You care only for your money, your wars, your possessions. Never for anything of worth."

"And what do the natum value?" Jes asked softly.

At their name, every creature in the room looked at her in surprise. Except for Darby.

"Yes, I heard you learned about us," he said in his raspy voice, his narrow black tongue flicking out. "I'll have to go visit that woman in Los Angeles after we do what we came here for and make sure I silence her."

Jes's mouth tightened. "You didn't answer the question. What do your kind value? What would motivate you to do all of this?"

On the wall, the clock was under four minutes.

"My people," Darby hissed, tilting his head this way and that, the shallow sockets where eyes should have been seeming to regard her. "My people are the only thing I care about and changing the world so they can come out from hiding and finally live in the way we were meant to."

Jake could see the look of confusion on Jes's face from where he stood. He didn't blame her. He had no idea what Darby was talking about either.

"We can survive underground in those rare places that are warm enough," Darby continued. Around him, the other natum looked almost pained at the words. "But we require sunlight to thrive and reproduce. Unfortunately, cool weather is our enemy and shortens our lives, so we can't live on the surface like humans." He motioned around the room at his fellow creatures. "The members of my tribe who came with me on this quest sacrifice their comfort—their lives even—to help me change this planet and make it more inhabitable for our kind. It is worth the pain for us to know that one day, our kind will wipe yours off the face of it."

When Jes still looked confused, he went on.

"There are no satellites in those rockets. Instead, each carries over twenty-two thousand pounds of chlorodifluoromethane, a chemical that, when dumped straight into the atmosphere, will rip a hole in the ozone layer almost as large as the entire northern hemisphere. The amount of radiation that will come through will kill a good portion of the human race at the same time the greenhouse effect will push average temperatures up as much as ten degrees over the next few decades—death for your kind and global warming on a scale you can't imagine. It's a win-win for us, as you humans are fond of saying."

The scientists in the room gasped in horror. Jes, on the other hand, didn't so much as blink.

"That's why we needed the convoluted Bilderberg

scheme," Darby added, pointing at each of his fellow natum in turn as he continued. "Arsenault gave us access and priority to the space center. Khan provided the needed chemicals. And Marconi got us the rockets. It was incredibly easy to implement our plan once we had the right humans to shapeshift into."

Jes gave him a smile. "Sorry to screw up your plans, but we've already disabled the other two rockets. When we take care of this one, your complicated scheme is going to go straight down the toilet."

Darby moved toward Jes so fast Jake could barely follow him. With a growl, he lifted his M4 and pulled the trigger, clipping the creature in the knees and dropping him to the floor. Then Jake quickly turned and aimed for the two natum holding Jes.

The other natum in the room immediately returned fire. Jake felt several rounds hit him, but he ignored them all, focusing on the only thing that mattered—freeing Jes so she could get the hell out of there. But the moment he took out the two creatures holding her captive, she scooped up the first weapon she could find and started shooting.

Jake should have known better.

The scientists ran for the doors, some of them trying to take out the creatures with nothing but their bare hands on the way. It was a brave attempt, but against the stronger, faster, and deadlier natum, it was wasted. But it gave Jake a few needed seconds, and he put round after round through the creatures' midsections.

Darby was on Jake in a flash, taking several M4 rounds in the chest in an effort to get close enough to knock his weapon aside. The creature was all jagged claws and sharp fangs.

Shit, the thing was fast—even faster than Damien. Within moments, Jake's forearms were a bloody mess, and he was so focused on defending himself that he never even saw the boot coming his way until it connected with his chest and sent him flying across the room to smash into the wall right under the TV screens. That's how he saw the countdown clock and the fact that it had somehow run down to less than a minute.

That knowledge scared the hell out of him, but not nearly as much as the image of Jes fighting Damien, the natum towering over her by almost two feet. Like him, Jes had lost her weapon and was trying to fend the massive creature off by hand, punching and kicking so fast it was almost a blur. But her blows seemed to do little damage.

He had to help her.

But Darby cut him off, claws shredding through his vest and shirt underneath, slicing his chest and shoulders, seemingly unfazed by the big chunks of flesh Jake ripped off him with his own claws. The natum was actually laughing, as if the wounds didn't bother him at all.

Jake was trying to come up with another plan, until he saw Jes go down, scrambling backward across the floor to get away from Damien. The idea that she was about to be killed drove every rational thought out of his head, and suddenly the only thing that mattered was killing Darby, then reaching Jes in time to save her.

Baring his teeth, Jake charged Darby. The natum ripped into him, but Jake ignored the pain. Catching the creature by the throat, Jake lifted him off his feet like a toy and shoved his clawed hand into the thing's abdomen with a growl that shook the room.

Dropping Darby with a snarl, Jake spun around to see Damien kneeling in front of Jes, his hands clasped over his stomach as oily blood poured out by the gallon. His features had barely started to change when the creature flopped forward on his face.

That's when Jake realized the shooting had stopped and the rumbling he'd thought were his growls still echoing in the room was something completely different. He glanced at the countdown clock to see that it had reached zero. On the TV screens, flames were already coming from the base of the rocket.

He hurried over to the computers. Maybe if he shot them up, they could still stop the launch. But the one scientist still left alive, his face covered in his own blood, shook his head even as he struggled for breath.

"Too late. Too late," he muttered in heavily accented English before he died.

Jake didn't stop to think. M4 in hand, he reloaded as he raced for the door. It was insane, but he had some crazy thought in his head that maybe he could shoot the rocket motor from this distance and make something good happen.

Flames billowed out from under the rocket now, and the ground around them shook like a frigging earthquake had hit. There was no way he'd hit even the rocket from here with a 5.56mm round. The range was too far.

"Get to the helicopter!" Jes shouted, running toward the door.

Of course! He could use the .50 caliber mounted in the door. He'd have to rip the thing out of the mounting supports to do it, but it would definitely give him more range. Probably still not enough, but better than what he had now.

When they got to the helicopter, the pilot was nowhere in sight. That sucked, since they needed him to fly the damn thing. But then Jes ran to the front left side and climbed in, and Jake found himself hoping just a little as he jumped into the bird and took the gunner position.

"Can you fly the thing?" he shouted, even as the rotors roared faster above them and the chopper began to pitch forward on the front of its skids.

She flashed him a beautiful smile over her shoulder. "We're going to find out."

Taking that as a yes, Jake checked the .50 caliber gun, loading a fresh round off the belt and holding on for dear life as Jes tipped the helicopter almost on its nose and took off like a frigging combat pilot.

Looking out the door, Jake saw that the rocket was already a couple hundred feet off the ground and building speed. "Take us higher. We have to get closer before the rocket gains too much velocity."

Jes complied and while the helicopter wasn't exactly stable, it was at least under control. "I can climb and fly pretty straight and level, but any kind of maneuvers are out. I'm not so sure about the landing part either."

Good to know.

"That's okay," he shouted back as they climbed and moved closer at the same time. They were probably at almost five hundred feet already and getting higher, but not nearly as fast as the rocket. "Just get us up there in time."

"Isn't it going to be bad to release all that gas when the rocket hits the ground?" she asked, slipping the helicopter sideways and giving him a good shooting angle.

"I'm hoping the fireball will consume everything." He

squeezed the double trigger on the big gun. "Hold on. This isn't going to end well."

Jake had half a second to see Jes's panic-stricken expression before the enormous Ariane 5 motor came apart in a flash of light and smoke.

The reaction was a hell of a lot more violent than he'd expected, and he almost fell out the open door as the entire helicopter got shoved sideways like a giant hand had smacked them. For a moment, he hung out over the skids in open air, his grip on the handles of the machine gun the only thing keeping him in contact with the bird. With a grunt, he swung himself back inside—barely—only to find Jes fighting with the controls and doing everything she could to keep them from flipping completely over in a barrel roll.

Jake thought for a minute they might have a chance... until there was a second explosion as the entire front of the rocket disappeared in a fireball brighter than the one the engine produced. The flames swatted the chopper like a bug, and Jake knew there was no chance they were going to stay in the air. No way in hell was he going down on another helicopter. Once was frigging enough for him.

Leaning forward, he got a hand on the shoulder of Jes's tactical harness, yanking her out of her seat and dragging her back against his chest. Holding on to her tightly, he leaped out the door of the helicopter as it spiraled downward. It was difficult to know exactly how high they were, but it had to be at least fifty feet. He knew impact with the ground was going to hurt like a son of a bitch, but he wrapped himself around Jes as best as he could, bracing for impact and praying she'd survive even if he didn't.

Because while he was a werewolf, living through this wasn't a given.

By the grace of God, he hit the ground feetfirst. Even so, it felt like every bone in his body broke at once as he tumbled and rolled, doing everything he could to protect Jes.

Jake had a fraction of a second to realize they were both alive when he caught a flash of movement above them. Cursing, he scrambled to the side just as the remains of the helicopter smashed into the ground where they'd been mere moments ago. Even though it hurt like four guys were beating him with baseball bats, he kept moving to avoid being crushed by the falling metal and burning fuel.

He finally stopped when he felt water lapping at his crushed knees. He'd be damned. Somehow, he and Jes had come down on the beach. Fire, smoke, and wreckage from the helicopter was everywhere, just like the crash he'd survived in Afghanistan. Somewhere in the distance, the rocket was back on the ground and burning like a frigging small sun.

The pain in his body was everywhere and so overwhelming that all Jake wanted to do was pass out and make it go away. But he fought against the curtain of blackness trying to sweep over him. He needed to check on Jes first.

Jake turned his head to find her leaning over him, bruised and battered but blessedly alive. Giving him a smile, she bent down to kiss him gently on the mouth. She murmured words he couldn't make out, but that was okay. Her arms were around him and that was good enough. The worst of the pain slowly faded, and before he realized it, Caleb, Harley, and Misty were there. Caleb and Harley helped him to his feet, supporting him between them as they slowly headed toward the boat sliding up on the beach.

It wasn't until they were all safely in the boat and on their way back to the hotel and he was once more cradled in Jes's arms that Jake realized one of their teammates were missing.

"Where's Forrest?" he murmured.

On the other side of the boat, Misty began to sob softly. A tearful Harley put her arm around the girl, while Caleb turned his head and looked off at the horizon, blinking rapidly.

"Still in London," Jes said softly, her eyes glistening with tears as she gazed down at him. "We need to go bring him home."

Tears stung his own eyes then.

Damn.

Jake wanted to tell Misty how sorry he was, but right then, talking took more energy than he had. So instead, he let the darkness wash over him as he melted into his mate's embrace.

CHAPTER 19

London

JES HUNG BACK WITH MISTY AND HARLEY AS JAKE AND Caleb led the way down into the basement of the Lanesborough Hotel. McKay had pulled a buttload of strings to get them a direct military airlift out of South America and back to London, a Metro Police escort from Heathrow, and full access to every part of the hotel.

"I want to be up there with Jake and Caleb," Misty said brokenly, barely holding back tears as they walked down the steps, maintenance staff, Metro Police, and paramedics trailing behind. "I need to be there for him."

As they walked through the basement, Jes put her arm around Misty's shoulders, partly to lend support and partly to keep her from charging ahead and seeing something she should never have to see. "Let's stay back here until they find Forrest, okay?"

Misty looked at Jes, the tears she'd been holding back rolling down her face. No one had said it in front of Misty, but they didn't have to. It had been over four days since the natum had attacked Forrest. Even if he'd somehow made it through whatever the creature had done to him, four days was a long time to keep himself alive. Since none of the hotel workers had found him, it almost certainly meant the natum had moved him. Or disposed of his body.

The flight from Kourou to London had been excruciating for all of them. Jake had slept until his inner wolf healed itself, which ended up being most of the journey. He'd broken nearly every bone in his body when they'd hit the ground, while she'd barely gotten bruised. Jes still didn't know how he was alive. She was just glad he was.

When he finally did wake up, Jake spent the time beating himself up about not figuring out the reason Forrest smelled like a natum had nothing to do with the blood that had gotten on him but because he was one of the creatures. Harley and Caleb shared his pain on that front. Misty cried for hours, wanting to know how she hadn't realized the thing that had been with them for days wasn't the real Forrest, the man she loved.

"He wouldn't even kiss me," she said over and over. "I should have known there was something wrong."

Jes prayed for Misty's sake they were all wrong and that, somehow, Forrest was alive.

"I have his scent," Jake said from up ahead.

The trail took them on a meandering path through a basement that looked like it was the disjointed amalgamation of a hundred years' worth of additions and renovations. Several times, locked doors got in their way. When the maintenance people said they'd have to go find the key, either Jake or Caleb kicked them in, much to the hotel workers' obvious dismay.

Jake and Caleb stopped in front of a heavy metal door with a sign that read *HVAC. No Entry Allowed.* They exchanged looks and surged forward, slamming into the door together.

Misty tried to follow them into the room, but Jes held her back.

"He's here!" Jake called. "And he's alive!"

Misty was through the door in a flash.

Jes hurried after her into the dimly lit and cluttered room. Loud air-conditioning and heating units as big as Jes's apartment filled the space, and for a moment, she couldn't figure out where Jake had gone. Then she caught sight of him motioning at them from behind a big metal unit. Jes quickly followed Misty down the narrow passageway between the unit and the wall.

It was pitch-black in the tight space, but with the help of a flashlight, they soon found Forrest shoved into the very back corner, naked except for socks and his underwear. Down on one knee beside him, Jake looked up at her and Misty in disbelief.

"He's definitely alive," he said with a grin, then gestured to the dirty, metal tube that came out of the back of the nearest AC unit. "I think he's been drinking the condensation dripping out of the pipe."

On the floor, Forrest groaned.

Jake quickly got out of the way to make room for Misty. She was crying again, but they were happy tears this time.

As Misty leaned down to gently hug Forrest, Jes saw several gashes across his chest and arms. He'd stuffed dirty rags and foam insulation into the wounds to keep them from bleeding. Water wasn't the only thing that had kept him alive. On the floor beside him were several empty packages of shortbread cookies.

Misty gently kissed him, then sat back on her heels, not bothering to wipe away her tears as Forrest smiled weakly up at her.

"There you are," he said in a soft voice. "I've been waiting for you to realize I was missing and come back for me."

Misty cupped his stubble-covered jaw. "I'm sorry we didn't figure it out sooner."

Forrest put a gentle finger to her lips, shushing her with another smile, stronger this time. "Don't be sorry. I'd wait forever for you."

Misty kissed him again, only pulling away when Caleb touched her shoulder. Carefully picking Forrest up, Caleb carried him out of the room to the waiting paramedics, Misty hurrying after them.

Grinning, Jake held out his hand to Jes. "Let's go home."

Returning his smile, she took his hand, and together, they walked out to join their teammates. After what she'd just witnessed, she thought that maybe werewolves weren't the only ones to have soul mates.

CHAPTER 20

JES WAS STANDING AT THE GRANITE ISLAND THAT separated Jake's kitchen from the living room, pouring tortilla chips in a bowl and getting more guacamole out of the fridge, when the doorbell rang.

"I got it," Jake called out from the far side of the room, wading across the crowded floor to get to the door.

When he pulled it open, a cheer went up from the rest of the team as Forrest and Misty slowly walked in. Well, Forrest moved slowly. Misty stuck to his side like she was afraid to ever let him out of her sight again. Jes didn't blame her. After everything that had happened two weeks ago, Misty had a right to be overprotective.

Jes slipped into the living room long enough to drop off the chips and dip in front of Caleb and Harley—who would probably inhale the entire bowl before anyone else got a bite—and went over to give the latest arrivals a hug. It was obvious Forrest was still recovering from his ordeal at the hotel. She could tell from the hug that he'd lost some weight as well as some muscle. Being stuffed in a corner with your chest ripped open for half a week could do that to a person.

"I'm so glad you two made it," she said, noticing Misty looked a lot more relaxed now than she had the last time Jes had seen her. "I was afraid the hospital would want to hold on to you for a few more days."

Forrest shook his head with a chuckle. "What, and miss our very first post-mission celebration? Not a chance. I had Misty hack into the hospital's computer system and fake the doctor's signature on my release, and then it was hasta la vista, baby!"

Jake threw Misty a panicked look. "Please tell me he's kidding. You didn't do that, did you?"

Misty shook her head, throwing a disapproving look at Forrest. "Of course not. In fact, I was the one who triple-checked with the doctor to make sure he was good to go. If there had been a second of doubt, I would never have let him leave."

Forrest made a face suggesting he hated being taken care of like that, but it was obviously an act. The man loved having Misty look after him.

Jake crossed his arms over his chest. "Well, you might have been cleared to leave the hospital, but that doesn't mean you need to stay on your feet any more than you have to. You guys find a seat while I get you something to drink."

Jes watched Misty and Forrest weave their way across the living room toward Harley and Caleb, being careful to avoid the twins and their FBI agent crushes, who were play-ing with Sam and Dean on the floor. By the time the two had found their seats, Jake was already on his way back from the kitchen, a Sprite for Misty and a beer for Forrest. He'd been deprived of alcohol during his entire hospital stay and looked like he was in heaven after the first sip.

Within minutes, everyone was laughing and joking, with-out a single peep of shoptalk. Of course, with the twins and their boyfriends there, it wasn't like they could talk about the mission. The entire thing had been classified out the wazoo. But it didn't matter anyway. After being back for two weeks, there was very little that needed to be said. Everyone had gotten caught up on what they'd missed during the fight, including how Misty had helped Harley and Caleb disable the second rocket, how Jes had gotten grabbed the second she got close to launchpad three, and how everyone found Jake and Jes on the beach after the helicopter crash. They'd even all gone to the hospital together to re-create the entire mission at the space center in Guiana word for word for Forrest so he wouldn't feel left out.

It had taken a while to figure out how the hell STAT was going to cover up everything that had happened down there, but with almost all the witnesses to the events dead, it seemed the world was more than ready to believe the rocket explosion had been caused by criminal recklessness because the Bilderberg Society had tried to go too fast. No one even asked why there'd been so many environmental cleanup teams needed to disassemble the two remaining rockets. Word of the ozone-depleting chemicals that had been in there never slipped out.

Nothing on the natum either, even though the general consensus was that at least some of them had gotten away during the fighting. In a way, Jes felt kind of sorry for them. Not necessarily Darby and the ones who'd tried to kill her and everyone else, but their species as a whole. Knowing there were more still living underground that might try something like this again was a terrifying thought, but at the same time, she could understand how much they wanted to live on the surface. If they ever ran across them again, a part of her hoped there'd be a way to help them. Naive of her maybe, but still, anything was possible.

Jes walked into the kitchen to grab a wine cooler when she felt a pair of strong arms wrap around her waist and tug her close. The heat from Jake's chest warmed her all over, but not nearly as much as the lips that came down to nuzzle at her neck.

"You need some help in here?" he asked, his voice husky in her ear.

Something told her he wasn't talking about getting a drink from the fridge.

She turned to face him, wrapping her arms around his neck and pulling him down for a kiss. "No, I'm good in here. But I can definitely use a hand or two later after everyone leaves."

Jes said that last part as softly as she could, well aware there were werewolves in the other room—including Zoe and Chloe—who could overhear everything she and Jake said if they wanted to.

Jake chuckled and kissed her again. His mouth tasted so good it was hard not moaning out loud. Maybe no one would notice if they slipped into his bedroom for a few minutes and closed the door?

While Jes hadn't officially moved in or anything like that yet, she might as well have, since she'd been staying at his place every night since getting back from the mission. She couldn't stand being separated from Jake, and the feeling was mutual. Fortunately, the twins were thrilled to have her in Jake's life and theirs. As for her, she simply adored the girls.

"Do you have any idea how much I love you?" Jake murmured, not bothering to lower his voice. Not that he needed to. Everyone knew about their relationship.

"Yeah, I'm pretty sure I do," she said, trailing her mouth over to his ear and nibbling on all the tasty parts along the way. "Since it's exactly as much as I love you."

A few days after getting back from London, she and Jake

had sat down with McKay to talk about their relationship. They let him know they were going to be together whether he was okay with it or not. They'd already agreed they'd walk away from the team before they ever walked away from each other. Surprisingly, McKay had been extremely open to the idea.

"I know the legend of *The One*," he'd told them. "As long as you two can continue to work as a team, I don't have a problem with you being together."

That had been music to their ears and exactly what they'd been hoping he would say.

She and Jake stopped kissing when Caleb asked if they could come up for air long enough to grab him another beer.

Laughing, they grabbed a couple beers from the fridge— one for Jake and the other for Caleb—then went back into the living room to find some seats.

"It's nice having the whole team here together," Jake said softly as they sat together on the couch.

"You mean the whole pack, right?" she asked teasingly, nudging his shoulder with hers.

Jake considered that for a moment, then flashed her a smile that lit up the room…and her heart. "Right. The whole pack."

He looked like he would have said more, but his cell phone rang before he could. Pulling his cell from his pocket, he checked the screen to see who was calling, then thumbed the green button and put it to his ear.

"McKay," he said. "What's up?"

Every werewolf in the room—including the twins— stopped what they were doing to focus on Jake. It took a moment for her to realize they were listening to what

McKay was saying on the other end of the line. Man, she'd love to have their hearing. She couldn't pick up anything he was saying and she was sitting right beside Jake.

Jake hung up and looked at them. "We have a mission—possible human trafficking involving our specialty."

Since Austin and Colt didn't know what their team specialized in, Jake couldn't say, but Jes knew what he meant. Human trafficking with a supernatural angle.

"Our plane leaves in two hours," Jake added, getting to his feet.

She and the rest of the team—the Pack—stood as well, Harley and Caleb already heading for the door.

"Where are we going?" Jes asked.

He grinned. "Paris."

Paris, huh? As she and Jake hurried into the bedroom to pack, Jes wondered if they might slip in a romantic dinner while they were over there. In between saving the world, of course.

ACKNOWLEDGMENTS

I hope you had as much fun reading Jestina and Jake's story as we had writing it! When we decided to write a spin-off from our SWAT: Special Threat Assessment Team Series, we wanted to keep all the fun things that made it part of the SWAT world while making it different at the same time. That's when we came up with the idea of taking our werewolves international, à la *Mission Impossible*. Making Jake Huang, the werewolf we introduced in *Wolf Instinct* (SWAT), the hero and alpha of the STAT pack was an easy choice. And a special shout-out to our real-life friend and author, Jestina, for inspiring the heroine!

This whole series wouldn't be possible without some very incredible people. In addition to another big thank-you to my hubby for all his help with the action scenes and military and tactical jargon, thanks to my fantastic agent, Courtney Miller-Callihan; thanks to my editor and go-to-person at Sourcebooks, Cat Clyne (who loves this series as much as I do and is always a phone call, text, or email away whenever I need something); and all the other amazing people at Sourcebooks, including my fantastic publicist and the crazy-talented art department. The covers they make for me are seriously droolworthy!

Because I could never leave out my readers, a huge thank-you to everyone who reads my books and Snoopy Dances right along with me with every new release. That includes the fantastic people on my amazing Review Team, as well my assistant, Janet. You rock!

And a very special shout-out to our favorite restaurant, P.F. Chang's, where hubby and I bat story lines back and forth and come up with all of our best ideas, as well as a thank-you to our fantastic waiter-turned-manager, Andrew, who makes sure our order is ready the moment we walk in the door!

Hope you enjoy the next book in the STAT: Special Threat Assessment Team series coming soon from Sourcebooks, and look forward to reading the rest of the series as much as we look forward to sharing it with you. Also, don't forget to check out the action-packed series that started it all—SWAT: Special Wolf Alpha Team!

Happy Reading!

Read on for a sneak peek at the next book in
Paige Tyler's enormously popular SWAT series

UNTAMED WOLF

Coming soon from Sourcebooks Casablanca

THE MOMENT THE MAN IN THE EXPENSIVE SUIT AND
Italian loafers walked into the diner, Bree Harlow was
sure she recognized him. She couldn't remember where
they'd met, but she was certain they had. In fact, she was
so sure, she stopped mid-conversation with her teenage
son, Brandon, to give him a smile and a wave. But before
she could so much as lift her hand, the man walked up to
the table where the two police officers were sitting and shot
them.

Without saying a single word.

Without even waiting for them to notice him.

He'd just…shot them.

Before Bree realized what was happening, she and
Brandon were on the floor trying to stop the bleeding while
the man in the suit was ranting and raving about monsters
and voices in his head.

She'd taken Brandon out to breakfast this morning so
they could relax and, hopefully, talk. Bree knew her son was

dealing with some stuff and she desperately wanted to help. But between the nightmares that had him ripping up his sheets and the way his brown eyes flashed yellow whenever he got upset—which seemed to be all the time lately—she had no idea what to do.

No matter how many times she tried to get her son to tell her what was wrong, he wouldn't. If anything, he became even more withdrawn. Bree thought having breakfast at the diner that made his favorite chocolate chip pancakes might put him in a talkative mood, but then the guy with the gun had shown up and keeping those police officers alive had become the only thing that mattered to her at that point.

Hope flared bright when a big cop walked in. Diego's presence commanded the room, and Bree found herself believing there was nothing he couldn't do. When he convinced the guy in the suit to release the injured officers and four other people, she started thinking the whole thing would ultimately end okay.

Then the guy grabbed Brandon and Bree watched in horror as the humanity left the man's eyes and he'd lifted the gun to her son's head. Terror flashed yellow gold in Brandon's eyes, tearing her heart out.

If her son died, she'd die, too.

Bree would have done anything she had to do to save Brandon's life—even putting herself between him and the gun—but it felt like she was buried in Jell-O, unable to close the distance between herself and the man threatening her son, no matter how hard she tried.

All at once, a blur of movement caught her eye, then a SWAT cop was knocking Brandon and the guy with the gun to the floor. A split second later, three more SWAT cops came through the windows. Screams of fear echoed in the diner, but the only thing she could focus on was getting to her son.

She'd just reached Brandon when she heard Diego shouting for the guy with the gun to drop it. She grabbed her son to protect his body with her own, even as her gaze went to the scene playing out a few feet away. When the guy placed the gun under his chin, every instinct she had begged her to look away, but she couldn't, and the sight of him taking his own life was the most horrible thing she'd ever witnessed.

The overwhelming chaos in the diner disappeared, replaced by silence and time seemed to slow.

There was so much blood.

Bree had no idea if seconds passed—or hours—but then she heard something so out of place with her surroundings that it immediately snapped her back to reality.

Growling.

Low, soft, pained…growling.

And it was coming from Brandon.

She looked down to find him gazing up at her with vivid gold eyes, half-inch-long fangs visible over his bottom lip.

Bree had always considered herself to be a strong person. She'd gone through a lot in her life and dealt with it. But she couldn't ignore the obvious. The accumulated stress of this situation had been too much for her. She was having a mental breakdown. Because there was no way she was seeing what she thought she saw.

Suddenly, Diego was at her side, pulling Brandon up and talking to him in a slow, calm voice, telling him to relax and breathe, that everything was over and he was going to be okay at the same time he used his big body like a shield, keeping other people in the diner from seeing her son's face. His voice was the most soothing and calming sound she'd ever heard in her life and even though he wasn't talking to her, she found herself breathing in time with his instructions—in through the nose, hold it for five seconds, and out through the mouth.

Bree watched in stunned fascination as the yellow glow slowly receded from her son's eyes and the fangs disappeared. At the same time, his panicked breathing and frantic features relaxed, and she realized it was the first time in months he didn't seem tense.

There was a commotion behind her and she glanced over her shoulder to see the other officers quickly moving everyone outside, herding them in such a way that they didn't have time to look at the body on the floor…or Brandon.

It was like they were all working together to keep anyone from seeing what was happening with her son. Like they all somehow knew something unexplainable was going on.

"There you go, kid." The SWAT cop's deep voice made her turn back around and she saw him standing there with his hands on Brandon's shoulders. "Just a few more deep breaths and you'll be good to go."

Diego was right. A few seconds later, Brandon was completely fine, and Bree found herself wondering if everything she'd seen was a figment of her confused mind.

It could have been, right?

She felt a gentle hand on her arm and looked up into the warmest brown eyes she'd ever seen, a little overwhelmed by the concern she saw there. Diego didn't even know her and yet he seemed genuinely worried.

"Let's go outside," he said, nodding toward Brandon. "This place is about to be crawling with cops, crime scene techs, and general-purpose gawkers. I'd rather be somewhere else before they show up. I think we have a lot to talk about."

She was about to ask what he meant by that, but then it hit her. Everything she'd seen had been real. Diego had seen it, too. And now he wanted to talk about it. Because that's what cops did. They dug into stuff until they knew everything.

Bree's heart began to thump hard all over again as she realized the danger her son might be in now. What if Diego revealed what he'd seen? Brandon would be treated like a freak. From the look on Brandon's face, he realized the same thing and was on the verge of freaking out.

"Relax," the cop said softly, looking first at Brandon, then her. "I'm not a threat to your son. I promise."

Gaze locked with hers, Diego's eyes flared vivid yellow gold. The color was only there for a second before it disappeared, but it was impossible to miss. Or mistake it for anything other than the same thing she'd seen in her son's eyes. The cop looked at Brandon, earning a wide-eyed gasp. Bree had no idea what any of this meant, but it had to be a good sign...right?

"Like I said," Diego murmured. "We have a lot to talk about."

Bree nodded, her head spinning as she tried to understand what was going on. What was happening to her son and how could a cop they'd just met know what it meant?

ABOUT THE AUTHOR

Paige Tyler is a *New York Times* and *USA Today* bestselling author of sexy, romantic suspense and paranormal romance. She and her very own military hero (also known as her husband) live on the beautiful Florida coast with their adorable fur baby (also known as their dog). Paige graduated with a degree in education, but decided to pursue her passion and write books about hunky alpha males and the kick-butt heroines who fall in love with them.

Visit Paige at her website at paigetylertheauthor.com.

She's also on Facebook, Twitter, Tumblr, Instagram, Tsū, Wattpad, and Pinterest.

NIGHT OF THE BILLIONAIRE WOLF

USA Today bestselling author Terry Spear
brings you a shifter world like no other

Lexi Summerfield built her business from the ground up. But with great wealth comes great responsibility, and some drawbacks she could never have anticipated. Lexi never knows who she can trust... And for good reason—the paparazzi are dogging her, and so is someone else with evil intent.

When Lexi meets bodyguard and gray wolf shifter Ryder Gallagher on the hiking trails, she breaks her own rules about getting involved. But secrets have a way of surfacing. And with the danger around Lexi escalating, Ryder will do whatever it takes to stay by her side...

"Fun, flirty, and super sexy."
—Fresh Fiction for A Silver Wolf Christmas

For more info about Sourcebooks's
books and authors, visit:
sourcebooks.com

YOU HAD ME AT JAGUAR

First in the new Heart of the Shifter series from *USA Today* bestselling author Terry Spear

They're not the only ones on the prowl... but they're the most dangerous...

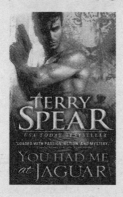

The United Shifter Force gives jaguar agent Howard Armstrong an impossible task—to protect fierce she-jaguar Valerie Chambers, when the last thing she wants is protecting. They're going international to take down a killer, and he can guard Valerie all day long. But guard his heart? He doesn't stand a chance.

"Packed with adventure...magnificently entertaining."
—RT Book Reviews TOP PICK
for *Billionaire in Wolf's Clothing*

For more info about Sourcebooks's books and authors, visit:
sourcebooks.com

WICKED
COWBOY WOLF

Cowboys by day, wolf shifters by night—don't
miss the thrilling Seven Range Shifters series
from acclaimed author Kait Ballenger

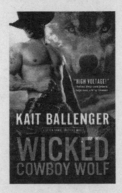

Years ago, Grey Wolf Jared Black was cast from the pack for a
crime he didn't commit. Now, he's the mysterious criminal wolf
known only as the Rogue, a name his former packmates won't
soon forget. But when a vampire threat endangers the lives of
their entire species, Jared must confront his former packmates
again, even if that means betraying the only woman he's ever
loved...

"This story has it all—a heroine with grit and a
hero who backs up his tough talk with action."
—Fresh Fiction for Cowboy Wolf Trouble

For more info about Sourcebooks's
books and authors, visit:
sourcebooks.com

Also by Paige Tyler